Sitting on Top of the World

of the

CHERYL KING

Published by Purple Marble Press

Copyright © 2021 by Cheryl King

Second Edition

ISBN: 978-1-7377858-0-4

Cover artwork by Jamie Hitt

Dedication

To my family. Family is everything. With family you can do anything.

Like write a book, get it published, have your publisher go belly up and run off without paying royalties, and then republish it yourself.

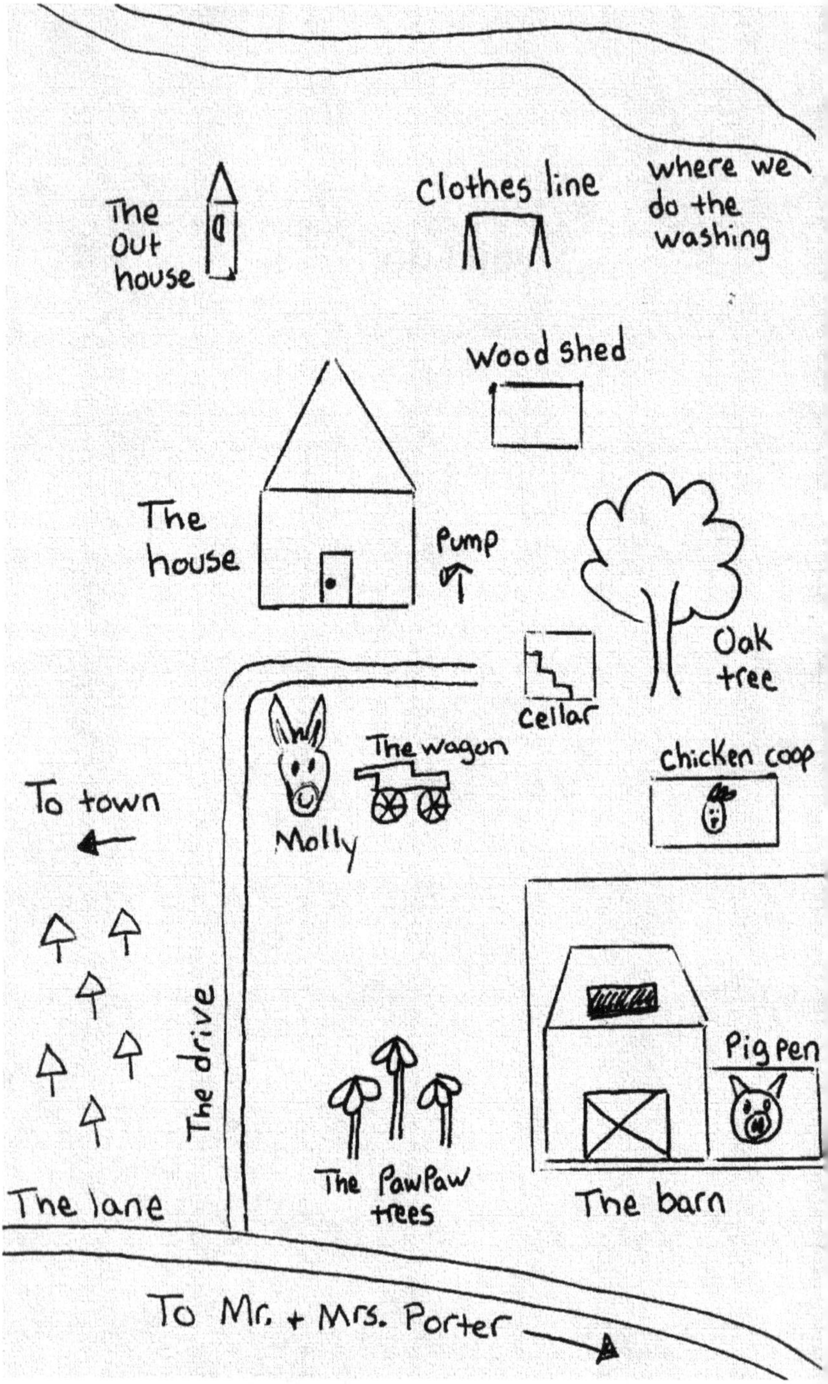

The out house
Clothes line
where we do the washing
Wood shed
The house
Pump
Oak tree
Cellar
The wagon
Chicken coop
To town
Molly
The drive
Pig pen
The PawPaw trees
The lane
The barn
To Mr. + Mrs. Porter

The woods

Josy's traps

The creek

Corn

The Depression Trees

Carrots

Cow + goat Pasture

Green beans

Strawberries   Onions

1

Jump!

May 1933

I can smell the hobo camp before I can see it. Pungent sweat and sweet tobacco mingle with dew-dampened leaves, and I scrunch up my nose and breathe through my mouth. I can hear it, too. Raspy coughs, deep and ragged laughter, clinkin' of tin, cracklin' of fire.

As I edge farther into the woods toward a clearing, the tents appear suddenly. Small tents and cardboard shacks, barrels, tree-stump stools, crates, moonshine bottles litterin' the ground, and men everywhere. There must be twenty or so men, some of 'em young, just boys. But they're all as different as can be. I skinny up behind a tree and watch.

Some of 'em are old and scary-lookin', their faces lit up by the light of the fire, and they got long, scraggly beards and missin' teeth, and they laugh with their whole faces, chins droppin' down like someone's yankin' on their beard. Others are dressed like they're headin' to a day at the office, suit coats and slacks and fedoras on, and they're sittin' proper-like, waitin' on somethin' that must be important. The young ones are gathered around a firepit, cookin' somethin' that sizzles and pops. Everyone's drinkin' and chattin' and eatin', and for a split second it feels like home, and I wonder if I've made a mistake.

I tuck a piece of my short hair under my cap and think back to when my best friend, Margaret Ann, cut it for me. She'd said it was the only way I could do this – disguised as a man. "A teenage girl pretty as you ain't gonna find nothin' but trouble in a hobo camp full of men, June, you know that," she'd said. "Gun or no gun, you gonna be a target."

I hug my pack in close to me, caress the bulge of the gun, and think about how I got here. How I got to this point of no return. And my thoughts turn to Josy and the day we got the news that he'd been beat up out on the rails. We didn't know how bad it was 'til Pate and Charlie came hobblin' up the drive with Josy lollin' between 'em nearly bleedin' to death.

They laid him in his bed, and Mama and Daddy fussed over him while I stood frozen in the corner, watchin'. Couldn't hardly recognize him. They said the bulls got him. Not animal bulls, but people bulls. They're the mean ol' men who catch train hoppers and either arrest 'em or beat 'em silly. I sure wish they'da just arrested Josy.

Josy's my older brother – name's Joseph, but I cain't remember a time I didn't call him Josy. He's the best big brother I coulda ever wanted. Always took real good care of me, and Mama and Daddy, too. He helped Daddy on the farm up until we couldn't sell nothin' no more and most of the crops went bad.

I helped Mama with the sewin'. I cain't remember a time Mama didn't have a sewin' needle in her hands, 'cept o'course when she had a skillet in 'em. She could sew quilts, aprons, and real pretty bonnets, and we'd sell 'em at the market. But things got so bad, she said cain't nobody 'ford to buy pretty things when the economy's so ugly.

When the crops went bad, it was a good thing Daddy and Josy were handy-like. They could build outhouses and sheds and barns. But Daddy said it was just like with Mama's sewin' – nobody could spend what little money they had on anything extra when they had to put food on the table. I said, "Well, what if they ain't got no table to put the food on?" He didn't have an answer for that, but wouldn't you know it – Daddy and Josy started buildin' tables and chairs and stools, and they traded 'em for things we needed, like shoes and winter coats. They was always used, o'course, but we didn't mind none, so long as we had somethin' to keep our feet dry in the rain and our bodies warm in the winter.

Soon Daddy had to start sellin' off the animals. He sold all the goats and some of the cows, and we ate the pigs – that's a day I'll never forget, 'cause I was so sad about them silly pigs gettin' slaughtered, never mind the fact that bacon's about the best food in the world. Anyway, all's we had left after that was two good milkin' cows, the mule to pull the wagon, and a handful of good layin' hens. That way we always had our own milk and butter, and we could eat eggs any old time. And we had stuff to trade.

One time, Mama took a dozen eggs to Mr. and Mrs. Porter down the lane, and they gave us eighteen potatoes. For quite some time after, we had potato hash, mashed potatoes, potato soup, stewed potatoes, potato pancakes, and I don't know what all else. And we never did get tired of them potatoes, 'cause we knew what it felt like to not have any.

Soon me and Josy couldn't go to school no more, 'cause we had to help Mama and Daddy, 'specially after Daddy's accident – another day I'll never forget 'cause there was so much blood. I sure was sad to not go to school with my friends and learn and study no more. But Josy said I should feel proud 'cause we's a hard-workin' family.

But sometimes I still wish things was different. 'Specially the day Josy went to ride the rails. Then when Mama got sick, things sure took a turn for the worst. You'd think we was the unluckiest family in the world, after all that went wrong, but it ain't all bad, not really. I just wish the Depression never happened and people didn't have to hop trains to find work and nobody got sick and nobody got hurt just tryin' to live.

I know they ain't really animals, but I cain't help it – every time I think about what them bulls did to Josy, I imagine giant hairy beasts with horns and metal rings through their noses, and I cry and cry and cry. I think if it had been the animals, Josy wouldn'ta had no problems. He's real good with animals.

So, how did I get here? It started the summer of 1930, just before I turned twelve. That's when everything went absolutely haywire. And if I knew then what I know now, things'd be different. So different. See, the thing about me is, I notice things. I notice things but don't think nothin' of it 'til later, and then I think, *Aw, crumbs! I knew it!* Or *I shoulda seen that comin'.* Like that little twitch in Margaret Ann's left cheek when she ain't tellin' the whole truth. Or the hitch in Mama's throat when she's tryin' to put on a brave face but inside she's fallin' apart. And, mostly, the darkness that shadowed Josy's eyes for a split second that day in Knoxville when we felt like we were sittin' on top of the world. Lord, were we happy that day.

I wish I could go back to that day and hold onto Josy, keep him from goin' out on the rails. Better yet, maybe I could go back to the day we got eighteen potatoes from Mrs. Porter, back when all we had to worry about was food and clothes. 'Cause, like I said, the world just kinda fell apart like wood rot.

But that's the past. Cain't change it. All I can do now is make things right. I have to, 'cause this Depression's bleedin' us dry, and we're runnin' outa time. I gotta find work so's I can save the farm and take care of Mama and Daddy. I'm gonna make Josy proud even if it kills me to do it. That's what I think.

And that's what I'm thinkin' 'bout when I'm darn-near fallin' asleep right up against this ol' tree and a commotion startles me back to life. There's a rumble in the distance and all the men are busy packin' things away and clearin' up and cleanin' up. The train's comin'. Bits of conversation tell me that some of the men are stayin' back, but most of them are hoppin' this train when it gets near.

This is it.

I try to think of everything ol' Jimmy Mack told me about hoppin' onto a train, but my mind goes blank. The train whistles, and the clackety-clack of the train cars on the rails is gettin' louder. I reposition my pack across my other shoulder and scoot up behind a tree closer to the tracks, and I see men approachin' the tracks and crouchin' in wait.

Now the train appears, and it's goin' much faster than I imagined. *How'm I gonna jump onto that?*

Then I see the hobos runnin', so I run up after them, and one man half jumps, half climbs up into an open boxcar, and then another jumps up into the boxcar next to it, and all the others are runnin' beside the train, and one by one, they're jumpin' on and helpin' the others up. I'm runnin' faster now, my pack bouncin' against my hip, and I got one hand holdin' my cap on my head, and one hand reachin' up toward the train car, and a big, beefy hand reaches for me, and men are hollerin' at me, but I cain't hear nothin' over the roar of the train that swallows the drummin' of my heart.

"JUMP!"

2

The Crash Heard All the Way in Maynardville

June 1930

I notice four strange things on this Friday morning in June, and it starts right when I step offa my front porch to head to my best friend Margaret Ann's house. Margaret Ann lives closer to town, near the schoolhouse. It ain't but a twenty-five minute walk from here if I don't dawdle.

So any time I go to town, I stop by Margaret Ann's place. She shows me her newest doll clothes 'cause her mama makes them outa old tea cozies and doilies. I show her my newest scrape or scab 'cause I'm always gettin' new ones. I cain't remember a time I wasn't climbin' the old oak out front or

6

swingin' from a rope on the barn loft or some such business. And sometimes we gossip 'til the sun's about to go down and I remember what I came out there for in the first place.

On Fridays in June, I wake up 'fore the crack of dawn and milk the cows by the light of one measly old lantern, pick strawberries, then wash up and go to town to help Mama with the shoppin'. She usually comes too, and we hook Molly, our mule, up to the wagon, but today Mama ain't feelin' too good, so I'm goin' by myself, and I don't mind none, 'cause I just love walkin' to town. I'm goin' to Macafee's Market and General Store to get Mama some thread for her sewin' and then next door to the Piggly Wiggly to get some flour and sugar.

The Piggly Wiggly is new and everybody was excited to see it go up in Maynardville, 'cept Mr. Macafee, o'course, who says that ol' Pig is gonna run him outa business, but it surely ain't done it yet, 'cause Macafee's has been in Maynardville since before I was born, and I cain't imagine it goin' nowhere. I'm just pleased as punch to be goin' to town by myself like a real grown-up. I wasn't always allowed to walk all the way to town by myself. Josy used to have to come with me, but now that I'm almost twelve, Mama and Daddy say it's alright, long as I'm real careful and watch out for snakes.

Most people'd say there ain't much to see between our farm and town, which is Maynardville, which is the biggest town in Union County, Tennessee, but that ain't sayin' much 'cause Maynardville ain't nowhere big as Knoxville, which is almost an hour's wagon ride away. But most people don't know nothin', 'cause walkin' the twenty-five minutes to Margaret Ann's, I can see just about every form of landscape there is, 'cept ocean.

This part of the Tennessee Valley blesses us with woodlands and mountains on both sides, creeks and farmland in between. I can smell the sweet breath of fish and crawdads from Norris Lake and hear the musical ruckus of mallards flittin' from stream to pond to lake to creek. Here, you walk anywhere long enough and quiet enough, you're bound to come across somethin' of interest. I cain't remember a time I didn't come upon a turtle, a rabbit, or a family of foxes on my walk to Margaret Ann's. And that twenty-five minute walk turns into thirty-five easy, 'cause I cain't help but sit and watch 'em for a spell.

So, like I said, I notice four strange things on this Friday in June. The first thing is the blue summer skies of Tennessee done clouded over like nobody's business, and there's a chill to the air that just ain't natural on a June day, even if it is mornin' time.

June's my favorite month, by the way, and not just 'cause of the warmth of summer, but 'cause it's my name, too. Mama says she named me June 'cause when I was born I was a right breath of sunshine. I'm glad of that, 'cause she said I coulda been named September since that's the month I was born, and I don't know why she was dead set on namin' me after a month to begin with. If Josy'd been named after the month he was born, he'da been named December. Mama too, and Daddy's name would be February, which is hard enough to say, but to spell, forget it. Margaret Ann would have the most beautiful name of April. These are the silly things I think about on my long walk to Margaret Ann's house, 'cept when I'm distracted by a toad or a bluejay or a spiny lizard.

I spot Mr. Tomlinson's big ol' car bumpin' down the road, kickin' up dust. He toots his horn at me and slows down and waves out the window. "Where ya goin', li'l Miss June?"

"Hiya, Mr. Tomlinson. I'm headed to town to go to Macafee's and the Piggly Wiggly, but first I'm stoppin' by to see Margaret Ann Murphy," I tell him.

Mr. Tomlinson's got to be the nicest old man I ever did know, other than my own daddy and granddaddy and anyone else related to me. He's on the town council and lives up toward the lake. He drives down this way from time to time "to wave hello to the townspeople," he says. He also has a beard that hangs clear to his belly, which makes me laugh.

"Well, you do be careful, dear; it looks like a storm's comin'," he says, lookin' up to the sky as if he can see things written in the clouds.

"I will, Mr. Tomlinson." I wave and he waves and off he goes and off I go.

The second strange thing I notice is when I get to Margaret Ann's, ain't nobody home. I cain't remember a time that I come here and at least one person ain't been around. She got a big family, Margaret Ann does. Five brothers and sisters, and o'course her mama and daddy.

Now, Margaret Ann's mama, she's a piece of work, no offense. She likes to think that since they live close to town, they're smarter than us farm folk. But I'll tell you somethin' that don't make a lick of sense: That woman got six children, and every one of them got two first names. There's Margaret Ann, then Jenny May, then Sally Lynn (which ties up a tongue so bad that her own kin cain't say it right, so everyone calls her Say-Lynn), then there's Michael Ray, Johnny Joe, and Richie Lee, who's still in diapers. And that ain't even the worst of it. They all got two middle names, too. They all got Reynolds as one middle name 'cause that's their mama's before-she-was-married name, plus another one. So Margaret Ann's whole name is Margaret Ann Flora Reynolds Murphy. And Jenny

May is altogether Jenny May Caroline Reynolds Murphy. And I cain't remember all the rest, but don't you know that when any one of them gets in trouble, Mrs. Murphy says their whole darned name. I've heard it happen a time or two, and my own jaws get tired just hearin' her say those long names.

And here's the funny thing: You know what Margaret Ann Flora Reynolds Murphy's mama's name is? Bee. That's it. Bee. May as well be just one letter.

Anyhow, they also got three big coon hounds (who each have just one name, I think), and I don't hear not a one of them barkin'.

I run up onto the porch and pound on the screen door. Then I open the screen door and pound on the real door. This time of year, if the doors are closed, ain't nobody home. I scooch over to the window and peek in, but I cain't see nothin'. Margaret Ann's family got a car, but it ain't here neither.

We ain't got a car, but Mama said we could probably get one if we had a little bit more money. Daddy says right now ain't nobody got much money 'cause the economy is goin' straight to hell in a handbasket. I don't rightly know what that means, but when Daddy says it, he sounds real mad-like, and that ain't like Daddy, so I believe him.

I'm still thinkin' about that handbasket and goin' to hell when I reach the town, and that's when I see the third strange thing. People are lined up at the bank, which should be open by now, but the door's closed, and the people are lookin' real antsy-like, like they may just start beatin' down the door.

I step into Macafee's, down the road from the bank, and Mr. Macafee is at the counter. I go straight over to him, but he's talkin' to Mrs. Linder, who just so happens to always know everybody's business from Maynardville to Memphis, so I wait over to the side a bit, not starin' or clearin' my throat or anything. Josy's been teachin' me grown-up manners and all. But I cain't help listenin' even if I ain't starin'.

Mr. Macafee and Mrs. Linder are whisperin', but it sounds urgent-like, and I can hear them talkin' 'bout a crash and money, and I wonder if Margaret Ann's family got in a car crash and that's why ain't none of them home. But that don't explain why the dogs ain't there. Maybe they had to take the dogs to the animal doctor in Knoxville. Sometimes the animal doctor comes out to the farm when we got a problem with one of our animals. Like the time one of the cows was birthin' a calf and somethin' wasn't right.

Mrs. Linder finally folds up her sack of whatever she bought and says goodbye and turns to leave, smilin' at me on her way out. "Hi, Miss June. Lovely to see you out so early this morning," she says. Mrs. Linder buys Mama's sewing sometimes. "I hear your mama's not feeling too good, so you tell her I said to get well."

"I will, Mrs. Linder." I smile real big at her, 'cause when Mrs. Linder smiles, every single tooth in her mouth shows, and I wonder if it hurts her mouth to smile that big. Her teeth almost make me forget what I was 'bout to ask Mr. Macafee, but when he hollers hello at me, I remember.

"Mr. Macafee," I say, scooting up to the counter. "What's goin' on at the bank? Why's near everybody in town lined up out there like that?"

Mr. Macafee frowns and sighs. "Well, Junebug," (He calls me Junebug. I cain't remember a time he didn't call me Junebug.) "the stock market crash got everybody in a tizzy." I musta scrunched up my face or somethin', 'cause he clears his throat and explains. "People are anxious to get their money outa the bank before all the banks run out. It's happening all over the state – the country, even."

11

I think about that for a spell, then nod and amble over to the sewin' supplies shelf, still wonderin' what all that means. It musta been a pretty big crash to make all those people wanna take their money outa the bank. Again I wonder if Margaret Ann's family was involved.

I cain't imagine how all the banks could run outa money. I may be almost twelve, but I don't know much about how bankin' works and where the money comes from and where it goes. I got a piggy bank Daddy gave me when I was just about five years old. I think I got at least thirty pennies in it, plus a nickel or two. I wish I had enough to share with all those people lined up at the bank. I'm thinkin' so hard about money that I forget what I'm supposed to be gettin' for Mama. Mr. Macafee comes up beside me, and that's when I remember, 'cause he says, "Your mama need more thread, Junebug?"

I pick out three spools – two white and one yellow.

"Here, let me package those up for ya," Mr. Macafee says.

I find myself dawdlin', lookin' at the sewing patterns hangin' on hooks at the end of the shelf. Flowery blouses, flowy dresses, and a ruffly apron. That one catches my eye 'cause it don't look like any apron Mama has made before. "This new, Mr. Macafee?"

He nods from the counter. "Just got that in yesterday, matter of fact. Think your mama'd like it?"

I finger the coins in my pocket and wish I had brought some of my piggy bank money. "How much is it?"

"That one's forty-five cents."

I let out a low whistle. That's almost twice as much as the other patterns. I turn to go back up to the front of the store, not wanting to take my eyes offa that apron pattern. Mama'd sure like that.

"This is all I got," I tell Mr. Macafee, my coins tinklin' down onto the counter. "And I still need to go next door and get flour and sugar."

"Tell you what, Junebug," Mr. Macafee says real quiet-like. "You go get that pattern and take it to your mama. I'll write down what you owe, and you can bring it next time."

"Really, Mr. Macafee?"

I don't even wait for him to nod; I just run right back over to the pattern hooks and grab the envelope with the frilly apron on the front, then run back over to the counter. "Thank you, Mr. Macafee, really, thank you! Mama will be so happy! We'll pay you just as soon as we come back to town."

Mr. Macafee chuckles and says, "Of course, Junebug. No worries. No worries at all. I know your mama will be good for it. She doesn't normally run a tab."

After he puts the pattern in a sack with the thread and hands it to me, I think about the line of people at the bank, and I ask, "How come you ain't in that line? Don't you need to get your money out?"

He leans way over toward me and says, "You know, June, I'll be honest with ya." And now he's whisperin' like he's tellin' me a secret, and that makes me feel real special. "I think those people may be overreacting, and I think everything's gonna be just fine." Then he smiles from ear to ear and tells me to say hello to Mama and Daddy for him.

I grab my shoppin' sack and skip next door to the Piggly Wiggly. The flour and sugar take all the rest of my money, and it sure seems like the price of things is gone way up. When I walk back by the bank, I notice the line is gone. I peek in the doors and see everyone inside at the teller's desk, and they still don't look none too pleased. I decide I'll ask Daddy about it when I get home. I don't remember Mama and Daddy sayin' anything about gettin' our money outa the bank.

When I pass back by Margaret Ann's house, their car is still gone and the hounds are still gone, too, so I chew my cheeks and wonder where they went and when they're comin' back.

Margaret Ann is the best best friend I could ever ask for. I cain't remember a time when we weren't friends. In school, we sit next to each other every chance we get, 'til Miss Glass makes us separate 'cause we giggle too much. At lunch and recess, we eat together and walk together and spy on Jimmy Mack together. (Jimmy Mack is only the cutest boy in Union County.)

Margaret Ann's daddy let me ride in their car two times, and Margaret Ann is always excited to ride in our wagon for some reason, even though ridin' in a car is about a hundred times more fascinating than ridin' in a mule wagon. Margaret Ann is good at math, so she helps me with my math work, and I help her with readin' 'cause that's surely my favorite thing in the world besides watchin' nature.

And I'm thinkin' so hard about school and Margaret Ann that I almost step right on a king snake. I yelp and jump about a mile high, and he slithers real fast-like over to the creek, where he belongs. I know I said I love nature, but I can do without snakes forever and ever. Even though the ones by the barn keep the rats away. But they also go after the chickens and their eggs, so it's six in one hand, a half-dozen in the other, as Daddy likes to say.

The wind picks up and thunder rumbles in the distance, so I run the rest of the way home, as fast as my worn-out little shoes will take me, wishin' I had knotted my long hair up in a bun. By the time I get home, it's a tangled mess.

The fourth strange thing happens when I get home. I run in the front door, lettin' the screen door slam the way Mama always tells me not to, but I cain't wait to show her the apron pattern I brung her. I bound over to Mama, who's sittin' at her sewin' table. She stops the spinning wheel and looks up, her hazel green eyes smilin' just as big as her mouth.

"Mama, I got your thread and lookwhatelseIgotforyou!" It comes out in one big jumble of words, I'm so excited, and I thrust the apron pattern into her hands.

And here's the strange thing, and I think it must be stranger than the line of people at the bank. Mama's smile turns into a frown, a real serious and sad frown. She holds the pattern, her thumb runnin' over the picture of the frilly apron on the front. "How much did this cost, baby girl?"

And I know somethin' is really wrong, 'cause Mama only calls me baby girl when there's some kinda bad news she's 'bout to tell me. It's what she called me that day I'll never forget three years ago when she told me I wasn't gonna have a baby sister no more, and her stomach went flat, and then she cried and cried for two weeks straight.

"Forty-five cents, but Mr. Macafee said we can bring him the money ..." and I don't even finish, 'cause the look on Mama's face is scarin' me.

"June," Mama says, "we gotta start bein' real careful with our spendin' money." Her eyes lock on mine. "We have to tighten our belts."

I'm pretty sure I know what she means, but I ain't even got a belt, and at least with this pattern she can make aprons and sell 'em for a whole lot more than forty-five cents. I tell her so, and that's when I start to understand about the stock market crash.

"June, people are losin' their jobs and businesses all over the country. And even here in our small piece of Tennessee, people are startin' to feel it. They're scared. Not too many ladies want to buy my aprons or quilts or bonnets right now."

"Is that why they were lined up at the bank this mornin'?"

Mama flinches and blinks. "What?" She grabs my shoulders and asks with a shake, "What did you say?"

My voice is wobbly 'cause she's scarin' me somethin' awful now. "They– a whole bunch of folks from Maynardville was lined up outside the bank this mornin'. Mr. Macafee said they all wanted to get their money outa the bank before it runs out."

Mama lets out a small cry and lowers her head, her hands goin' up to her pale face, gettin' paler by the second.

"But Mr. Macafee said he thinks they're overreactin' and that everything's gonna be just fine. He said so." I want Mama to say the same thing, but she doesn't.

"Mama, are we gonna have to get our money out too?"

She doesn't answer me, but she stands up, smooths out her skirt and heads out the door to the barn, where I know Daddy and Josy are, and I think I hear her say on her way out, "It may be too late."

3

Secrets

When Mama and Daddy come back, me and Josy are sittin' at the kitchen table playin' with a big ol' jar of marbles. Them marbles is one of my favorite things in the world. I love lookin' at the swirls of colors melting into each other. I love the feel of 'em when I dip my hand in the jar to scoop a bunch out, the clicking sound they make as they knock together, the weight of 'em in my hand, the silky smoothness of them as they roll in my palm, the clunk-clunk-clunk as I drop them gently to the table and hold out my arms to stop them as they roll every which way.

Me and Josy made up a game with the marbles. First we divvy 'em up so's we each have the same amount – 'cept there's an odd number, so I close my eyes and pluck one out of the pile and put it back in the jar, then set the jar under the table where we cain't see it. Then, without lookin', we each grab a marble from our pile and hold it up at the same time, and whoever has the prettiest marble wins both of 'em. And we keep goin' like that 'til one person has all the marbles.

17

Most of the time, it's clear enough which marble is prettier, 'cause there's always one that stands out for some reason or 'nother. Today my favorite one has blue and green swirls, like water meetin' God's green earth, and it makes me think of peace and calm. But last time we played, my favorite was one that's so clear you can almost see through it, 'cept for an orange and white swirl right in the center that reminds me of the orange ice cream they got at the Sweet Shop & Soda Stop in town, which I ain't had in so long it makes my mouth water just lookin' at that marble.

Sometimes it ain't so easy to decide who has the prettiest marble. If Mama or Daddy ain't busy, we let one of them be the judge, but most of the time, we just argue and argue 'til one of us finally says, "Okay, you take 'em then!" The best part of the game comes at the end, when we're down to one marble left each. Whoever is losin' can choose to use the extra marble we hid away in the jar under the table instead of the one they got left, and with that'n, they can win the whole lot. It's a gamble, 'cause we weren't lookin' when we put the extra marble in the jar, so we don't know what it's gonna be. Truth is, though, we been playin' with these marbles so long, we 'bout got 'em memorized, so if we's payin' attention, we know exactly which marble is in that jar.

Josy's gloatin' about winnin' a round with a flashy purple and blue marble against my plain cloudy white and gray one when the screen door screeches open and we look up to see Mama, pale as ever, and Daddy, straight-faced and tense behind her.

They stand there a moment before Josy says, "Well, what happened?" (Josy thinks just 'cause he's fifteen he's grown up, so he ain't afraid to just come right out and ask about what happened at the bank.)

Daddy's holdin' a piece of paper so tightly that it's crinkled and creased on the one end. He holds it out toward Josy, who scrambles up outa the chair and goes to look at it. I look at Mama with questions in my eyes, and she looks about ready to pass out. "The bank's all out of money," she says, barely above a whisper, grabbin' for a chair to sink into. "It's closed down."

Daddy pats Mama on the shoulder all calmin'-like and says, "They gave us an IOU. Said to try the bank in Knoxville. Otherwise … could be weeks, months before we can get our money."

And here's where it gets real scary, 'cause brave, brave Josy has tears in his eyes, and then I look at Mama, and she's cryin', then everybody's cryin', includin' me, even though I don't understand what any of this means, and all I want is for Josy to sit back down here and finish our game of marbles.

And just then, lightning flashes and the sky opens up. It rains and rains and rains.

Spring and summer on the farm are downright busy, the busiest, most hard-workin' times of the year. Me and Josy stay home from school startin' in April and we don't go back 'til after the fall harvest in August. We already planted the carrots and onions, corn, strawberries, and green beans. Now we're harvestin' the strawberries and it's almost time to harvest the green beans. After that, we get a little bit of a break before we have to harvest the first batch of corn, then the carrots and onions and the second batch of corn, and I'm tellin' you, it is hard work full of sweat, dirt, and not a whole lotta sleep or play. So me and Josy try to have fun whenever we can.

There's a creek that runs behind the house where we do the washin', and thank God for that creek, 'cause in the hot summer, me and Josy splash around in it to cool off, and we splash each other too, and get to gigglin' so much that Mama comes stompin' outa the house tellin' us to get back to work. Sometimes during plantin', we play hide-and-seek or Marco-Polo in the corn field 'til Daddy comes to find us and hollers for us to get back to work. And sometimes when we're workin' in the field or in the barn, Josy pulls a handful of pretzels outa his pocket and we sit on a haystack and savor the taste, salt-side down on our tongues, until someone tells us to get back to work.

We each got chores aside from the gardening, too. I milk the cows, churn the butter, help Mama with the washin' and the sewin' and the cookin'. Josy cleans the barn, feeds the animals, and helps Daddy with the fixin' and the buildin' and the sellin'.

And when we ain't in school, Mama makes us study and practice our readin' and writin'. I don't mind that one bit, 'cause I love readin', but Josy'd much rather be sleepin' or out carvin' wood or somethin'. He's teachin' me how to whittle things from pieces of pine with a pocketknife. I've whittled a duck head and a turtle, and I intend to keep workin' on the turtle 'til it's perfect, and then I can give it to Daddy for a Christmas gift.

Josy says I'm a natural born whittler, and it makes me feel real proud when he says things like that. Most people treat girls like we're small and cain't do things, but not Josy. Josy makes me believe I'm a giant, always has.

I remember when I was little, he used to lift me up to pick fruit off the pawpaw trees over by the barn, and he'd hold me up so high. That patch of pawpaw trees has always been one of Josy's favorite places in the world to go. In the fall before it gets too cold, we pick the fruit and sit up under their shade and eat 'em right then and there, and we pretend we're on a tropical island, the tangy juice of the pawpaw fruit drippin' down our chins.

We got secrets, me and Josy. Every strawberry season, when we go out pickin', we look for the reddest, plumpest, sweetest lookin' one, and instead of droppin' it in our buckets, Josy cuts it in half, and we prop ourselves up against the fence, and we eat that strawberry together, savoring the velvety sweetness of it. Then we wipe our mouths off with a rag we carry in our pockets, and every single time, Josy holds up a finger to his lips, like "Shh, don't tell no one," like it's our top secret.

On Saturdays during the harvest, we load up the wagon with sacks of all the vegetables we got, jars of peaches, tins of strawberries, packets of butter I churned myself, and baskets of eggs (minus the bit we pack in the cellar for ourselves), and we all four of us head out to the farmer's market, which is in a big field a little ways from Macafee's. Mama also brings aprons and bonnets and whatnot that me and her sewed, and Daddy packs whatever he and Josy built that can fit in the wagon, like small stools and medicine boxes.

Daddy drives Molly, and Mama sits right beside him, and me and Josy scrunch up in the back with all the food, and that always used to be a real tight fit 'cause the wagon was packed full. Nowadays, we got room to spare 'cause we got less and less to sell – fewer crops are growin' and Mama's doin' less sewing, and I don't mind none 'cause that just means there's more room in the wagon for me and Josy to stretch out 'steada bein' all cramped up.

But this time Josy looks worried, and he don't talk much the whole way into town. And he don't sing like he does when it's just me and him, neither.

"Whatcha thinkin' about, Josy?" I ask him, and I absent-mindedly reach for a strawberry, like we always do every time we ride to market, and Josy puffs up and reaches out and slaps the strawberry from my hand and back into the tin, and he yells, "Put that back, June!"

"What'd you do that for?" It don't hurt none, but the surprise of it stings, so I'm starin' at him with my mouth wide open.

"This stuff's to sell at the market, you know that."

"But we always eat a strawberry or two on our ride into town."

"We cain't do that no more, June," Josy says, all serious-like. "We need every penny we can get now, and don't you forget that." Then he looks away and I'm still shocked, and we don't say another word the whole rest of the way.

After sittin' all the livelong day at the market and watchin' so few folks come through shoppin' and then seein' how much we still have left on the ride home, I see I coulda eaten that strawberry and it wouldn'ta made no difference anyhow. Josy sees it too, and the look in his eyes says *I'm sorry, but still.* Then he hands me a purple coneflower he musta found in the grass at the market, and he smiles, and I smile 'cause purple is my most favorite color in the whole world, and I weave the long stem into my hair and tuck it behind my ear.

Long Saturdays at the market, and packin' up the bit that didn't sell, then helpin' with supper and evenin' chores leaves me plumb tired and lookin' forward to Sunday. I cain't remember a time that Sunday wasn't my most favorite day of the week.

The first thing I love about Sunday is that we get dressed up in our only nice clothes and shoes, which we call our Sunday dress 'cause there ain't no other time 'cept maybe a funeral or a weddin' that we wear our Sunday dress. And we climb into the wagon and go to church, and I love church 'cause we see all our friends from town and school and all around Maynardville, and it's like a big ol' family reunion, and we all cram into the little ol' Lutheran church, where we pray and kneel and sing and kneel and stand and kneel over and over again until it's over. And that's the best part, 'cause when it's over, there's almost always a box of doughnuts for the children in the sanctuary, and we eat a doughnut and chase each other around while the grown-ups visit. Then we ride home feelin' so refreshed like Jesus done washed all our cares away, and that's a feelin' that I won't never forget.

Sundays on the farm are for restin' and relaxin'. We still gotta tend to the animals and wash the clothes, but besides that, we just sprawl out on the porch, try to tune somethin' in on our old battery-powered radio, and sip on some fresh-squeezed lemonade that Mama makes.

Other times we splash around in the creek, pick gooseberries at the edge of the woods, or fly kites that we make from Mama's scrap cloth and switches we find on the ground. They don't generally fly much, but it's still fun tryin'. In the evenings we sit on the edge of the porch, swingin' our legs, and we watch the purple-orange sun sink behind cotton candy clouds.

And every Sunday night, after the biggest supper of the week, when we say our prayers and tuck into bed, I pray that every day could be like Sunday. But then I wake up and it's Monday, and I say *Aw, crumbs!* and there's so much work to do.

Like I said, it's my job to milk the cows, but one of 'em is so ornery, she huffs and puffs and stomps her hooves like she's havin' a downright temper tantrum, and sometimes she looks at me like I'm the devil, and she won't give me no milk. I call her Miss Priss. I don't know what she got against me, but I don't want to disappoint Daddy, so I keep tryin', and I talk all nice-like to her and try to settle her, which works sometimes, but other times it's just no use.

On those days, Josy comes and takes over for me. He sends me out to feed the goats, which is fine by me, 'cause I got me a favorite goat – Li'l Belle – and she sees me comin' up the hill and starts runnin' toward me, never mind that I got the bucket full of feed. She butts her little head up against my hip and sings, and I sing right back to her. When Josy's done with Miss Priss, he comes up the hill and we trade buckets, and he holds up one finger to his lips, "Shh," like it's a secret he done my chore for me, and I trudge down the hill to the cellar with my bucket of milk.

About the middle of June, me and Josy are workin' our way down the rows of green beans, squattin' down and snappin' 'em off the vines and plunkin' 'em into our buckets. It's quiet and warm this morning. Mama's in the house sewin' and cannin' and cookin' up a strawberry pie, all at the same time, and I think it's amazin' how she can do everything she does, and I hope one day I can be an amazin' mama just like her. Daddy's over at the barn, patchin' up the side where some of the wood's rotted out. All's we can hear is the distant ping of a hammer, the songbirds, and the whistle of the wind in the trees.

Pickin' green beans is real tiring 'cause we're down on our knees or hunched over in a squat, and our backs and legs start to ache, and our hands get sore, even with gloves on. It's hard work that takes a long time, but it's quiet and peaceful. There's lots of time to think when you're pickin' green beans, and that's why I'm thinkin' about the bank and the IOU.

"Josy," I say, when we're gettin' close to halfway down the rows, "what's gonna happen to us? I mean, with the bank and all?"

Josy stands and shakes dirt offa his gloves and says, "Aw, Junie, you ain't gotta worry 'bout that now. Everything's gonna be fine."

"That's what Mr. Macafee said that day the bank closed down, but then all them people at the bank looked real angry-like, and you and Mama and Daddy was cryin'. Shoot, even ol' Mr. Tomlinson looked mighty worried 'bout somethin', and I don't think it was the weather."

Josy winks at me, then scoots over and pinches my shoulder. "You're too smart for your own good, Junie June." But his smile fades then, and he squats down to pick more beans while he talks. "Things are gonna change around here, and it may be scary for a time. But we'll be alright."

I kneel down beside him. "Are we gonna lose all our money?"

"Stop it now, that ain't gonna happen."

"But—"

"Just keep pickin'. Get back to work, now." Then he reaches down to grasp a bean, but instead comes up with a bug perched on his finger. He holds it up in front of my face. It's a perfectly round, perfectly red ladybug, and it looks like it's lookin' right at me. I extend my finger to touch it, and it flutters its little wings and flies right up and lands on my shoulder.

"That's good luck, June," Josy says. "You remember that."

Later that day, I'm in the kitchen helpin' Mama can peaches from the trees out back, and Josy hops in like a jackrabbit.

"Hey, June, I'm takin' Molly to town to the feed store. Wanna come?"

I jump up and down like a kid on a pogo stick. "Can I, Mama? Can I?"

Mama rolls her eyes and sighs, then pops me playfully with a kitchen towel. "Go ahead. I'll finish up here. But you got some math to do when you get back, don't forget." And I'm takin' off my apron and runnin' toward the door faster than a fox toward a chicken coop.

"Joseph, wait," Mama calls to Josy. She digs some coins outa her coin purse and hands 'em to Josy. "Can you pick up a can of baking powder and a roll of tinfoil?"

"Sure thing, Mama," Josy says, and he kisses her on the cheek, and then we're climbin' into the wagon.

Josy pops the reins and Molly ambles off, and not two seconds later, Josy turns to me with a sneaky smile and says, "You know where we're sittin', Junie?"

It's another one of our secrets, thanks to our rickety, staticky ol' radio, and I smile real big and say, "Why, Josy, we're sittin' on top of the world, we are." And then we're singin' our favorite song, by the Mississippi Sheiks, and just hummin' when we don't know the words, which is most of it, truthfully. But all's we need to know is that it's about bein' happy, and these days we can use a little more happy in the world.

We're singin' and hummin' all the way to Margaret Ann's house, and I beg Josy to let me hop down and run up to her porch and check to see if she's back yet, but their car still ain't there and everything looks dark and lonely even though it's the middle of a bright summer day, and I fret the rest of the way into town, 'cause what if Margaret Ann don't never come back?

Goin' into town with Josy is one of my favorite things to do, 'cause he lets me go into the Sweet Shop, and even though we cain't buy nothin', I breathe in the sugary scents and look at all the colors of candy and sodas and ice cream, and sometimes, if Miss Jane is workin', she lets me have a little taste of somethin' for free. Thinkin' about the Sweet Shop is the only thing that takes my mind offa Margaret Ann.

When we get to the feed store, Josy loops Molly up to a hitchin' post and we go inside. Both me and Josy stop short and stare in shock when we see that many of the shelves are bare.

"Heya, Joseph, June," Mr. Clay nods to us, and we nod back, unsmilin'. I ain't sure what to say, and I can tell Josy ain't neither. I cain't remember a time when the feed store looked this empty.

"Mr. Clay," Josy says as he steps to the counter. "You got a bag of chicken feed?"

"Only just," Mr. Clay says. "Down to my last bag."

"I ain't never seen it this empty," Josy says, lookin' around the small store while I stand there fidgeting. I feel all nervous-like, and I ain't sure why.

"Welp, that's the way of things now-days, I guess. Lemme throw this in your wagon for ya." Mr. Clay heaves the bag up over a shoulder and we leave the money on the counter and walk out to the wagon.

"Thanks, Mr. Clay," we say at the same time.

"Yep. Y'all take care, now."

Me and Josy look at each other, wide-eyed and disbelieving.

"Why's it so empty?" I ask Josy.

He shrugs. "Let's just go get Mama's bakin' powder and go on."

When we step into the Piggly Wiggly, I 'bout have a heart attack, 'cause the grocery store looks almost as empty as the feed store, and I can feel that emptiness in the pit of my stomach. We walk together to the bakin' goods aisle, and it looks darn-near empty, just a few boxes of some mix or another, some oil, and one bag of powdered sugar, but we don't see no bakin' powder or tinfoil. Me and Josy look at each other with worried and confused eyes.

"Come on, June," Josy says, "Let's see if Macafee's has what we need."

Macafee's Market generally has tools and cleanin' supplies and paper goods and things you cain't find at Piggly Wiggly, and I don't expect to see bakin' powder and tinfoil there, but then again, after what I seen, I don't rightly know what to expect, so I follow Josy to Macafee's.

"Hiya, Junebug," Mr. Macafee says when we bound through the open door into the hot store. Mr. Macafee's got all the windows open, but there ain't no breeze. "Hiya, Joseph. What can I do for ya?"

Our eyes scan the market shelves, and my shoulders sag when I see so much emptiness here too.

"We need a can of bakin' powder, sir," Josy says.

Mr. Macafee shakes his head. "I'm sorry, son, but I don't carry baking powder. Got to go next door for that," and he tilts his head toward the Piggly Wiggly.

"They're all out, Mr. Macafee," Josy says. "What about tinfoil? Got any of that?"

Mr. Macafee clicks his tongue. "I usually do keep a few rolls of tinfoil around, but I'm all out."

"Mr. Macafee, why's it so empty everywhere?" I ask.

"The cost of things has gone up so much, it's gettin' harder to get food and supplies here," Mr. Macafee says, "and folks buy it up so fast. All the shops 'round here are hurtin', and not just here, neither. Knoxville and Nashville too."

He sees the worry in my face and adds, "But don't you worry, Junebug, it'll turn around. I got a shipment comin' in a few days, and that store next door'll surely be restocked soon too."

I like Mr. Macafee a lot, but I get the feelin' he ain't tellin' the whole truth, and I start to say so, but Josy interrupts me.

"Junie, go on and wait in the wagon for me," Josy says. I turn to go, but my eyes flick over to the sewin' shelf, and I see there ain't but a few spools of thread and maybe a few packs of pins and needles, and there ain't no sewing patterns. My eyes water up and threaten to spill over, and there's an emptiness in the pit of my stomach as I climb up into the wagon. I ain't never seen nothin' like this. It's one thing to not be able to buy what you want at the market 'cause you ain't got much money, but it's a whole 'nother thing entirely to not be able to buy what you need at the market 'cause there's nothin' left. And it makes me scared for our family and even our whole town.

Josy comes outa the store with his hands shoved deep into his pockets, then unhitches Molly and climbs up and takes the reins in one hand. The other hand he holds out to me, fingers closed over somethin'. "Gotcha somethin', Junie." He unfolds his fingers, and in his hand is my most favorite of all time penny candy, a soft, luscious, scrumptious, individually wrapped cube of caramel. I take it and try to smile, but I ain't sure my smile goes all the way to my lips, and it sure don't go all the way to my eyes, 'cause I'm too scared and sad to smile for real, but I unwrap the caramel and pop it into my mouth, and we bump along in the wagon in silence.

We're almost home when I spot somethin' movin' around in the brush on the side of the dirt road. I grab Josy's arm. "Stop the wagon." My eyes are glued to the spot where I saw the movement.

"What is it, June?" Josy gets Molly to slow down and then stop, not that she was goin' that fast in the first place. Molly don't go nowhere fast, and it's a good thing we ain't never been chased by marauders or ne'er-do-wells, 'cause we'd lose that race for sure, with Molly clompin' around slow as a snail.

"I saw somethin' over there, and I want to see what it is." I climb down and tiptoe over to the spot, and that's when I hear it. A soft, tiny cry.

Josy comes bouncin' up behind me, makin' all kindsa noise with his boots. "What is—"

"Shhh!" I shush him and flap my hand at him. "Listen. You hear that?"

We crouch down in the tall grass and listen, our ears pointed toward the brush and thorny woods. Whatever it is cries again, and our eyes follow the sound, and that's when I see it – a teeny tiny baby kitten, fluffy and gray, just sittin' there in the leafy underbrush at the edge of the woods, and I scoop it up and pull it to my chest.

"Awwww, look at him!"

Josy looks about as dewy-eyed as I feel, and he scratches the baby's head and ears, and it's shakin' like a leaf, and I just know this is a sign from God that this little kitten needs me and I need it, and I say, "Josy, we have to take him home and take care of him, or he'll starve to death out here. He ain't got no mama!"

"June," Josy says, all serious-like, "you know we can't keep this cat. Mama and Daddy won't allow it. How we gonna feed it? You saw what the stores were like, never mind the fact we ain't got extra money to be wastin' on no cat."

"But, Josy, he'll die!"

Josy looks around, fists on his hips, like he's lookin' for the kitten's mama.

"Come on, Josy," I beg, "we can keep him in the corner of the barn, by the haystacks, and I'll feed him milk 'til he's big enough to have a little of my dinner scraps. And then soon he'll be big enough to chase the barn mice, and Mama and Daddy'll be grateful for that."

I'm nuzzlin' the kitten under my chin and battin' my eyes up at Josy and pokin' my bottom lip out, 'cause I know how to persuade Josy of anything that way. He's shakin' his head, and he's clickin' his tongue and sighin', but then Molly gets impatient like she's gonna head on home without us, so Josy finally throws up his hands and says, "Come on."

We get in the wagon, and I nestle the kitten into an empty feed sack, and I cuddle it and cuddle it, all the while Josy's shakin' his head, but there's a hint of a smile on his face. I decide to name the kitten Bug, 'cause I'm June, and this is my kitten, and together we're June and Bug, and that fits just right, and thinkin' about havin' my very own kitten all of a sudden like this makes me forget about the scary emptiness of the feed store and the grocery store and Macafee's Market, and for a while, I feel like everything is gonna be just fine.

Josy drives Molly right up to the barn, and I scamper down and set up the kitten's home with haystacks for walls. Then I run into the cellar and fetch a bowl and pour some milk in it, and I grab a little wool blanket so the baby'll have somethin' soft to lay on. I scurry back to the barn as fast as I can without spillin' the bowl of milk, and I breathe a sigh of relief when I get there and see the baby kitten, cute as can be, curled up in the corner, just sleepin'. And there's Josy leanin' up against the wall, arms crossed like he's mad, but he's just grinnin' and watchin' me and Bug.

This is another one of our top secrets.

4

Everything's Different

July comes and goes like a whirlwind, and if it wasn't for the Maynardville Fourth of July Picnic, we wouldn'ta slowed down at all, 'cause besides harvestin' the vegetable crops, cannin' fruit with Mama, milkin' cows, doin' the washin' and everything else there is to be done, we have to start preparing for winter soon. But nobody in Maynardville ever misses the Fourth of July Picnic, no sir. Everybody in town and lotsa folks outside of town bring somethin', and we all get together in the field by Macafee's.

Mr. Tomlinson always brings a big ol' tent, and Mrs. Tomlinson hands out paper fans she makes herself. Mrs. Linder brings the best desserts (and the best gossip), and Mr. Clay brings horseshoes, and once the fellas get started playin' that, it gets real competitive. Jimmy Mack and some of the other boys set up a stage and play the fiddle and the trumpet, and all the kids dance the Lindy Hop (or at least try to) 'til we're too tired and thirsty, so we sit and eat watermelon and sip lemonade.

Then as soon as the sun even thinks about settin', the firecrackers and the sparklers come out, and by that time, the grown-ups done smoked so many cigarettes and drank so much hooch (secretly made by Mr. Clay, don't tell the sheriff) that they're wobblin' around and singin' at full volume, and the whole thing is just enough cheer to make us forget about farm work and hard times and sad times.

But the fifth of July always jumps up and bites us in the rear end, as Daddy likes to say, and it's back to work. On top of all the work I gotta do, I have to look after Bug in secret. I sneak over to his corner of the barn every chance I get, and I feed him milk 'til he can eat scraps, and I brush him and play with him, and I even make him a toy out of a little jingle bell I got from a Christmas wreath in a box in the shed. I wrap it in a small piece of scrap cloth from Mama's fabric basket and stitch it shut. Before I close it all the way, I stuff in a few crumbles of sun-dried oregano from Mama's herb garden.

Nobody ever suspects about Bug almost the whole month of July. But he gets so big he can jump right up on the haystacks and go anywhere he wants to go in the barn. Sometimes I go in there in the mornin' and find him curled up under Miss Priss, and it's a wonder she don't stomp him to death, 'cause that ol' heifer's just as ornery as can be.

But one day, 'bout the end of July, Josy and me are sittin' at the kitchen table finishin' up breakfast, when Daddy comes into the house. He got a shovel in one hand and he's holdin' Bug like a football in the other. "Why's there a cat tryin' to get into my chicken coop?" Daddy asks.

I gulp and look at Josy, and Josy looks at me, and Daddy's lookin' from me to Josy and back to me again, and finally, I say, "Why would I know anything 'bout that?"

Then Daddy leans the shovel up against the wall and reaches into the big pocket of his overalls. "I found this in the barn," he says and pulls out the toy I made for Bug. "Along with a whole lotta smelly cat mess."

My eyes go real big and Josy shrugs and sighs and says, "Junie, you might as well fess up now."

I drop my shoulders and turn to Daddy, who, incidentally, don't look mad at all, so I take that as a good sign. "Daddy, that's a poor little kitten we found stranded in the road, and he was all alone with no mama, and he coulda died, so Josy and me rescued him, and I been takin' good care of him all month long. Please can we keep him, Daddy?" I flash my best sweet, innocent, beggin' look.

Daddy plops Bug and the toy down into my lap. "Sorry to disappoint you, June," he says, and all of a sudden, I feel like cryin' 'cause I know he's gonna say we cain't keep him, but instead he says, "but this cat's not a *he*, it's a *she*. And if she helps keep snakes and rodents away, I'm mighty obliged to her." Then he looks at me and points, all serious-like and adds, "But don't let her get in my way." Then he grabs his shovel and trudges out the door. Before I have time to squeal for joy, I hear him holler, "And keep her away from my chickens!"

I hold the kitty up to my face and tickle her nose with mine. "Bug! You're a girl!" I squeeze her close in my arms and Josy's laughin' and I'm so happy I could dance, and that's just what I do. I carry Bug like a baby and waltz out the door with her toward the barn, and Josy's laughin' so hard I can hear him all the way there. Or maybe that's just the happiness in my head and in my heart.

I'm mighty relieved to not have to sneak around with Bug no more. That was a right hard secret to keep. And it'd be especially hard now that the harvesting season is over and me and Josy are goin' back to school.

This whole summer I been checkin' on Margaret Ann and still ain't seen her, and after a while, I got so used to her bein' gone, and I was so busy that I forgot to worry 'bout it. So on me and Josy's first day back to school in the second week of August, I'm surprised as a newborn chickadee when I see Margaret Ann standin' out at the end of the lane, just awaitin' on me. I run as fast as I can to close the distance between us, and we just about knock each other down with our hugs and we talk all at once, her sayin' it's so good to see me, and me askin' where she's been, and Josy hollers from the road, "You two don't be late, now." And he walks on ahead.

I have so many questions for Margaret Ann, I don't even know where to start. First thing I see is their car ain't behind her in the drive where they usually park it, and the second thing I see – or don't see, more like it – is the dogs ain't jumpin' around in the yard. And the third thing I see is all her little brothers and sisters ain't crowdin' around to walk with us to school, which is two blocks down the road from their house. But first I want to know where she's been and why she's been gone so long. So we start walkin', and I start askin'.

"Where you been, Margaret Ann? You been gone so long, and I sure did miss you!"

Margaret Ann looks down, a little sad-like, like all her spark done burned out. "We went out to stay with my aunt and uncle in Memphis for a while, that's all."

She looks like she don't wanna say much more, but I'm burnin' up with questions, and I want to know everything, but

I say, "Well, I'm just so thrilled you're back, and I hope you don't never stay gone that long again!"

I look behind us and still don't see Jenny May or Say-Lynn or any of the boys, so I ask, "Where's your brothers and sisters?" and at the very same time, Margaret Ann is askin' me, "How's Josy been?" But I know ain't nothin' changed a bit with Josy, and there ain't a single reason why I need to answer that question 'fore she answers my question, so I just look at her, and we're walkin' slowly, and she's pickin' at a blade of grass she's holdin', and then she drops the grass and turns to look at me, and she got tears in her eyes.

"Daddy lost his job at the mill," Margaret Ann says, and her voice is so quiet I scoot up closer to her so's our shoulders are almost touchin'. "That happened back in March, and we been gettin' by, but he hasn't been able to find work…" Her voice trails off and she's just starin' off into nothin', and I'm confused 'cause that don't answer my question 'bout where all her brothers and sisters at.

I'm lookin' at Margaret Ann lookin' all sad, and I'm scared for her, and then she says, "Jenny May and Say-Lynn and Michael Ray are stayin' with my Aunt and Uncle in Memphis. And the little ones are stayin' with other relatives around there. Daddy took a train out west to try to find work, and he won't be back likely 'til Christmas. So it's just me and Mama here now."

And just like that, we're at the stoop of the schoolhouse and Miss Glass is hollerin' for us to come in, and I don't have even a second to think about everything Margaret Ann just said or even to squeeze her hand or tell her it's gonna be alright.

I step into the schoolhouse, which always feels a bit strange after bein' gone so long, but this time the strangeness is the strangest it's ever been. The school looks the same, but inside, things feel different. The first thing I notice is that Miss Glass is rushin' around settin' out biscuits and sausages on all the desks, and she's hummin' a happy tune while she's doin' it. Now, Miss Glass always been known for hummin', but she ain't never served food at school before. She looks up and sees me starin', and she says, "Welcome back, Miss June! I made some breakfast for everybody. Homemade biscuits and sausages cooked just right. Come sit down."

I find my usual seat next to Margaret Ann, and that's when I notice the next strange thing. Everybody in the school, includin' Margaret Ann, looks like skin and bones, and I don't remember any one of them bein' so skinny.

There's fifteen of us, now that Margaret Ann's brothers and sisters ain't here, and half the kids look like the cat drug 'em in, and some of them ain't wearin' shoes. Most of 'em are shovelin' the biscuits and sausages into their mouths like it's the only meal they gonna get all day, and that makes me think of how lucky me and Josy are that we live on a farm, and we got enough food, even when the store shelves are empty. We get by; Mama and Daddy see to that. And as I slowly pick at my biscuit and sausage, I wonder if I can bring some food from home to share, like Miss Glass does.

Margaret Ann nudges me with her elbow, and I snap outa the trance I musta been in, and everybody's finished with their breakfast but me, and I let Margaret Ann eat mine.

Every day after that, Josy and me bring a little somethin' from home, and we share it with all the kids, and we give 'em our share of what Miss Glass brings, 'cause it surely looks like they need it a whole lot more than we do. And Mama sews some moccasins outa feed sacks and hog hide that we had in the cellar, and I bring those for the kids that come to school barefoot. It ain't the same as real shoes, but at least it's somethin'. Me and Josy been puttin' cardboard in the soles of ours 'cause there's holes in 'em, but at least we got somethin' to wear. None of the kids mind takin' handouts, 'cause, as Miss Glass says, we all in this together, and we all here to help one another the best we can.

Pretty soon, Miss Glass cain't bring breakfast no more 'cause her pay got cut, and I worry 'bout what'll happen to all the kids, and me and Josy try to bring as much as we can, but shoot, it just ain't enough to go around.

I get back into the routine of school real fast. I cain't remember a time I didn't love school. I love the smell of freshly sharpened pencils, notebooks, and textbooks. I love the sound the wooden chairs make when they scrape across the wood floors, and I love the sound of Miss Glass writin' on the chalkboard.

Some of these things are different now too, though. We ain't got new pencils, and there's only a few good ones left, so everybody scrambles to get to the good ones first, and then pairs of kids end up sharing one pencil. But most of the time, not everybody makes it to school. The Paulsen brothers live the farthest away, clear down to Luttrell, so they gotta walk more than twice the distance me and Josy do, and they don't always got shoes to wear, and Mama's little ol' moccasins ain't strong enough for them to make that walk every day. So sometimes, they just don't come to school. And Catherine gotta stay home and take care of her little brothers and sisters sometimes. Some days it's just about five or six of us.

Another thing that's different is that we ain't got new books, and our old ones are wearin' out fast. The schoolhouse serves as the Maynardville Library, and the shelf on the side wall that has all the library books is lookin' mighty bare 'cause folks don't always return the books they check out, and no new books have come in for a long time. Even the chalkboard is different 'cause Miss Glass is down to one tiny piece of chalk and one dirty eraser, and the board is all scratched up and stained, and she says she tries to keep it clean, but it's just wore out, and the city cain't give us a new one right now. Times are real hard, she says, but we'll make do with what we have just fine, and I love how cheerful Miss Glass is, no matter what.

One thing that ain't changed one bit is that me and Margaret Ann sit together and work together and spend recess together. We share a pencil, a textbook, and a notebook. And at lunchtime, she shares some of her mama's brownies with me, and I share strawberries or peaches from our farm with her, and we always real happy, even when it don't seem like there's very much to be happy about. We always got somethin' to talk about, too, even when we ain't supposed to be talkin', and Miss Glass gotta get onto us.

"I ain't seen y'all's car. What happened to it?" I ask her one day.

"Daddy had to sell it," Margaret Ann says, "but truthfully we don't need it anyway. We live close enough to town to walk everywhere. It's not like we're country bumpkins livin' way out in the middle of—" She blinks at me like she's worried she hurt my feelings, but I don't mind none. I do wish my family had a car, but we do just fine with Molly and the wagon. Don't need to go nowhere anyhow, do we? Where we gonna go?

Then that gets me thinkin' about Granny in Nashville and how we don't hardly see her no more 'cause she's gettin' too old to travel and we're too busy to travel. And we got cousins and other kin all over Tennessee. They come visit us when they can, and we have the grandest time, wadin' in the creek, chasin' the goats, sittin' out on a picnic blanket under the pawpaw trees eatin' nuts and berries.

I musta looked sad there for a minute, 'cause Margaret Ann grabs my hand and starts talkin' 'bout Jimmy Mack and seein' him in town with his huntin' dogs, which reminds me – "Hey, where are your dogs, Margaret Ann?"

"Oh," she says, lookin' down, "we couldn't keep 'em. Mama said it got too expensive to feed 'em and keep up with 'em." I don't ask her what they did with 'em, 'cause now she looks all sad-like, but I remember to tell her about Bug and how we found him – or *her*, I mean – on the road when she was a itty bitty thing, and now she's our barn cat, and Margaret Ann is so excited 'cause she's always wanted a cat, and we make plans for her to come home with me so she can meet Bug.

And just like that, Miss Glass is on the porch ringin' a bell, and our recess time is over, and we all scramble back into the small schoolhouse, take our seats, and look up to Miss Glass expectantly, 'cause we know it's readin' time now, and that's my favorite time of the whole day, and I know I cain't speak for everybody, but it sure seems like it's everybody else's favorite time of the whole day too.

Miss Glass claps her hands and the young'uns crowd around her for about the fifteenth read-aloud of *The Velveteen Rabbit*, the older ones open their fallin'-apart *Sherlock Holmes*, and us middle ones settle in with our *Sixth-Grade Reader*, and since we're readin', all is right with the world.

5

Sold and Slaughtered

fter school, Josy runs up ahead of us, but me and Margaret Ann mosey along slow as molasses so's we can talk while we walk, swingin' our clasped hands to and fro.

"Do you miss your brothers and sisters?" I ask her, thinkin' 'bout how quiet and lonely it must feel in their house with most everybody gone.

"I miss my sisters the most," she says. "That room sure feels empty now."

Margaret Ann shares a room with her sisters, and the three boys sleep on a blanket in the front room, but in the heat of the summer, they all sleep out on the porch. Now Margaret Ann and her mama got the whole porch to themselves.

"But with them gone, me and Mama have less cookin' and

cleanin' to do, and there's a little more food — not much, but still more."

Then she looks kinda sad and I search her eyes for what she's thinkin', 'cause you can always tell what someone's thinkin' by the way their eyes look — twinkly, teary, cloudy, dark, or blank — especially your best friend. Finally, she says, "I'm real worried about my daddy, most of all. He was desperate to find a job, and he didn't just take a train out west, he *hopped* a train out west."

I musta looked blank or somethin' 'cause she looks at me with wide eyes and says, "Ain't you heard of train-hoppers? They don't have money to buy a ticket, so they sneak on, and it's real dangerous, 'cause they hop on and off when the train is movin'! And sometimes they hop on freight trains that ain't even supposed to have passengers, but they're goin' to try to find work somewheres else."

I cain't believe anyone in their right mind would do such a thing, but Margaret Ann swears that lots of people are doin' it nowadays 'cause they ain't got no choice. I think about that a spell, side-steppin' the spot in the road where I saw that king snake awhile back, even though I know it musta moved on by now — I cain't help but watch for it every time I pass by here. So now I'm thinkin' about trains and snakes, and before I know it, we're walkin' up the lane to the farm, and somethin' ain't right.

The first thing I notice is I don't see the goats on the hill, not a one. And I don't see the cows in the pasture, neither. I listen hard for the sounds of all the animals, and I don't hear a thing but the cluckin' of chickens.

"What's wrong, June?" Margaret Ann asks.

I drop her hand and run toward the barn, and she follows me. Maybe all the animals are snug up in the barn together for some reason. But the only ones in the barn are Miss Priss and the other milkin' cow.

Bug prances over and rubs up against my leg, mewlin' like nobody's business, and Margaret Ann coos and picks her up and hugs her, but the excitement of introducin' her to the cat has left my mind, replaced by confusion and worry.

The second thing I notice is I don't see Molly or the wagon anywhere. I peek around behind the barn, and not only are Molly and the wagon gone, but the pigpen is empty too. "Come on!" I grab Margaret Ann's arm, and she drops Bug, who scampers away, and we run to the house, straight into the kitchen, where Mama's preparin' somethin' for supper.

"Mama!"

"Hi, baby girl," Mama says, and she sees Margaret Ann and says, "Oh, hi, Margaret Ann! I would hug your neck, but I'm covered in raw pork over here. How you been? It's so nice to see you!"

"I'm fine, Mrs. Baker," Margaret Ann says, but I'm pushin' my way over to Mama, my arms out like *What's goin' on here?*

"Where's all the goats and the cows and the pigs?" I practically shout it, and Mama's eyes tell me to simmer down, so I lower my voice and ask again, "Where's the goats and cows and pigs?"

Mama wipes her hands on her apron and says, "Mr. Rowland, from up toward Morristown, came and bought the cows from us, and Daddy and Joseph took the goats to sell to some fella in town."

"And the pigs?"

Mama looks down and then her eyes flick over to the basin and back to me, and that's when I notice that the kitchen basin and the counter's stacked high with raw, bloody meat, and she real quick reaches out and says, "Now, Junie, remember what we been tellin' you about times bein' hard right now."

Tears flood my eyes and I cain't see, and Margaret Ann is shiftin' from one foot to the other, all nervous-like, and Mama looks half like she wants to soothe me and half like she wants to laugh, and I don't understand nothin' but that they gettin' rid of half our animals and slaughterin' the other half.

"Darlin', what'd you think we had them pigs for anyhow, just to look at?" Mama says, and I cross my arms and huff, and I know she's right but that don't make it any easier, and then Margaret Ann pops up and says, "Your cat's real cute, June," and that gives me the perfect opportunity to shout at Mama, "You gonna kill the cat too?" and I stomp off out to the porch, and Margaret Ann follows sullenly behind me, and now our day is ruined.

Margaret Ann stays for supper, and then Daddy and me drive her home in the wagon, and the wagon stinks to high heaven from havin' the goats all crammed in there. Daddy tells me we just couldn't afford to keep all those animals no more and it didn't make sense to anyhow when somebody'd pay good money for 'em.

I argue that we could make cheese and soap from the goats' milk, but Daddy says we got more bars of goats' milk soap in the cellar than we know what to do with and the cheese ain't good enough for folks to want to pay money for.

I sure am gonna miss them goats, though, 'cause they was the funniest little things, especially Li'l Belle. I get terribly sad thinkin' 'bout what that little goat's gonna do without me.

Margaret Ann says everybody's sellin' what all they can, just to make ends meet, and that makes me feel a bit better 'cause it shows me we ain't the only ones. Like Miss Glass says, we all in this together. Besides that, once I get a taste of the bacon-fat cracklings Mama makes, I ain't sad about them slaughterin' the pigs no more. Mama fries up all the pieces of pork and packs 'em in lard so they'll keep for a long time in the cellar, and I don't think I'll ever get tired of pork, no sir.

The end of August is a right hot mess 'cause Mother Nature never seems to know what she supposed to do. She cain't make up her mind between devil-swamp hot or chill-bumps cool, and we can tell that we don't got much time left 'fore it's wintertime, and wintertime on the farm can be downright miserable if you ain't well prepared.

So after school and on weekends, we're choppin' firewood, helpin' Daddy with cleanin' and repairin' the barn and all the fencing, cleanin' the chicken coop, cannin' fruit and wrappin' up meat and vegetables to put in the cellar for winter. And the whole next month, we'll be washin' and darnin' the winter clothes and patchin' up winter boots and beefin' up the bedding for the hens and the cows. 'Course since most of the animals are gone now, maybe it'll all go faster and easier.

But first, Mother Nature gives us one more swelterin' heat wave, and we're just about dyin' on our walk home from school, and we head straight for the creek and throw off our shoes, roll up our britches, and take a little dip and a little splash.

Then Josy hops up and says, "Come on, I wanna show you something," and he's off and runnin' and I'm chasin' after him, our shoes left behind like yesterday's news. We run along the creek toward the edge of the woods, and then Josy stops and kneels down next to some contraption that looks like a wooden cross but it's got a wire circle hangin' down, and it's

45

attached real tight-like to a switch from the tree right behind it, and there's half a carrot layin' on the ground in front of it.

"What is it?" I ask.

"It's a rabbit trap," Josy says. "See, the rabbit will come and eat the carrot, and when he puts his weight right here, this'll snap and the noose'll cinch around his neck."

"But Josy, won't that hurt the rabbit?"

"'Course it'll hurt the rabbit. That's the point, ain't it? So we can skin it and cook it, then use the fur for clothes or somethin', maybe even sell it." Then he points and says, "I got traps lined up all along here, and over there by the base of that tree. Maybe I can catch raccoons and squirrels too."

I don't really like the sound of that, number one 'cause I don't think it's right to take the life of the cutest of God's creatures, and number two 'cause I just don't think they'd taste that good. But Josy says we best be prepared, especially for winter, 'cause things just keep gettin' worse and worse.

And just then we hear Daddy hollerin', but it ain't his normal hollerin'; no, this sounds like emergency hollerin', like somethin' bad has happened, so we go runnin' and we find Daddy hobblin' into the house and there's blood. The blood is everywhere, and Daddy's holdin' his hands up to his chest like somethin's 'bout to fall off, and Mama's rushin' to him, and we're rushin' to him and screamin', "What happened?"

Daddy looks like all the blood that's supposed to be in his face and head done drained out, and he says he was splittin' logs for firewood with the hand axe and slipped up and got his fingers.

Mama rushes him to the basin, and now he's moanin' and Mama's shakin' and they're dippin' his injured hand into a bucket of water, and when he pulls it out, it's still a big ol' bloody mess.

I feel like I'm 'bout to pass out, so I lower myself wobbly-like into a chair and watch through my fingers as Mama and Josy wrap up Daddy's hand real tight in cheese cloth.

Then real fast, Mama leads Daddy out to the wagon, sayin' they gotta go to the hospital in Knoxville, and sayin' Josy's in charge while they're gone, and as soon as the screen door slams, I burst into tears and Josy's huggin' my shoulders and sayin' everything's gonna be okay.

To keep ourselves busy, we clean up the trail of blood from the porch to the kitchen, and I take the bucket of water outside and dump it out, clean out the bucket, and fill it back up at the pump. Josy hauls the firewood Daddy had chopped over to the side of the house and puts some in the wood stove firebox so I can cook supper.

I cut up some carrots and potatoes and bits of pork and throw them all into a pot with some water and salt and crushed herbs, then put the pot on the stove. While that's goin', I go outside and take the clothes down from the clothesline and fold 'em up into a basket and bring 'em inside. Then I decide to make some tea, and my hands are still shakin' from fright and the sight of all that blood and worry 'bout Daddy, and I set the tea kettle on the stove and stand there not knowin' what to do next, 'cause what do you do when your daddy's been rushed to the hospital likely bleedin' to death?

And that's when Josy comes to the kitchen table and holds up our jar of marbles and raises his eyebrows, and I smile and he smiles, and boy, that brother of mine knows just how to calm me down and cheer me up all at the same time. "How'd you get to be so smart, Josy?" I ask him, and I am dead serious, and he just shrugs and says, "I know how much you like playin' with these marbles, Junie, and we don't get to play with 'em that often during harvest season, do we?" And he opens the jar and lets me be the first one to dig my hand in, and he lets me divvy 'em up, and he lets me put the extra secret marble in the jar.

"Josy," I say, and I mean this from the bottom of my heart, "you're gonna be a real good daddy someday, you really are."

He just smiles, and then he commences to beatin' me in the first three or four rounds, 'cause that's one thing Josy never does is let me win on purpose. He says lettin' me win would make me weak, and I need to win for myself, even when I don't feel like a winner. He does concede to me a couple times when our marbles are just about equally beautiful, though, and in the end, he's the one who gets to pick the extra marble outa the jar, but I still end up winnin'. And even though normally I would gloat and dance and show off, I just don't feel like it this time 'cause my heart is too full of worry to have room for celebratin'.

By the time we're done playin', the stew's about ready and the tea kettle whistled long ago, but Mama and Daddy ain't home yet. We decide to go ahead and eat and leave most of it warmin' on the stove for them when they get home. I fetch some biscuits that Mama made this mornin' outa the breadbox and we eat in silence, both of us lost in a haze of exhaustion.

"Josy, you remember when Daddy hung up that ol' tire swing out back?" I say between bites.

He chuckles. "Yeah, and your wild behind done tore it up faster than we could enjoy it."

"Did not!"

"Did so. Dontcha remember you was always standing on it insteada sittin' down and swingin', and you'd jump on it like it was a pogo stick or somethin'?"

"Oh yeah, now I do remember that," I say, and I cain't help but smile and think on that a spell.

Then Josy says, "You remember when Daddy took us to the circus down in Knoxville a few years ago when Mama wasn't feelin' well?"

I perk up at that memory 'cause the circus was one of the most excitin' and disturbin' things I ever seen in my life, all at the same time. I got a kick outa seein' huge elephants right up close, and monkeys, too.

But then they had some strange things that sure 'nough scared me to death, like that man puttin' a torch of fire right into his mouth, and I cain't think of a single reason why anybody'd do such a thing. And they had a lady who was nearbout eight feet tall, and she had a full-grown beard. There were little men runnin' around, and I mean little – they weren't any taller than Margaret Ann's littlest brother, but they was grown-up men. And there were people doin' strange and dangerous things and wearin' bizarre makeup, and I ain't never seen no normal person that could bend their body like a pretzel and walk on their hands on a rope up high in the sky 'til that day. I had nightmares for a week after that, I surely did.

But the best part of that trip to the circus was bein' with Daddy. He works so hard all the time that we don't hardly get to see him have any fun. He surely made up for it that day, 'cause he was hootin' and hollerin' and buyin' us giant cotton candy cones and playin' all the carnival games with us so's we'd win a prize, and I cain't remember a time I seen him smile and laugh as much as I did that day. Besides bein' scared outa my mind, that's the main thing I remember is Daddy's laugh that shook his whole body, head to toe. And the way he scooped me up and put me on his shoulders to watch the fireworks and put his arm around Josy, and even though it was sad to not have Mama there with us, it was a joyful time with just the three of us that I will always remember.

For some reason, all this rememberin' got me feelin' much better for a while. We talk about the time Daddy grew out his mustache and looked just like Douglas Fairbanks in *The Mark of Zorro,* which Mama and Daddy took us to see on free movie night at the moviehouse in Knoxville a while back. We talk about the time a snake got into the house, and Daddy picked it up like it weren't nothin' and pitched it outside like he was Babe Ruth, and we watched it slide away, thinkin' how terrific Daddy was to have done that.

And we talk about the time it snowed more than it ever has in Maynardville, Tennessee, and we had a snowball fight out in front of the house, but Daddy picked up great big chunks of snow and ice packed together, and he threw those at us as we raced around hidin' behind trees with our socks for gloves. And by the time we got tired of doin' that, we was soaked right through to the bone. I cain't remember a time it snowed like that, before or after.

Josy and I are still gigglin' and sighin' over those memories when we hear Molly clompin' up the drive. We light the lanterns and run out to the porch and see Mama helpin' Daddy down from the wagon.

"Joseph, unhitch Molly and take her to the barn, please," Mama says. He looks at Mama and Daddy, questions in his eyes, and then his eyes go to the bandaged-up stump that was Daddy's left hand, and it looks like a big ol' clumpy club, and Mama says, "Hurry now, Daddy's alright." So Josy goes, and I move aside as Mama and Daddy come in.

"We saved you some stew and biscuits, and I made tea," I say, and Mama sits Daddy down at the table and ladles him out some stew and brings it to him.

"Thank you, June," Mama says, and Daddy just grunts, and then Mama gets busy scrapin' some ginger root into a cup of tea for Daddy, and she brings him that and a piece of willow bark to chew on for the pain.

"Are you alright, Daddy?" I ask, when Mama sits down and both of them are eatin' their supper, and then Josy comes in and sits down with us.

"Lost two of my fingers," Daddy says, "but I'll be fine once it heals up and I can use this hand again." Josy and I sit there stunned, and I think about that a spell, and I wonder how a person uses a hand that's missin' two fingers, even if it is his left hand. I start imagining all the things I do with my left hand – fastenin' buttons takes two hands and a lotta fingers, milkin' the cows takes two hands, and all the gardening we do takes two hands. Shoot, I cain't think of anything that'd be easy to do with missin' fingers, let alone just one hand.

"How long you gonna be bandaged up like that, Daddy?" I ask.

He shrugs and says, "A few weeks, maybe." He's lookin' like he's in a heap of pain but still smilin' anyway.

"Junie, you go get washed up for bed now," Mama says, and I don't even argue, 'cause I am one plumb-tired girl, what with all that done happened today.

In the mornin' I get dressed for school, and then I find Mama and Daddy and Josy all sittin' around the kitchen table right where they was last night, and for a minute I wonder if they even went to bed. But they look all serious-like, and Mama says g'mornin' and tells me to sit down, then she fixes me a plate of pancakes with a thick slice of bacon.

"Somethin' wrong, Daddy?" I ask, my eyes flickin' over to his bandaged hand, wonderin' if somehow it healed up already, or if maybe last night was all just a bad dream and none of that really happened and Daddy's hand is alright and ain't really missin' two fingers.

"Your mama and I been talkin', and with the economy the way it's been and now with my ..." and he holds up his stump like he don't know what to call it, "well, we think it's best if you and Joseph don't go back to school. We need you home to help on the farm, 'specially to get ready for winter. You can help Mama, and Joseph'll help me."

I start to protest, but then I see how Mama and Daddy look both helpless and hopeful at the same time, and I remember what Miss Glass says – we all in this together, and we're gonna help one another in whatever way we can. And then I start thinkin' about how much I'm gonna miss goin' to school and seein' everybody and readin' and learnin', and then I start thinkin' what about all the kids who need somethin' to eat?

And Mama must see that I got all these worries, 'cause she says, "Don't worry, Junie. I'll make sure you get time to read and write and practice your math. And on Mondays I'll pack up a basket of food we can take to the schoolhouse. And I'll make sure you get to see Margaret Ann as much as possible."

I nod and nod and nod 'cause everything she's sayin' sounds good to me, and I look over at Josy, and he looks downright puffed with pride that he's gonna be doin' more to help Daddy, like he's a grown man all the sudden. Then I look at Mama and Daddy, and they both are beamin' like happy days are here again for some reason, and then I got happy tears boilin' over and I just love my family so much my heart almost cain't take it.

The next Monday, me and Mama pack up a few vegetables from the garden and a little bit of pork sausage Mama made, and we head up to the schoolhouse in the wagon. The kids all come runnin' when they hear the clompin' of Molly's hooves, and Miss Glass sings a cheery hello. Me and Mama hop down from the wagon and Mama gives Miss Glass the pack of food. I tell her me and Josy won't be comin' to school no more, and she says she's sorry but that she understands, and that's when I notice I don't see Margaret Ann, so I ask, "Where's Margaret Ann, Miss Glass?"

She claps her hands and tells the kids to go inside and open their books, and she puts her arms around me and Mama and walks us away from the schoolhouse porch. She looks worried 'bout somethin', and she says in a whisper so soft I have to strain real hard to hear, "There's been an accident." My eyes go wide, and Miss Glass adds, "With her father. I'm afraid he's—well, he's…" and her eyes tear up, and she says, "Well, I think it's best if you stop by the Murphy house and talk to Mrs. Murphy and Margaret Ann yourselves. I'm sorry." And she runs back up the steps and into the schoolhouse.

Me and Mama get back in the wagon real quick, and we're over to Margaret Ann's house before you can snap your fingers. When Mrs. Murphy comes to the door, Mama takes her in a hug and they go off to the kitchen, and Margaret Ann sits with me on the porch, and she looks like she's been cryin' a spell.

"Margaret Ann, what happened?" I ask.

"My daddy was thrown off a train, and he got hurt, and he— he didn't make it." Tears are streakin' her face, but she's sittin' with her back high and her shoulders straight, and I think about how strong she is, how very, very strong. But then I think about all the questions I have, 'cause I don't understand.

"What'd you mean he was thrown off?"

"Railroad bulls – kinda like police who guard the trains to keep hobos and vagrants off. They threw him and a bunch of others off the train, while it was movin' fast and there wasn't no soft place to land." She looks down at her hands, and I see that they're shakin' somethin' awful, and I scoot up closer to her and put my arm around her, and we lean our heads together and just sit like that for a long time.

I don't ask her about what's gonna happen to her and her mama, or what's gonna happen to her brothers and sisters, who all live with other kin now. I don't ask her to tell no more of the story, 'cause I think if I was her, I wouldn't wanna say no more about it.

6

Becoming

a Woman

September dawns bright and cool, and even though June's my favorite month, the cool breeze of September brings promise with it and cools my soul. The best thing about September is that my birthday is comin' and I'm gonna be twelve, which to some people ain't a big deal, but to me it is, 'cause that means I caught up to Margaret Ann, who turned twelve in April, and for three months I'm only three years younger than Josy, 'til he turns sixteen in December. And I think bein' twelve will make me more of a grown woman, if I do say so myself.

Last year for my birthday, we had a picnic of fried chicken, and carrots with cinnamon and sugar, out under the pawpaw trees in the September breeze, and we played stick ball, just the four of us, me and Mama against Daddy and Josy, and Mama made a cake with my most favorite flavors in the whole world (besides caramel) – chocolate and strawberry – and then Margaret Ann came over and we got to have a sleepover, and we spent the whole night prankin' and teasin' Josy. And Mama gave me a pair of winter gloves that she made herself, and Daddy gave me my own pocketknife for whittlin', and Josy gave me a little owl that he whittled himself, along with a whole handful of caramel cubes.

Things are different this year, I know, and I don't expect nothin' special, but I do hope Margaret Ann gets to come over again, 'specially 'cause I ain't been able to spend much time with her since she told me about what happened to her daddy.

They had a little funeral, and then Margaret Ann was gone with family for a few days. I used to think that Margaret Ann had it so good, 'cause they live in town and had a car up until recently, and even though they lived three kids to a room, I always thought their house was so pretty, and couldn't nothin' go wrong for a family with a nice house and car like that. But now it seems like everything's fallin' to pieces for the Murphys, and that just makes my heart hurt. And it's a good thing we always got work to do on the farm so I don't have time to sit around and think about sad things.

We get so busy gettin' ready for winter, that for a while I almost forget that my birthday is comin'. Me and Mama are finishing the cannin', and we're sewin' blankets and darnin' the rips in old coats, and we're preparin' the chicken coop, and we're packin' the cellar with the vegetables that'll keep.

Josy and Daddy are workin' the crop fields and choppin' and haulin' more firewood and gatherin' and haulin' hay, and o'course Josy's doin' a whole lot more than Daddy now, 'cause Daddy's still healin' from his accident. Daddy's wound keeps openin' up, and he says we cain't afford for him to keep goin' back to the hospital in Knoxville, so Mama's nursin' him, and Daddy says it's a good thing she knows how to sew, and I don't even want to imagine that.

Mama changes his bandages every night, and I ain't seen what it looks like, but Mama says he's missin' his pointer finger and middle finger, and I cain't even imagine, 'cause that leaves him with just the useless ol' ring finger and pinky finger, besides the thumb, o'course.

Sometimes I fold down my pointer finger and middle finger and try to do things with my hand like that, but my silly ol' ring finger won't stay up and I have to hold my first two fingers down with my thumb, which ain't an accurate experiment 'cause Daddy still got his thumb. Anyway, I try that as best as I can, just to see what it's like to be missin' those fingers, but I guess it looks strange when I do it, 'cause when Mama catches me, she says, "June, what in the world are you doing?" Then I have to do a lot of finger stretches 'cause my hand's all cramped up.

Mama says we're runnin' low on things, like the soap we keep in the cellar and use for washin' clothes and takin' baths. We're even runnin' low on pork, 'cause we been eatin' a lot and givin' away a lot, and it's goin' faster than a roadrunner after a rattlesnake.

But Josy's rabbit traps are makin' up for that 'cause wouldn't you know it, at least one of his traps is full almost every other day. So Mama makes up some rabbit stew, and it tastes alright, long as I pretend it's chicken or pork. Josy's traps ain't caught any squirrels or raccoons yet, and I'm glad of that, 'cause I don't think I could pretend enough to make those taste good. After we skin and clean and cook the rabbits, we use the fur for our coats and hats – sew it right into the cuffs or the lining – and that'll be nice once it starts gettin' real cold.

Three peculiar things happen during my birthday month. The first thing is that one late afternoon I smell somethin' burnin' outside and I hear loud, angry talkin'. So I go outside, and Josy and Daddy are in the pasture throwin' I-don't-know-what-all onto a bonfire, and Daddy looks mad and Josy looks like he's in a hurry. I run out there and ask what's goin' on, and Daddy just grunts and he's throwin' dried up onions and shriveled up carrots and shrunken green beans into the fire.

Josy says, "These crops done gone to waste," and I ask why, and Daddy tells me that we just couldn't sell it all, and what we didn't wrap up and put in the cellar went bad.

I ain't never seen this happen before, so I ask how come we couldn't sell it all, and Daddy says folks don't have enough money to buy as much as they used to. He says next spring we'll be plantin' less, if we can even afford the seeds by that time. And I think about that a spell, and we all stand there watchin' the flames flick up to the twilight sky, and Josy and Daddy are huffin' and puffin' from their efforts and maybe from anger too. I cain't remember a time we ever let anything go to waste like this, and it makes me feel funny in my stomach, like the time me and Josy saw all the empty shelves at the stores in town.

The next thing that happens is that I'm on the front porch, stitchin' up socks with Mama, and I feel somethin' wet in my undergarments, like I peed my pants or somethin', which is really strange 'cause I didn't feel like I had to go. So I ask Mama if I can be excused, and I go out to the outhouse, which I ain't talked about yet 'cause outhouse business is private and unsanitary. But this is different. I go in and pull down my pants and undergarments and see blood. I don't panic or get scared or anything, 'cause I knew this was bound to happen sooner or later. Margaret Ann told me all about it 'cause she started her menstruation months ago. I run to tell Mama, 'cause even though I know what's happenin', I don't know exactly what I'm supposed to do about it.

Mama takes me into Maynardville to the drugstore, which is just another room attached to Macafee's Market, and we buy some Curads and a sanitary belt, and on the slow wagon ride home, Mama tells me stories about womanhood, and my cheeks burn hot as a cattle prod. Even more embarrassing is when we get home, Mama takes me into my bedroom and shows me how to wear the sanitary belt, and once I got it into place and I'm steppin' back into my undergarments, with Mama standin' there watchin' me, I wonder what's gonna happen when I have to start wearin' a bra for the first time.

The third peculiar thing that happens during my birthday month is that Bug starts actin' strange. For some reason, she starts bringin' creatures to the front porch. Every day it seems like I'm almost steppin' on some dead bird or mouse or baby possum or shrew, and there's Bug, sittin' there lookin' at me like *Ain't you proud of me?* It just about scares me half to death each time I see a new dead animal on the porch, but I'm grateful she ain't brought a snake up there – I think she just eats those.

And she's been extra clingy, too, for a barn cat, always rubbin' up against me and purrin' and mewlin' so loud and starin' at me like she want somethin' but cain't figure out how to tell me. And boy, she's gettin' fat, too, and that makes me wonder what all she's eatin', 'cause I sure don't feed her a whole lot.

One Monday after me and Mama get back home from takin' some food up to the schoolhouse, we're restin' a spell on the porch, and Bug comes prancin' up the steps and sets a dead bird at my feet. I jump up and holler, "Bug! Why do you keep on doin' that? I don't want no more dead animals!" I grab the broom, which is leanin' up against the wall behind the porch swing, and I sweep the dead bird off the side of the porch and sit back down, and all the time, Mama's just alaughin'.

I tell her it ain't funny, and Bug mewls and hops up into my chair, and Mama leans forward and squints up her eyes and says, "Junie? Bring me that cat." So I scoop up Bug and take her over to Mama, who runs her hands around Bug's belly and looks up at me with strange eyes.

"June, your cat is actin' strange 'cause she's gonna have kittens."

And I just stare at Mama with my mouth wide open. "What?"

"Bug is gonna be a mama."

"But that's impossible! I ain't seen a tomcat around here anywhere."

"Well, there must be one somewhere," Mama says, "unless this is the feline version of Mary, Mother of Jesus. And there's no tellin' where this cat goes at night."

"Well, I'll be. ... My little Bug, a mama." And I think on that a spell and then wonder where she's gonna have her kittens and how we're gonna take care of more cats, and I guess Mama's washed her hands of it, 'cause she shrugs and leans back and closes her eyes like she don't care none.

With my woman's menstruation and my pregnant cat as my first two birthday presents, I start lookin' forward to September the twenty-first, which falls on a Sunday this year, and I take that as a good sign. On the Saturday before my birthday, Mama's at the kitchen basin, scrubbin' the breakfast dishes, and she asks me what kinda cake I want her to make, but before I can say anything, she says, "Now, Junie, we're a mite short on sugar and flour, so it's gonna be a *small* cake."

I put my arm around Mama's waist and lean my head on her shoulder. "That's alright, Mama. What'd we need a big cake for anyhow? Maybe you can make whatever flavor you got the ingredients for. I'll be happy no matter what."

Mama wipes her hands on her apron and turns and grasps my shoulders and says, "Thank you for bein' my ray of sunshine, June. I'm really proud of you." And she pulls me into a tight hug, and even though I feel too old for hugs from Mama, I lean into it and close my eyes and breathe in the smell of her hair and the sound of her hummin' voice.

On Sunday morning, the twenty-first of September, my twelfth birthday, I wake up to the rich, smoky smell of bacon cookin', the sounds of it sizzlin' and poppin' in the pan, and the rumbly sounds of—*aw, crumbs, is that thunder?* I jump outa bed and scoot over to the window, throwin' the curtains aside. Sure enough, it's a gloomy gray out there, with big ol' dark rain clouds lit up every few seconds by lightning. That's just about the only thing that could ruin my birthday, is rain, and it looks like it's about to pour like nobody's business. I cain't remember a time it rained on my birthday. Before I get dressed, I holler out to Mama. "Mama! We still goin' to church in the rain?"

Mama hollers back, quick as a lightning bolt. "Does God still exist in the rain?"

I guess that's my answer, so I light my lantern so's I can see, and I pull my Sunday dress and my good shoes from my wardrobe and get dressed. I catch sight of myself in the mirror and linger there for a spell. I drag my brush through my scraggly brown hair 'til it's soft and shiny. My summertime freckles are already startin' to fade, and my eyes look darker blue than ever, as if they was lightened by the summer sun and now they're growin' dark for the winter.

I stand up straight and tall and I sure do think I grew an inch overnight, 'cause now that I'm twelve, I feel much more grown up. I wonder if anybody will notice and say, *My, how grown-up and mature you look, Junie.* And maybe Josy won't pinch my arms no more and Daddy won't tickle my feet no more and Mama won't set me in her lap no more, and now all the sudden I want to cry.

When I get into the kitchen, the first thing that happens is Mama and Daddy and Josy all come grab me into a big jostlin' hug and tell me happy birthday, and Josy's pinchin' my arm and Daddy's askin' if I feel older today, and Mama's sayin' I do look mighty old, and then we're laughin', and I lie and say I don't feel a minute older than yesterday.

By the time we finish breakfast, it's pourin' rain, so Daddy puts on his boots and a rain slicker and goes out to hook Molly up to the wagon, and Mama gets a tarp from the back porch that ain't no bigger than a baby's blanket. She says we all gonna squeeze in together in the front of the wagon and put this tarp over our heads, and I look out and see how hard it's rainin', and I don't know how that tarp's gonna keep us dry.

Daddy hollers, "Come on!" when he's ready with Molly, and Josy holds the tarp up over our heads and Mama and me are standin' on either side of Josy, and we make a run for it.

"Careful not to slip on the steps," Mama shouts over the roar of the rain. In just the three or four steps from the porch to the wagon, we already got mud all over our shoes.

Josy helps Mama up into the wagon, then he gets in, and last is me, and boy, that rain is cold, and my shoes are muddy, and it's hard work gettin' up into that wagon, and we are stuffed in there like sardines, and we all look at each other, and I don't know if we gonna laugh or cry. Daddy snaps the reins and tells Molly to "Get on!" and Molly struggles to pull the wagon through the mud. It is slow goin', I'm tellin' you, and at this rate it's gonna take hours to get to church. We ain't got halfway down the drive when the wagon gets stuck, and poor Molly is gruntin' and strainin' against the weight, and she just whinnies and gives up.

Daddy smacks his leg and throws down the reins and climbs down, hollerin' at Josy to come help him. Mama takes the tarp from Josy, and me and Mama squeeze closer together under it, and it's so wet it's saggin' down on our heads and water's drippin' all over us.

I look over and see Josy and Daddy, wet as soaked rags, heavin' and pullin' on one of the wagon wheels, tryin' to get it unstuck, and Daddy's hollerin' orders, and both he and Josy got mud up to their knees, and their white Sunday shirts done turned brownish gray, and their hair is plastered to their heads and faces. I poke my head outa the tarp and look up to the gray sky and I think, *I hope Jesus can see how hard we tryin' to get to church!*

It ain't been but a minute or two, but it surely feels like an hour gone by, and I beg Mama, "Cain't we go back inside now?" And I guess Daddy was thinkin' the same thing, 'cause right then, he unhitches Molly to take her back to the barn and hollers at us to go on back home, and he don't have to tell us twice, no sir. We are off and runnin' toward the house, slippin' and slidin' on mud in our Sunday dress, and we don't even bother with that dumb ol' tarp, we just high-tail it back to the house, screamin' and hollerin' the whole way.

And when we get to the front porch, I'm shiverin' and shakin' like mad, and the rain on my face feels like tears, 'cause I feel heavy in my chest, but then Mama starts laughin', and it's a deep laugh that gurgles up from her belly, and I ain't never heard her laugh like that, so I start laughin' too, and so does Josy. Daddy comes runnin' from the barn, and he thinks something's wrong 'cause the three of us are layin' on the porch and rollin' around laughin' so hard we're holdin' our bellies, and then Daddy scowls and steps over us and goes inside.

It takes a long time, but once we're all cleaned up and dried and sittin' by the warm wood stove, and our muddy clothes are draped over the back porch railin' and gettin' washed by God himself, Mama gets started on bakin' my birthday cake. She lets me lick the bowl after she scoops the batter into the pan, and that's one of the best parts about bakin' is gettin' to lick the bowl.

Since we didn't get to go to church, Daddy gets the Bible and he reads some from Isaiah, and truer words weren't never spoken, 'cause Isaiah Chapter 55 Verse 10 says, *For as the rain cometh down, and the snow from heaven, and returneth not thither, but watereth the earth, and maketh it bring forth and bud, that it may give seed to the sower, and bread to the eater*, and the rain sure did cometh down, and I don't know about bread, but today it brung chocolate cake!

After we eat my birthday cake, Mama disappears into her and Daddy's room, and when she comes back out, she's got a package wrapped up in a flour sack, and she hands it to me and says, "It ain't much, Junie, but twelve is a special year, and we wanted to do somethin' real nice for you."

Inside is a stack of books, and I cain't believe my eyes. "Mama! Where'd you get these books?"

On top is a cookbook, my very own cookbook! And there's *The Story of Dr. Dolittle*, and *Emily of New Moon*, and even some books that ain't for little kids, like *The Great Gatsby* and two by Virginia Woolf. Six books in all. I ain't never had this many books at one time, and my mouth is hangin' wide open, and Mama says, "I made a deal with Miss Glass. These are from the library. Miss Glass said you can keep 'em, or if you want, you can trade 'em back when you're done."

Mama reaches over and opens the cookbook, where there are some small cards in a pocket on the inside of the cover. "Look here. These cards are for you to write your favorite recipes down, and then you can give the book to someone else who wants it."

I jump up and hug Mama's neck, then Daddy's, and I'm burstin' with joy, and then Josy hands me a small velvet pouch, cinched closed with a satin ribbon. I open it up and inside are five perfect marbles with swirls of different shades of purple, and I cain't even squeal loud enough to show how happy I am.

Even though we nearly drowned in rain and mud, and even though we couldn't go to church, and even though Margaret Ann couldn't come over 'cause of the rain, this is the best birthday I could ever have, and now I don't even know what to do first – add my new marbles to me and Josy's jar, or read one of my new books, or find somethin' good to cook from my new cookbook.

In the end, I do all of 'em 'cept cook somethin', 'cause we don't have all the ingredients, but I do write down all my favorite recipes on the cards and hope I get to cook 'em someday.

7

Josy's Decision

The first snow falls on December eighth, which is perfect, 'cause that's Josy's birthday. He's sixteen now, which means he's darn near a grown man. He's way taller than Mama now, and just about as tall as Daddy. He's also grown more broody and ornery for some reason. Must be spendin' too much time with ol' Miss Priss.

Josy's been workin' real hard the past few months 'cause Daddy's got to where he cain't hardly use his left arm at all, and it just sorta hangs there, and he's in a lot of pain. So Josy's choppin' and haulin' all the firewood, cleanin' the barn, carin' for the cows and Molly, and I don't know what all. I help when I can, and so does Mama, but we got our whole list of chores too. Daddy's worried 'bout what's gonna happen when plantin' season comes around again.

We still ain't got our money from the bank, and the Maynardville bank is still closed down. Mama and Daddy went down to the bank in Knoxville with their IOU and Daddy says they 'bout laughed them outa there. Matter fact, he says, they started talkin' 'bout callin' up loans, so Daddy says they lit outa there and won't go back 'til this "depression" is over. That's what President Hoover calls it, and I have to say I rightly agree with that, 'cause we are downright depressed, not to mention tired. Tired from workin' so hard, tired of eatin' pork and beans all the time, tired of not makin' any money offa Mama's sewin' or Daddy and Josy's buildin', which is mostly Josy's now anyhow. And we're depressed from bein' so tired, and tired of bein' so depressed.

One bright spot in the middle of all this depression is Bug and her litter of kittens, which she gave birth to 'bout the end of November, right when we was all busy with Thanksgiving cookin' (one of the few times Mama said we could splurge on a big meal). I was scared the kittens would make a whole lot more work for me, but Bug is such a good mama, she does all the work. She cleans and feeds and looks after her babies and I don't gotta do nothin' but keep 'em away from the chickens.

Now that it's colder, they mostly stay in the barn where they can get warm, and Josy makes me help him clean the barn 'cause it can get mighty stinky back in the "kitty corner." Bug had six kittens, but one of 'em didn't survive, so there's five little ones runnin' around, and two of 'em got the most beautiful orange colorin', which is the strangest thing, 'cause Bug is mostly gray. Everywhere I go, I keep a lookout for an orange tomcat, but I ain't never seen him.

Mama and Daddy complain about all these cats everywhere, but I tell you one thing, we ain't seen a rat or a snake around here since we brought Bug home, not countin' the dead mice she brings to the porch for us, and ain't that worth somethin'?

Like I said, it's snowin' on Josy's birthday, and we gather up some snow, and Mama whisks it together with milk and sugar and vanilla to make ice cream, and it is just about the most delicious thing I ever tasted, besides caramel cubes. The first snow is the best for makin' ice cream, but even that don't put a smile on Josy's sour face.

Later I find him layin' on his bed, just lookin' up at the cobwebbed ceiling, and first I wonder what he's thinkin', and then I wonder why he's in here lazin' around. I cain't remember a time I seen Josy lazin' around on a day that ain't a Sunday.

"Whatcha doin', Josy?" I ask as I step cautiously into his room. Nowadays there's no tellin' when Josy might snap at ya, which really ain't like him at all, so I been real careful around him. He don't answer me or even look at me, he's so lost in whatever he sees on the ceiling.

I step closer to the bed, then real gentle-like, I sit down and put my hand on his hand, and finally he looks at me. His eyes look puffy and red like he's been cryin', but I don't think that's possible 'cause he's sixteen now, and I try to remember the last time I seen Josy cry, and it musta been back when Daddy got the IOU from the bank, 'cause I don't think Josy even cried when Daddy got his fingers cut off.

Josy sits up and scoots next to me and clasps his hands together like he's gonna pray, and he says, "Junie June, I gotta tell ya somethin'," and then I get scared 'cause he looks all serious-like, and this is the first time in a long time that he's really talked to me.

I look at him with questions in my eyes, but I don't say anything, and I think I'm not even breathin'.

"Things are real bad," Josy says. "We ain't got no more money, we're runnin' outa food, and we need new clothes."

I look down at my overalls, and for the first time I notice

how threadbare they are, how dirty, how small. I see the rips and tears in my shirt sleeves and the fraying ends of my britches. Josy's are the same, 'cept he's grown so much the past few months that he got a whole lotta ankle showin' below where his britches end. We got socks on 'cause it's wintertime, but our socks are thin and holey. For some reason, lookin' at our clothes makes me suddenly feel the cold air, and I shiver.

"We cain't buy new clothes," Josy says, and real quick I say, "Mama can make some," and Josy just looks at me, then says, "With what, June? We cain't afford cloth or thread. And even if we could, the market's always outa almost everything, and Mr. Macafee's raised the price of things so much."

Josy continues, "Daddy's havin' a real hard time and cain't do a whole lot. Come plantin' time, there ain't gonna be much plantin'."

"What are we gonna do, Josy?" I'm wrackin' my brain tryin' to think of how we can help, and I think of my piggy bank money, and I'm about to say so, when Josy says, "I know what you're thinkin', and don't you think we already thought of that? When's the last time you got out your piggy bank?"

I cain't remember the last time I took down my piggy bank. It musta been … I don't know, and I'm thinkin' real hard tryin' to remember, and Josy says, "I already used your piggy bank money. I'm sorry I didn't tell you, but we needed to buy paint for the barn, and the wagon needed repairs, and we just didn't have enough."

I blink away tears as I think about how bad things really must be for Josy to take my piggy bank money without tellin' me. It scares me somethin' awful.

"I know you woulda gladly given up your money if Mama and Daddy asked you to, but they wouldn't ever ask, so I took it, and they don't know where it came from, so don't tell 'em,

June, please. I just wanted to help." I wipe my cheeks and take a shaky breath, and I feel better knowin' that my piggy bank money was put to good use, but then I'm even more scared, 'cause if that's all gone and we don't have any money left at all, what are we gonna do? And I ask Josy that, and that's when my world collapses.

"I'm gonna take a train out west," Josy says, and I don't hear anything else he says, 'cause my head fills with panic and my heart is hurting, and I'm thinkin' about railroad bulls and Margaret Ann's daddy, who ain't never comin' back, and I don't know what good it's gonna do 'cause who's gonna help Daddy with the barn and the animals and everything else, and this cain't be happening.

"June!" Josy snaps his fingers in front of my face. "June, did you hear what I said?"

I look slowly into Josy's deep blue eyes, the ones that look just like mine. "What?"

"I said, you don't have to worry. I'm gonna take a train to Memphis, maybe a little further out, where I can find work, and I'll bring home money so we can keep the farm, and it's gonna be alright." He takes my hands and squeezes them.

I nod, but I don't feel like it's gonna be alright. "You tell Mama and Daddy? They said you can do this?"

"I told 'em," Josy says, and he looks away, toward the window, like he's lookin' for another way out, and I can tell by the way he looks that Mama and Daddy surely do not approve of his plan.

"How long you gonna be gone?"

He shakes his head. "I don't know. It depends on what work I find, but I'll try to come back for Christmas."

"Christmas! When are you leavin'?" Christmas is three weeks away, and no one in our family has ever been away from home that long, and I think, maybe he ain't leavin' for at least another week, and then he says, "Tomorrow."

After a night of dreams about railroad bulls throwin' people offa trains and animal bulls chargin' and stompin' people, I wake up in a panic, thinkin' Josy left without sayin' goodbye, so I jump outa bed and run out into the kitchen. Mama looks like she didn't sleep none either, and she's cryin' up a storm. Daddy's rubbin' her arm and talkin' softly to her. "Where's Josy?" I holler.

"He's in the cellar," Daddy says. "He'll be up shortly."

I want to scream at them. *How can you let him do this?* I want to remind Mama about what happened to Mr. Murphy. I want to beg them not to let him go. But what I see in Daddy's face ain't worry or fear or even sorrow. It's shame.

Daddy understands that we need Josy's help, and he don't like it one bit 'cause he's supposed to be the grown and strong one, and now he cain't be that no more. He's ashamed that he has to let his sixteen-year-old boy put his life in danger so that the family and the farm can survive. But he cain't *not* let him do this. 'Cause if Josy don't take this risk, what will happen to us? And I see all this in Daddy's face, and for a second, I hate him for it. Why'd he have to go and do a stupid thing like cut his fingers off with an axe, for Pete's sake? Why'd he have to let his arm go weak and limp like an invalid? And why cain't things just go back to normal?

Josy comes in from the cellar, and he's layered in just about all the clothes he owns, and he has on Daddy's work boots, and over his shoulder, he's carryin' a pack, which he says has some food in it and some bandages and peroxide, "just in case," and I'm thinkin', *Bandages and peroxide ain't gonna do you no good if them bulls throw you off a train like they did Margaret Ann's daddy.* But I don't say that.

Josy says he only has to walk as far as Knoxville, and from there he can catch a freight train goin' out toward Memphis. He says he heard there's work to be had out there and not to worry 'cause he's gonna bring home plenty of money and everything's gonna be alright. And Mama's up and wrappin' herself around him like she can keep him from leavin' if she holds on tight enough, and Daddy's pattin' him on the back and I can see Daddy's tryin' so hard to be strong, but his face is shakin' and he's blinkin' like mad. Josy's the only one who doesn't look scared or nothin'. Matter fact, he looks downright excited. After he's done huggin' Mama and Daddy, he steps over to me and grabs my shoulders, and he's smilin' so big.

"Junie June, don't you worry, now," he says, squeezin' my arms. "Don't you worry for a second, 'cause I know what I'm doin'. I'm gonna find work, and when I come home, we'll have the grandest Christmas feast you ever seen. I promise."

And I don't know what's happened to me, 'cause I cain't say nothin', cain't get my voice to work. I want to tell him I love him and I care about him and I will miss him, and I want to tell him to be careful and to watch out for them bulls. I want to tell him so many things, but it won't come out, and I cain't breathe, and then he's walkin' down the porch steps and he's wavin' bye, and Mama and Daddy are wavin' bye, and Josy's walkin' down the drive, and then he's beyond the fence, and I still cain't speak or breathe or move, and then Josy's disappearin' beyond the tree line, and that's when I finally feel my feet and they're runnin' and runnin' and my arms are flyin' and I'm runnin' and I'm cryin' and I cain't catch him 'cause he's already gone and I fall to the ground and I sob a voiceless cry of despair.

8

Happy Days

For three days straight, me and Mama and Daddy walk around in such a lonely, depressed silence that you'd think someone died. The space that Josy left behind is a thick fog that we trudge through day in and day out, watchin' out the window as if he'd be walkin' down the lane any minute now. Mama always looks like she's been cryin', and Daddy always looks like he's in pain, and I bet she has and he is, and I feel awful bad 'cause I don't know how to help them when I feel the exact same way.

Then one day I just sorta snap out of it, 'cause I remember that Josy ain't dead, and he's strong and smart and he's workin' hard to bring home money for us. And I remember that while Josy's gone, I gotta do the barn work and help Daddy as much as I can, and I gotta check Josy's traps and help Mama with the cookin' and cleanin' and sewin' and everything else. So how I see it, we ain't got time to be all sad and mopey. When I figure that out, I cain't wait to spread my knowledge and wisdom to Mama and Daddy, and I'm positive they will appreciate it.

One good thing about Josy bein' gone is that me and Mama are spendin' a lot of time together and gettin' closer, like good talkin' friends 'steada just parent and child, and I bet that has a lot to do with the fact that I'm twelve now and I can do a lot of things to help her 'round the house.

A few days before Mama's birthday, me and her are sittin' in the front room and sewin' up some moccasins using rabbit fur and pig skin. We plan to take the moccasins up to the market and either sell 'em or trade 'em. They're nice and soft, and I'm sure somebody'll like to have 'em since it's gettin' to be real cold out now. It's quiet in the house, 'cept Mama's got the ol' radio on, and it's tuned to some big band music with static every now and then. Daddy's out in the woodshed workin' on some project or 'nother – he's been makin' some hen nesting boxes and wagon hitches, and everything takes him twice as long 'cause he's workin' with one good hand and without Josy.

"You check Joseph's traps today?" Mama asks, and it's the first time she's said his name out loud since he left.

"Yes, ma'am," I say after a pause. I wonder if now will be my chance to cheer Mama up about Josy bein' gone. "There wasn't nothin' in 'em yet."

She opens her mouth like she's gonna say somethin' else, but it's a long time before she does. "It's mighty quiet around here without him bouncin' around, isn't it?"

I look real close at Mama 'cause I wonder if she's gonna start cryin'. Her lips ain't shakin', and her eyes don't look all red and wet, but I never know these days. "Did I tell you 'bout the time I was climbin' a tree and I fell down and scraped up my hands and knees?"

Mama's lookin' at me like I just told her I'd broken my head wide open and never told her about it. "Josy was right there when it happened," I continue, "and you know what he did? I'll never forget this, 'cause instead of coddlin' me, he told me to stand myself up, and he showed me how to break open the aloe plants that grow along the fence and rub the juice on my scratches. And the whole time, he was lookin' hard at me, like, 'Don't you cry, June.' And then he marched me right back over to that tree and made me try again. And he told me, 'When you live on a farm like we do, you gotta be strong and tough, and bein' strong and tough don't mean you don't ever fall down. It means when you fall down, you get right back up and try again.'"

Mama smiles, and she's lookin' past me, through me, lost in thought.

"Mama," I say, "Josy is strong and tough. He is."

She nods, and her eyes fill up, but tears don't fall. She straightens her shoulders and gets back to sewin', and I get back to sewin', and we work quietly, listenin' to Ben Silvin and his Orchestra play *Happy Days Are Here Again*.

Mama holds up a finished moccasin to inspect, and then she asks as if she just remembered, "Did you ever make it up that tree, Junie?"

"What? Oh, no, Mama, wouldn't you know it, I fell down that darned tree about fifteen times!"

And she looks at me and purses her lips like she's holdin' in a laugh, but it bursts out, and then she's laughin' and I'm laughin' and we're laughin' so hard the tears really start fallin'.

From that day on, Mama seems a whole lot happier, and since Mama's happier, Daddy is too, and we can finally breathe a little easier, and we start talkin' about Josy without gettin' all sad. We still worry, o'course, and sometimes I cain't stop thinkin' 'bout what happened to Margaret Ann's daddy, but it helps to think about what Josy might be doin' at that very minute – is he on a train, or is he workin' on somebody's farm, or is he buildin' things for somebody?

On Mama's birthday, she teaches me how to make a cake just like the one she made for my birthday. And I make supper from one of the recipes I wrote down outa my cookbook, and I serve it to Mama and Daddy like they're at a fancy restaurant, with candles and everything. First is the steamed salad, which I make from dandelions that are always growin' by the back porch and mint from Mama's herb garden. Then is the stew with a little bit of pork, potatoes and onions. And last is the birthday cake, and we sing happy birthday to Mama, and then I put on the radio and Mama and Daddy dance around the front room together, and the wood stove is goin' and it's nice and warm, and our bellies are full, and our hearts are full too.

Then Mama and Daddy pull me into the dance, and I start thinkin' about how when I was little, I used to stand on Daddy's feet and he'd dance around the room with me on his feet, and I'm wonderin' if I'm too big now to do that, and he taps his foot, an invitation. So I step gently onto his feet, and he holds my hands and carries me in a waltz, and I don't even notice his missin' fingers 'cause right now ain't nothin' missin', nothin' at all.

Three great things happen in the weeks before Christmas. The first thing is that I seem to have a breakthrough with ol' Miss Priss. It starts when I see a big ol' jacket hangin' on a hook in the barn, and I know Josy used to wear that jacket, so I put it on, and when I sit down to start milkin', Miss Priss don't make a sound, like maybe she thinks I'm Josy since I'm wearin' that jacket. I like to think that it's 'cause she knows things are real hard right now and she knows I need her to cooperate.

Animals got a sixth sense about those kinds of things. Like just when I'm startin' to feel real down and worryin' about Josy, Bug comes up and nudges my leg and purrs. Even the chickens been easier on us, layin' more eggs and not squawkin' up a fuss all the time, and it makes me feel like God's watchin' over us, and if he's watchin' over us, he surely must be watchin' over Josy. I ain't even gonna try to figure out why he wasn't watchin' over Margaret Ann's daddy, 'cause that's just too hard to think about.

The second great thing that happens is that me and Mama start sewin' shirts and knickers outa flour sacks and feed sacks, and I never woulda thought they'd look as good as they do. We trade eggs for spools of thread from Mr. Macafee, and we got enough feed sacks to just about make clothes for an army. We only got one sewin' machine, though, so I do the measurin' and pinnin' and cuttin', and Mama does the sewin', and once we have an armful of shirts and knickers done, we take 'em to Macafee's.

There ain't no farmer's market in the winter, but lotsa folks set up tables in Macafee's to sell and trade their wares, and Mr. Macafee don't mind none, since a lotta his shelves are generally bare anyhow. He says at least folks are comin' into the store, and if folks got somethin' to sell or trade, the more the merrier.

The only bad thing about ridin' to town in the winter is the wagon is so cold and Molly goes so slow. She's gettin' old, so each year, she's slower and slower, and I wonder what's gonna happen when she's too old to get along. We throw a blanket over her back so she's not so cold on the ride into town, and we wrap ourselves up too.

The third great thing that happens is that we run into Margaret Ann and her mama at Macafee's, and her mama and my mama agree to let us have a sleepover, and we decide to have it over at her house 'cause it's been a long time since we done that.

Things I love about Margaret Ann's house are: 1. She got lotsa magazines to look at, like *Ladies' Home Journal* and *The Saturday Evening Post*, and I even like lookin' at *The American Boy*, which they still have at her house even though her brothers don't live there right now. 2. They got an icebox, and in the summertime, that means we can have cold water and even frozen treats like popsicles. Even though the icebox don't do us much good in the wintertime, I still like seein' it 'cause we ain't got one at my house. 3. Margaret Ann's got glamorous posters of movie stars on the walls of her bedroom, like Bebe Daniels and Mary Pickford and Greta Garbo, and she even has real makeup, so we like to do up our faces and prance around like we're Hollywood beauties, and I tell you what, it's so much more fun without them boys runnin' around her house, no offense.

For supper, Mrs. Murphy makes corned beef hash and prune pudding, and we drink powdered milk, which I ain't never had before 'cause at home we drink milk from our cows, and it don't taste half bad, to tell the truth. We bundle up next to the wood stove, but we keep the lantern on and stay up real late tellin' ghost stories and talkin' about Jimmy Mack, and Margaret Ann says she's bored of Jimmy Mack so if I'm sweet on him, I can have him if I want to. Then she grabs one of her magazines and flips to a page and starts readin' somethin' to me all about "dating."

"It says here," Margaret Ann says, makin' her voice all high and proper like a lady 'til I'm gigglin' and she's shushin' me, "that to be desirable to a man, a lady must be well-dressed and well-groomed, and ... let's see ..." Her eyes scan the page 'til she finds somethin' else important to read to me. "The lady must pay her man suf-sufficient attention and never look bored when he is speaking."

Boy, according to that article, I got a lotta work to do to make myself desirable to Jimmy Mack, or any man, but I decide that magazine can stuff it, 'cause I don't need to change myself for nobody, and for some reason that reminds me to tell Margaret Ann all about getting my womanly menstruation, and we giggle all night long 'til Mrs. Murphy tells us to go on to sleep.

I go to church with Margaret Ann and Mrs. Murphy in the mornin' and go find Mama and Daddy and sit with them, and this is the first time that I actually listen real hard to Pastor Klein's sermon and hear it with my heart 'steada just my ears. The reason I hear it is 'cause Pastor Klein is talkin' 'bout mamas, and he says, "Mothers are called upon by God to love and care for their children, but they take it upon themselves to be servants unto all, to selflessly meet the needs of their family, friends, and community before their own."

And he tells a story about his mama, who was always the first one to wake up in the mornin' and the last one to go to bed at night because she was takin' care of everybody from dawn 'til dusk, and only when everybody else's needs were met did she put her feet up and take care of her own needs. Pastor Klein's mama died last Wednesday, and he says she lived a full life, raisin' five children and helpin' take care of twelve grandchildren, twenty-three animals, two houses, a barn, a greenhouse, and darn near everybody in the little town they grew up in, and his only wish was that she had taken more time for herself.

Pastor Klein ends his sermon by saying, "Mamas in the church house, we love you and we appreciate you, and this

Christmas, I want you to give yourselves a gift – the gift of time to yourself, because you surely deserve it." And that message makes my heart feel real full, and I grab Mama's hand and squeeze it tight, and I think about ways I can give her the gift of time to herself.

9

On My Own

Two weeks have passed since Josy left, but somehow it feels like a million years, and we're all lookin' forward to Christmas as if on that day everything will magically return to normal, even though we don't even know for sure that Josy'll be back on Christmas. Me and Mama have settled into a comfortable routine, but Daddy ain't been dealin' with Josy's absence as good. He mostly stays holed up in the woodshed or the barn, even when it's freezin' cold and even when it's snowin' and even when it's dark. He's made some milkin' stools to sell or trade at the market – sell on a good day, trade on a bad day – and he looks after the cows and Molly, but he's workin' a whole lot slower nowadays.

One day, Daddy ain't in the woodshed or the barn, and I find him in his bed in him and Mama's room, and Mama's worryin' over him, and it don't take but two steps closer to see how come. Daddy's hand, which just ain't never healed right since the accident, is all swollen and reddish-purple, and Daddy's shakin' and lookin' affright, and Mama says he got a high fever. She's holdin' a wet rag to his forehead, and she tells me to run and get a bowl of snow, which we dip his bad hand into, but that don't seem to help much.

Mama gets up and gets her coat and says she's goin' to get the doctor. We got one doctor in Maynardville, Dr. Jamison, and as far as I know, he can treat stomach aches and the common cold; anything more serious than that, ya gotta go to Knoxville. I sure hope he can do somethin' for Daddy. I help Mama hitch Molly to the wagon, and off she goes, and remember how I said animals seem to have a sixth sense about things? For the first time in my life, I see Molly gallopin' down the lane, the wagon bouncin' along behind her, and I ain't never seen that silly ol' mule go that fast, like she surely does know it's an emergency.

When Mama comes back, the doctor's in his car, right behind her, and they pull up to the house. I wait out in the front room, pacin' back and forth and wringin' my hands, while Mama and the doctor are in with Daddy. After a while, they come out, and I can hear Dr. Jamison whisper to Mama, "Mizz Baker, y'all gotta get him to the hospital. The medicine I gave him will calm his pain, maybe reduce the swelling, but that won't be enough."

I scoot closer so I can hear Mama's reply. "But Doctor, we can't pay…" and Mama looks helpless, and she's shakin' her head, and I get real scared.

Dr. Jamison puts a gentle hand on Mama's arm and says, "Down in Knoxville, right offa Main Street, on the river side, there's a clinic that'll take him, and you won't have to pay. Ask for Dr. Green." And now Mama's noddin' away the tears and she looks hopeful again, and I finally breathe out.

The first day they're gone, I take care of the chickens and do the milkin', but most of the time, I'm pacin' the front room.

It's just a few more days 'til Christmas, and what if Josy comes back and Mama and Daddy are still gone? Or what if no one ever comes back and I'm left here all alone for the rest of my life? Those are the crazy places my mind is goin', so I decide I better get busy.

I find a nub of a pencil and a notepad, and I make a list of things that need to be done to get ready for Christmas.

1. *Present for Daddy – turtle carving*
2. *Present for Mama – handkerchief*
3. *Present for Josy – shirt*
4. *Christmas tree*
5. *Christmas meal*

The first three things on the list are already done – I finished whittlin' my turtle for Daddy a long time ago, and it's hidden in my wardrobe. I stitched a needlepoint handkerchief for Mama with pretty purple flowers usin' thread that I got from Mr. Macafee in exchange for just a few strawberries last summer. And me and Mama made Josy a shirt out of a feed sack, and I know he's gonna love it.

Now for the Christmas tree. We got plenty of pine trees around here, but I ain't about to go chop one of those giants down by myself, not to mention they'd all be too big to put in the house. So I bundle up in my coat and scarf and head out for the treeline where Josy set up his traps. Out there, I seen some little ol' red cedar trees that I could probably chop down with no more than a hatchet, but I get Daddy's axe from the woodshed, just to be sure.

Choppin' down a tree is a whole lot more work than I expected, even though it is a small tree – and that's the main problem, really, 'cause I gotta chop way low down to the ground, and all its limbs are in the way, but somehow I figure it out without losin' any of my own limbs, and I hang the axe in my overalls belt loop and trudge back to the house, draggin' the tree behind me. I set the tree in a corner of the front room in a bucket filled with rocks to keep it steady.

By the time I'm done, me and the floor both are covered in dirt and melted snow and red cedar needles and juniper berries. But, boy, that smell is heavenly. Then I go to the shed and find the box with Christmas ornaments in it. We ain't got many, and they're 'bout as old as Santa Claus himself, but once I get the tree decorated, I'm startin' to feel the Christmas spirit, even with all my frettin' about Mama and Daddy and Josy.

Lastly, I pull out the Christmas wreath, which is dusty and shabby and bent outa shape and missin' a few of its jingle bells 'cause I been usin' 'em to make cat toys. I shake it like a tambourine and dust motes fly around like fairy dust. I hang it up on a big nail over the front door, then come back inside and stand with my hands on my hips, inspectin' my tree work and wonderin' what to do next.

Last on the list is the Christmas meal, and I need to sit and think about that a spell, but before long, I got a bunch of ideas and a plan so solid that I wish Josy was here so I could tell him about it.

I'm so excited that I'm runnin' around like a chicken with its head cut off, first to the chicken coop to package up some fresh eggs to trade with Mrs. Porter for some potatoes, then to the cellar to package up a bit of ham to trade to Mr. Macafee for a turkey, then to the woodshed for some firewood to trade to Mr. Tomlinson for one of his pumpkins that he always brings to Macafee's during fall and winter, then to Josy's traps for a rabbit to trade at the bakery for a loaf of bread.

Cheryl King

And with all that, my next two days are busier than a bee in a honeycomb, and I'm sprawled out on the floor by the wood stove, plumb tired, when I hear Molly and the wagon clompin' down the lane.

I hop up and run out to the porch, and my heart is so full of relief at seein' both Mama and Daddy in the wagon, that tears just burst outa my eyes, and I'm laughin' and sobbin' at the same time, and when the wagon gets close enough, I see Mama and Daddy's faces and I fall silent.

They look more exhausted than I coulda ever been, even with all the work I done by myself, and they look full of hope and regret at the same time, and I cain't figure out why, 'til I see that Daddy's bandaged-up hand don't look like a hand no more. Matter fact, it looks like Daddy don't even got a hand no more 'cause his left arm looks shorter than his right and it just sorta ends halfway below his elbow, and he sees me lookin', and they're climbin' the porch steps, and Daddy hugs me with his good arm, and all he says is, "They had to take my hand."

10

What Josy Brung Home

The fact that Daddy had to have his hand cut off brings about some confusing emotions for a while. Daddy says it was either his hand or his life, and the doctor at the clinic in Knoxville said that if Daddy had gotten there even just an hour later, he coulda died. Plus, Daddy says he ain't in so much pain no more. So there are the things we say out loud: *Thank God we got him to the clinic in time. It's better to have Daddy with no left hand than to have no Daddy. We are so blessed.* But underneath that, there are the fears we all have but nobody's sayin' out loud: *How's the farm gonna survive if Daddy cain't work? What's gonna happen come plantin' season? How's Daddy gonna take care of us — or himself?*

So, like always, we bury those fears, and to keep 'em from bubblin' to the surface, we get busy. On Christmas Eve, we wake up early and go to church, and it feels good to have all our friends from town prayin' over us and blessin' Daddy. Then we go home and take care of some of the chores, like the washin'. In the wintertime when it's too cold to wash the clothes down at the creek, we bring the washboard in and clean the clothes in the washtub, then hang the clothes up on the back porch. Mrs. Porter down the lane makes lye soap, and we trade eggs, potholders, or pork sausages for the soap we need for the washin', and it smells real good the way Mrs. Porter makes it 'cause she puts in some lavender.

Once we get the clothes washed, me and Mama start makin' the dough for the pumpkin pie. Mama was real impressed with all the things I done to get ready for Christmas, by the way, and both Mama and Daddy ooh'ed and ahh'ed over the little ol' Christmas tree. Daddy said, "You cut that down by yourself?" with a big ol' grin, and Mama said all the things I got for the meal are just perfect.

So we're makin' the dough for the pie, and Mama makes it stretch by using a little less flour than usual, and when we make the pumpkin filling, we use a little less sugar than usual, but Mama adds honey and vanilla beans, and I just cain't wait to have a taste.

Daddy's restin', which is a new thing around here and kinda hard to get used to. I cain't remember a time I seen Daddy restin' in broad daylight, 'cause there's always work to be done on a farm, or so he likes to tell us.

And just when we get the pie into the oven, our ears perk up and we all look at each other, 'cause we hear the rumble of an engine. We step out onto the porch, and down at the end of our drive, three men are jumpin' outa the back of a truck, and the truck turns around and heads back on up the lane, and the three men are trudging up the drive toward the house.

Daddy looks like he's wonderin' if he needs to get his rifle, but I scoot closer and squint my eyes. "It's Josy!" I holler that over and over and then I'm runnin' down the porch steps and Mama's followin' behind me and Daddy's hangin' back on the porch with a big grin on his face.

I practically run him right over, I do, and he scoops me up and says, "Hey, Junie June! Told ya I'd be back for Christmas!"

Then Mama's huggin' him and cryin' without tears, and then Josy spots Daddy on the porch and waves, and Daddy waves, and then we're walkin' back up to the porch and Josy motions toward the two men with him and says, "This is Pate, and this is Charlie. They been lookin' out for me real well this whole time."

Mama says, "How d'ya do?" to both of 'em, but I'm starin' and cain't say nothin' 'cause Pate's got skin the color of chocolate puddin', and I ain't never seen no one the color of chocolate puddin' this close up before, and Josy nudges me with his elbow and tells me to stop starin'.

Then we get to the porch and Josy notices Daddy's missin' hand, and he's askin' what happened, and Daddy's tryin' to smile and laugh about it, but Josy looks dead serious and stricken like somebody stole somethin' from him.

Mama rushes around to get everybody a cup of coffee and apologizes that it's gonna be real weak coffee, but I don't think she needs to apologize none 'cause these fellas look like they ain't ate nothin' in days, let alone drunk good coffee.

I take Josy and the men's hats and coats and plop 'em down on Josy's bed, and Josy pulls the dining chairs into the front room for him and his friends to sit in, and then Mama sits in her chair and Daddy and me sit on the couch, and Josy and his friends sit in the dining chairs, and we all sit there and stare at each other for a spell, but I especially stare at Pate.

Now that I'm gettin' a good look at these fellas, I see how rough they look. Charlie is tall and lanky like Daddy, and he looks almost as old, dark red in the face, with lots of dusty hair all over, and dirt and soot settled into deep lines. Pate, the color of chocolate puddin', cain't be much older than Josy, and in the middle of a craggy face are deep brown eyes, kind eyes that twinkle. But mostly he looks real uncomfortable, and I suppose that could be 'cause we're all starin' at him.

"So, where are you fellas from?" Mama asks.

Charlie answers for both of 'em. "Pate here's originally from Memphis, and me – I come from Kentucky, but the railroad's been my home for a while now." Pate nods, and then Josy explains that there's a whole world out there of train hoppers that been hoboin' since before the Depression begun.

"Pate and Charlie helped me out, showed me the ropes," Josy says, "and the best part is, we found work just outside of Nashville, digging ditches and unloading coal cars." Then he reaches down and starts diggin' in the pack he was carryin', which is a whole lot fuller than it was when he left, and I notice his hands are rough and calloused and dirty and scratched up. My eyes wander up his arms and to his face, and I see that the whole rest of him is rough and calloused and dirty and scratched up, too, and he got hair on his face that he didn't have when he left, and he's a sight thinner, smaller somehow, like in just three weeks he grew into a hero and shrunk at the same time.

Josy pulls a stack of dollar bills outa his bag and hands 'em to Daddy and says, "This oughta be enough for the mortgage payment for a while, plus some extra for new shoes for June and maybe some clothes for you and Mama."

Our eyes go wide, and Daddy looks disbelievin', like maybe he's wonderin' if Josy come by that money honest, and

Josy knows he's wonderin' that, 'cause he says real quick, "I worked hard for this money, every bit of it."

Daddy nods and he's tearin' up, and he says, "I know ya did, son." And I'm thinkin' Daddy feels ashamed again, both 'cause he thought for a second that the money coulda been stolen and 'cause he needs his own son to support the family.

Charlie reaches over and pats Josy on the back and says, "You got a good son, here, Mr. Baker. He's a real hard worker indeed." Everybody nods to that, and I look at Mama, who looks a million shades of relieved 'cause Josy came through and maybe we won't lose the farm and maybe we'll be okay.

Now I'm starin' at Pate again, and he's just starin' straight ahead and sittin' down real tight in the wooden chair like he wants to dissolve into it and be invisible. We ain't never had a colored person in our house, but if you ask me, he's just like us, only different. And that difference is enough that the whole house feels tense, and everybody seems nervous, and that's the silence we sit in for a spell.

Mama clears her throat after a while and asks, "How did you all meet?" And then it's a cacophony of talkin', with Josy recountin' his first time jumpin' up into a freight car and Charlie describin' how he grabbed Josy when he was about to fall back down and Charlie talkin' 'bout how innocent little Josy and scared little Pate hit it off real good, and both Josy and Charlie laugh and laugh like they've just had the grandest time out there on the railroad. But Pate just sits there and nods, and I wonder about his life. He looks so young but with a lifetime of scars, and he's so quiet that I begin to wonder if he can talk at all, so I turn to him and ask, "How'd you end up train hoppin', Pate?"

Pate shrugs and looks down and says, "Didn't have nowheres else to go, I guess."

Then Charlie nods toward Pate and says, "Pate's mumma died and he didn't ever know his daddy. He come wanderin' into our camp one night, and some of the other guys don't take too kindly to colored folk, so they was bein' mean and tryin' to chase him off. But I seen he was just a kid – that was 'bout a year ago – and I took up for him and been lookin' after him ever since."

And then Charlie launches into more stories about Pate and what all they been through since the two of them met, and I drift off into a daze, and I know this is gonna sound bad, but I guess I wasn't real interested in the answer to my question; I just wanted to hear Pate talk, and now that Charlie's doin' all the talkin', I ain't interested no more.

"Somethin' smells real good, Mama," Josy says suddenly, and Mama jumps about a mile high and shouts, "The pie!" and we sure are relieved that it ain't burnin' or ruint, but it's ready to come outa the oven, and when it does, the whole house smells like heaven, if heaven is made outa pumpkin and vanilla. Josy and Charlie come gather 'round the pie and Mama has to shoo them away and tell 'em it's for tomorrow. And Pate's still sittin' in his chair and starin' ahead, and I start to feel sad for him 'cause he looks like he might feel kinda lost.

Mama makes Josy and Pate and Charlie take off their dirty clothes after scroungin' around for somethin' for them to wear so's we can wash their clothes and they can get cleaned up, and that takes nearbout an hour 'cause they're so dirty. We hang their wet clothes up on the back porch to dry, and then we have a supper of bean soup and spicy carrots.

When Charlie and Josy thank Mama for the supper and for doin' the washin', I holler, "I helped!" and they all think that's funny for some reason, and all the sudden I feel like a little kid when just two days ago I was fendin' for myself and choppin' down a Christmas tree like a grown adult. And I decide that I cain't wait 'til I'm thirteen, 'cause bein' twelve is nothin' but goin' back and forth between feelin' like a grown-up and feelin' like a child, and it's exhausting.

Daddy grabs a lantern and takes Josy and Charlie out to the woodshed to show 'em what he's been workin' on, but Pate doesn't follow; he just stays in his chair at the table, starin' straight ahead 'til Mama asks if she can get him anything else, and he shakes his head. I decide right then that I'm gonna do somethin' to cheer him up, 'cause I don't know what all he's been through, but I do know he must be real lonely without a mama and daddy, so I go get me and Josy's jar of marbles and scoot my chair right up next to Pate's. I take the lid off and hold the jar up under Pate's eyes. "You wanna see our marbles?"

Pate sits up a little and looks down into the jar but don't say nothin'. I reach in and grab a couple and hold 'em out in my palm.

"I love lookin' at marbles. No two are the same, like snowflakes," I say.

Pate nods and then looks right into my eyes for the first time, but only for a split second, then he's starin' ahead again, like he ain't supposed to look no one in the eye.

"You can take one out if you want," I tell him, but he don't make a move, so I dig around in the jar for my favorite one, which is now one of the purple ones Josy gave me for my birthday. When I find it, I smile real big and hold it up to Pate's eyes. "This here's my favorite one. Look at how that purple spot right there sparkles."

And I turn it 'til the light from the lantern on the table shines on it just right, and I hold it there and look at Pate, and he looks like he might almost smile.

"Me and Josy made up a game we play with these marbles. Wanna play?" I don't even wait for an answer; I take the jar and scoot around to the other side of the table. I explain the rules and then we start playin', and even though Pate don't talk much, I can see that he's real nice. He lets me win almost every round, 'cept once when he's holdin' up a plain clear marble and I got a real pretty pink and green one, and he says his is the winner.

"You jokin'," I say. "Mine is most definitely prettier than that one. It's plain."

And he says, real low and quiet-like, "It ain't plain; it's pure. You can see right through it. It's almost invisible. That makes it somethin' special." And that's the most words I've heard him speak since they got here, so I let him have that round.

When Josy comes back inside he says all scoldin'-like, "You makin' poor Pate play that game with ya? Sorry 'bout that, Pate," and I feel like a kid again.

Daddy and Josy go and bed down the animals, and me and Mama set up the front room with blankets on the floor for Pate and on the couch for Charlie, and we all go to bed, glad to have Josy back home, bellies full of supper, heads full of dreams, and hearts full of hope.

Christmas morning is bright and sunny, and Mama's already up cookin' the turkey, and the front room is so hot with the wood stove goin' that me and Mama go to sit out on the porch to cool off, steppin' quietly over Pate on our way out. He and Charlie and Josy are all still sleepin'. Mama says they need their rest 'cause they probably don't get much of it these days. Daddy comes up from the barn and sits with us on the porch for a spell.

"You alright, Daddy?" I ask. We ain't talked much since he and Mama came back from the clinic in Knoxville.

He reaches over and squeezes my arm. "Better than ever, Junie," he says. "It's a real good thing what Joseph done. I know we were mighty worried and all, but what he brung back to us is a gift from God, and we should be thankful."

"I am, Daddy," I say. "When are they leavin'?"

Daddy looks out toward the horizon, like he's watchin' for a train that'll be comin' up any minute now. "They gotta leave tomorrow, early mornin'."

Me and Mama sigh and nod, then we get up and go back inside, where the smell of food cookin' has got the army stirred. I butter the biscuits that Mama made and take a plate in to Pate and Charlie.

"Here ya go," I say to Pate as I set the plate down on a table next to the couch. He nods and rubs his eyes and tucks into two biscuits at once. Josy comes out and joins them, and I sit and listen to stories of the railroad. Charlie got a funny way of talkin', and Pate got a funny way of not talkin', and Josy's just Josy but a little bit different, and the whole thing makes me laugh inside.

Then silly ol' Bug makes an appearance, mewling on the front porch like she knows Josy's home, and Josy's happier than a pig in a mud bath, and he runs out there and scoops Bug up and then hollers, "Where's all her kittens?"

So we put on shoes and coats and go tromping around, lookin' for the kittens, which ain't little kittens anymore, I remind Josy. We only find three of 'em – two in the barn, and one in the woodshed. I hand one to Pate to hold, and he looks scared of it, and he's holdin' it with his arms stretched out in front of him and a grimace on his face that sets all of us to laughin'. And I tell Pate, "You ain't gonna get warts from it like a toad or somethin'," and I show him how to hold it up close and snuggly-like, and it takes some coaxing, but eventually, he's cuddlin' the kitten and almost smilin', at least for a second, before he puts it down.

Mama gets Pate to help her in the kitchen and Daddy gets Charlie to help him in the barn, and me and Josy take the wagon to say merry Christmas to Margaret Ann and her mama and make sure they're alright. I take a handkerchief I stitched for Margaret Ann, and Mama sends along a loaf of strawberry bread. I sure been thinkin' about Margaret Ann and how she must feel horrible to have Christmas without her daddy, and without her brothers and sisters, too, but at least they're still alive and may someday come back home.

She's excited when she sees us clompin' up to her house, and she runs out in her stocking feet and hugs our necks before we even get up to her porch. Mrs. Murphy comes out and thanks us as we hand over the loaf of bread and say merry Christmas, and her eyes are puffy and red, and I feel real sorry for her.

Margaret Ann gives me a little bow to wear in my hair, and she says she knows I don't normally wear bows but maybe I could wear it to church, and I put it right on, and we get to talkin' and gigglin' and Josy says, "Come on, Junie, we gotta get back now." Even though it was just for a little while, I'm real glad I got to see Margaret Ann on Christmas.

Later, we gather 'round the little ol' Christmas tree, and I make sure to tell Josy that I chopped it down and hauled it into the house by myself and put all the decorations on, and Josy ruffles the top of my head and says what a grown-up I am, and Charlie laughs, and I look over to Pate, and he's noddin' like he's impressed.

We weren't expectin' Josy to bring anyone with him when he came back, so we don't got gifts for everyone, and that makes us feel a little sorry 'bout passin' around our gifts to each other, but Charlie says feedin' them and washin' their clothes is gift enough for them.

I was right about Josy loving the shirt me and Mama made for him, and he puts it on right away. Mama cries into the handkerchief I made her, and Daddy crows about the turtle I whittled. Mama gives me some potpourri that she made herself and says I can put some in my bedroom and in the outhouse to keep everything smellin' nice. Josy drops a whole handful of caramel cubes into a bowl, and I hoot and holler and dance around and then hand one to everybody, my mouth already full of two of 'em.

Then we all go outside, where Daddy says he's got somethin' for me, and what he gives me is a pistol. Daddy says it's a .22 Colt Army revolver and he's gonna teach me to hunt with it and it'll be better than tryin' to use a big ol' rifle. Mama goes back into the house to tend to the turkey and potatoes, and all the men take turns tryin' out the gun with a target that Daddy set up, and they show me how to load it and how to aim and how to shoot, and it turns out I'm mighty good at shootin'. All the sudden I don't feel like a kid no more.

Even though I know Josy's gotta go back out on the train and Daddy's missin' a hand and Margaret Ann is missin' a daddy and the whole country's in a heap of trouble, this just might be the best Christmas I ever had.

Since correct

Cheryl King

11

Honest-to-God

Lies

Our house feels heavy with dread the next morning, knowing Josy's leavin' again. Mama loads Josy and Pate and Charlie's packs up with as much food as we can spare, and there's no shortage of hugs and kisses and pats on the back. I been thinkin' 'bout the way Pate played the marble game with me even though he didn't have to and maybe didn't want to, and the way he took a shine to that clear marble, which I still say is downright plain, but he surely did like it a lot. And the next thing I do, and I honestly don't know why, but I go and dig that plain clear marble outa the jar and I secretly slip it into a pocket in Pate's pack when no one's lookin'.

I don't know if he'll find it in there or what he'll do with it or what he'll think about it, 'cause honestly, what does a

97

teenage-boy-almost-a-man need with a marble when he's out ridin' the rails, but I hope that someday he'll discover that marble and will understand it's a thank you for bein' kind.

"When will you be back, Josy?" I ask when they's all ready to leave.

"Well, I may be gone a little longer this time, June," he says, lookin' from me to Mama and Daddy. "There's word of some folks out near Memphis that pay real good for handymen during winter, and if we stay on long enough ..." He trails off and we're all lost in our heads, thinkin' on that and rememberin' how hard it was to be without Josy for three weeks.

And then just like that, Josy's gone, hoofin' down the lane toward Knoxville, toward a dangerous life on the railroad, riskin' his life so that our family can survive.

Just like the last time he left, me and Mama and Daddy sulk around a bit, but soon we get back to work. There's a lot of cleanin' to be done after havin' houseguests, Mama says, and I think about ol' Charlie and Pate and I'm real glad Josy's got friendly folks to look after him out there on the railroad. I wonder if Margaret Ann's daddy'd still be alive if he had folks to look after him. And that's what I'm thinkin' about as me and Daddy head to the feed store.

I'm drivin' the wagon for the first time, 'cause Daddy cain't hold the reins no more. Well, he could hold 'em with one hand, but he says it's about time I learned anyhow, and he's sittin' next to me and tellin' me what to do and what not to do. It's real easy. Molly's a good mule, and she's walkin' nice and slow, like she knows she gotta be careful since it's my first time drivin'. I steer her real cautious-like around that spot where I saw the king snake awhile back, and Daddy just looks at me like I'm crazy, which I probably am, but I don't want to be drivin' over no snake. Besides, I've seen Molly get spooked by snakes before.

We park at the feed store, but Daddy lets me go over to the Sweet Shop, just to look and smell, not buy anything, but the first thing I see through the window before I can even open the door is Margaret Ann sittin' at a table with Jimmy Mack, and they're sittin' real cozy and smilin' at each other. I sneak up closer and peek in, keepin' against the wall so they cain't see me. They're sharin' a soda, like an honest-to-God boyfriend-girlfriend couple, and I don't know why, but my heart is beatin' real fast and heat is pulsin' through my body and up to my face. I put my cold hands up to my cheeks to quell the burning, but I cain't shake this feeling of betrayal. I turn and go back to the feed store, ready to get on home.

"That was fast," Daddy says. "How was the sweet shop?"

"Aw, fine. I mean, I guess. Can we just go home?"

I spend a long time thinkin' about Margaret Ann and Jimmy Mack, and there ain't no reason why I should be upset or jealous. He ain't my boyfriend. I don't want a boyfriend anyhow. But didn't she say she was bored of him and I could have him? Yes, she specifically said that. And she knows I been sweet on him for a long time. I cain't remember a time I wasn't dotin' on Jimmy Mack. But that don't make him my boyfriend, does it? Well now I guess I'll never know, will I, 'cause Margaret Ann got her paws on him. Listen to me, how silly I'm bein'. I ain't got no right to be this way. Margaret Ann's been my best friend forever and ever, and she always will be, so I need to just snap out of it.

And once the first real cold snap hits – and I do mean cold, 'cause December's little ol' snow ain't got nothin' on January and February's freezin' weather – I do snap out of it, at least for a while. Me and Mama double down on sewin' up things that folks need in the wintertime, and we do alright sellin' scarves and mittens, but they don't go for what they used to since nobody got that much money these days.

One blustery day, Mama sends me to town to deliver a scarf and a pair of mittens to Mr. Macafee, and since I'm passin' by Margaret Ann's house, I decide to stop in and say hello. I'm takin' the wagon by myself and this'll be the fourth time for me to do that, and I already feel like an ol' pro, a real grown adult. I think Molly likes me drivin' better than anyone, 'cause she whinnies at me to pet her, and I give her lots of attention, talkin' to her the whole way there and the whole way back, and now without me even tellin' her, she sidesteps the spot in the road I like to call the snake spot.

Margaret Ann looks real happy to see me, and she don't act like anything's wrong or nothin', and we stand there on her front porch shiverin' and talkin' about nothin', until finally I ask, "You seen Jimmy Mack lately?"

She wrinkles up her nose, and there's a twitch in her cheek when she says, "No. Why would I see Jimmy Mack?" And that's all she says about it, and that's all I say, and then I gotta get on to town.

I start thinkin' maybe it wasn't Margaret Ann that I saw in the window. Maybe it was some other girl who looked like her. But no, I think I'd be able to tell the difference between my best friend and somebody else. But why would she lie to me? I just cain't think of a reason and it starts to make my head hurt tryin' to figure it out, so I just get my delivery done and get back home and try not to think about it.

Back at home, after I've helped with the chores, I lie back in my bed and read by the light of my lantern 'til suppertime. I've already read all the books I got for my birthday, and now I'm readin' 'em for a second time. I just love Virginia Woolf, and *A Room of One's Own*, even though it's a sight challenging for me, inspires me to do things, to stand up as a strong girl who's almost grown up and is worthy of respect from all people, just as much as men are, and I love this feeling this book gives me. It's amazin' to me that a book – a collection of words on paper – can make a person feel powerful and important and invincible.

Winter stretches out her long, icy fingers across eastern Tennessee, and in the darkest days of winter, the only good thing we got to look forward to is Josy comin' home, and finally, near the middle of February, he does, just in time for Daddy's birthday. He brings Pate and Charlie with him again, and they stay a couple days to get clean, get some rest, and to get some good cookin'. Josy don't have as much money this time around, but he gives what little he earned to Daddy, and he gives me a handful of caramel cubes. He also gives me some work gloves he bargained for, and a nice church hat for Daddy.

Pate don't say nothin' to me about the marble I put in his pack, and we don't play the marble game neither. They all seem too busy while they're here, spendin' all their time in the woodshed and the barn, and the time goes by so fast that before I know it, they're gone again.

They leave us with three new milkin' stools for Daddy to sell, and I feel so grateful to Pate and Charlie for helpin' with that for free, and I know Daddy does too, 'cause he offers to pay them for their work, but they repeat what they said at Christmastime, that feedin' them and cleanin' their clothes is payment enough.

I get so full of different emotions when Josy comes home and then leaves so soon, that I'm exhausted from it. And I guess Mama is too, 'cause the mornin' after they leave, she stays in bed for a long time past breakfast, so long that I go in to check on her. She says she ain't feelin' too well, and she sure don't look well to me neither, so I make some soup and bring it to her, and then she stays in bed all day long, almost 'til supper time.

Whatever Mama's come down with don't keep her from wantin' to go to church, even though the cold wind bites into our faces and sets her to coughin' up a storm.

I see Margaret Ann and her mama at church, but she don't come to talk to me, or even look at me, which I think is real strange. The next Sunday, she's ignorin' me again, and I cain't think of a single reason why she would act that way, 'cause she's the one who lied to me about Jimmy Mack, so if anyone should be ignorin' somebody, it should be me ignorin' her.

So after the service, when all the kids are standin' around wishin' there were doughnuts ('cause there ain't been doughnuts after church for quite a while), I march over to Margaret Ann, ready to give her the whatfor.

But when I approach her, she's got a funny look on her face. She motions for me to follow her, and we step into a corner where there ain't no one around, and this is when I figure she's gonna fess up about her and Jimmy Mack, but what she actually says, is, "June, my mama says I can't be your friend anymore," and she's lookin' like she might cry, and she continues, "'cause y'all got that colored boy stayin' at your house sometimes."

And I just stand there, the words caught in my throat, 'cause I don't understand or even know if I heard her right, and before I can say anything, she's bouncin' back through the crowd of churchgoers to stand by her mama.

I stand there in that corner for the longest time, feelin' like I've lost my very best friend in the whole world for no good reason.

When I tell Mama later that night about what Margaret Ann said, Mama clicks her tongue and shakes her head. "I'm sorry, June," she says, "I'm sorry." And she hugs me close to her while tryin' to suppress a cough.

"But why? Pate's a good person, and he's been real good to Josy. Why would anyone have a problem with that?" I'm beggin' Mama to make sense of this, 'cause I don't understand why a perfectly good friendship should be thrown away just like that.

Mama shakes her head. "Well, June, I don't have the answer you want. But I can tell you that maybe in your lifetime, the world will change. In the meantime, you can choose hatred, or you can choose kindness. I want my family to choose kindness."

I nod, but then I wonder if other people in town's gonna have a problem with it too. "Mama," I ask, "are we gonna get in trouble for havin' Pate over?"

She shakes her head, but her eyes don't look too certain. "I don't think so, baby, but we'll cross that bridge when we come to it."

She pats my hand and then she says, "And June, please don't hold this against Margaret Ann. She can't help the rules her mama sets. And her mama can't help the way of things, either."

I think on that for a long time, and even though I don't rightly agree, and even though Margaret Ann surely lied to me for some reason, which makes me think I cain't trust her, I decide that I will do as Mama says, and I will choose kindness, no matter what.

12

Fresh Air
and Exercise

Afte r the last frost, me and Daddy do our best with planting the carrots and onions, but even with a reduced crop, we cain't keep up with just the three hands between us and with Mama still sick. Seems like Mama's always been prone to comin' down with illnesses, and no matter how strong she is, she has a real hard time with gettin' sick. But this time is worse. She has barely enough energy to hold a broom, let alone a cast-iron skillet, so we're stayin' hungry longer and stayin' dirty longer, and that's just how it goes.

We haven't had much meat in a long while 'cause we used up all our pork. I gave up on Josy's traps a long time ago. Most of 'em's all twisted up and broken, and besides that, I keep forgettin' to set 'em with bait. I don't much like wrestlin' those poor rabbits outa the snares anyhow, and sometimes by the time I get around to checkin' the traps, whatever was caught in 'em is already ate up by ants or some other predator. The only way we get meat nowadays is to sell somethin', trade somethin', or shoot somethin'.

Daddy's been takin' me huntin' with my new pistol. We go way out deep in the woods behind the creek and behind the pasture. The first time we went out was a disaster 'cause I didn't want to hurt any animals. So he agreed to let me do target practice before tryin' to shoot real animals again. We painted a bullseye on a piece of wood, and each day we'd move it further out or hide it among brush and trees to make it harder to see. It didn't take me no time at all to start hittin' the bullseye every time, so Daddy said that was enough play shootin'. It was time to get us some meat. The last time we went out huntin', I got us two wild turkeys, which we ate on for three or four days, and I used the feathers to make some cat toys.

I still ain't seen all the kittens, which are all grown up now, and I guess they're just goin' their own separate ways. Bug still hangs around the most, and three of her babies are usually stalkin' around somewhere, but two done gone plumb missin', and I don't know if they've been killed by somethin' or starved to death or just run away. I just hope they all don't turn up pregnant, the ones that are girls, anyway, 'cause we don't need a million cats around here, and the way things are goin', Daddy's liable to shoot 'em and put 'em in a stew.

Josy comes home with a bit of money in the middle of plantin' season, but it ain't enough to do a whole lotta good, and I start wonderin' if it's even worth him bein' out there on the railroad. But the best part about it is that he brings Pate and Charlie with him again, and they help out with the corn, which is our most important crop 'cause we can sell it, cook it, grind it up for cornmeal, or feed it to the hens, so it goes a long way. They also help with some projects Daddy wanted done – stuff we can sell and repairs to the house.

And the really best thing is that every time Josy comes home, whether he made a little money or a lot, no matter what, he always has a few caramel cubes to give me. I don't know where or how he gets 'em, but they sure do cheer me up.

Josy's real scared about Mama's condition, 'cause she looks weak and has trouble breathin', so he talks her into lettin' him take her to see Dr. Jamison. Me and Mama and Josy pile into the wagon and Daddy stays behind to keep workin' with Pate and Charlie. The whole way there, Mama's carryin' on about how we cain't afford this and she'll be just fine with some rest and hot tea. But when we get there, it don't take Dr. Jamison no time at all to figure out Mama's got the consumption. Tuberculosis.

He says she can drink some cough syrup, but the best way to get rid of the consumption is to get outside in the fresh air and to exercise and let it run its course. Mama just laughs at that 'cause she ain't got enough energy to stand up for too long, let alone exercise. But she does take some of his advice, and we help her move her bed out onto the porch so she can be outside in the fresh spring air.

We make her a cough syrup outa honey, lemon juice, and whiskey that ol' Charlie carries in a hip flask. Pate comes up to the porch and checks on her 'bout a million times while they're here, and she tells him he needs to go on and quit makin' her laugh 'cause that makes her cough, and ain't we tryin' to get her to stop coughin'?

The fresh air and cough syrup seem to do some good after a couple of days, and Mama gets up and about a little more. Once Josy and them leave, she ain't got much choice in the matter, 'cause "the work ain't gonna do itself," she says. One night I get real worried, though, 'cause Mama coughs into her handkerchief, and when she pulls it away, I see blood on it.

"Mama, ain't there anything else we can do?"

She shakes her head and says, "Oh, sure, if we had money, I'd go to one of those fancy hospitals where they keep tuberculosis patients isolated and give 'em fancy treatments, maybe even surgery. They got one out in Nashville, I hear."

"Do you want to go, Mama?"

"Hush, now, June, you know that's not even an option for us. I'll follow Dr. Jamison's orders and everything'll be alright." As if to prove a point, Mama stands up and spreads her arms out and says, "Look, I'm feelin' well enough to exercise now." And she does a jumpin' jack right then and there. Then she sits back down, coughin' and huffin' and puffin'.

It frightens me somethin' awful to see her so sick, but she laughs it off and says she's more worried about gettin' us sick and maybe she should start wearin' a mask over her mouth, but I tell her if we were gonna get sick, we'd already done so 'cause we been around her germs all this time. So she uses her handkerchief when she's gotta cough, and we go about our business the best we can.

Over the next coupla months, Mama loses a lot of weight, so much that she looks more of a child than I do. Some days she sleeps almost the whole day 'cause she's up at night sweatin' so much she looks like she just took a bath. The air's gettin' a lot warmer out there now, so I go out on the porch and fan her with a big hand fan. It's days like this that get me real scared about Mama dyin'.

There's a place in the woods I like to go when I'm feelin' down. It's a clump of twenty or thirty birch trees real close to the creek with trunks so thin I can wrap my hand right around 'em and my fingers touch. Me and Josy call 'em The Depression Trees, 'cause they're skin and bones just like everybody else nowadays. I go and weave myself in and out and around The Depression Trees, wrappin' my hands around the trunks, and I can hear the bubblin' sounds of the creek and the tweetin' of the birds, and after a while, I feel at peace.

Mama has good days, though, and I guess I oughta focus on those rather than cryin' about the bad days. When Mama's feelin' good, we cook breakfast and supper together, and we play the radio while we cook, and we sing and try to see if Mama can get through a whole song without coughin'. One time she does, and we dance a little jig to celebrate, but then she has to sit down and rest a spell. Sometimes when we're sewin' together, I count to see how high I can count before Mama coughs again. One time I got up to five hundred and thirty-seven.

Mama's been sewin' a lot more lately 'cause she can do that while sittin' down, and it's easy work. Her stitches ain't as straight 'cause she's coughin' and shakin' a lot, and she goes a bit slower, but she's still able to make nice things. She stopped makin' aprons and bonnets a while ago, 'cause nobody wants to spend their money on those types of things nowadays, but she can make a little money with mittens and quilts, which she can sew without any patterns to follow.

I help her as much as I can when I ain't helpin' Daddy out on the farm, and I do all the clothes washin' now, and most of the cleanin'. I'm plumb wore out most nights, and I look at Mama, who's tryin' so hard to keep on goin' while she's in pain, holdin' her chest and holdin' in coughs and still holdin' it together with a smile, and I think about how amazing she is and I hope I can be that strong someday.

"You already are, June," she tells me.

13

Sittin' on Top
of the World

The fall harvest is the most depressing thing I ever did see. I cain't remember a time we had such a paltry harvest. Daddy says we wasn't able to take care of the crops like we used to do, and some of those that did grow good went bad before we could get to 'em. Without Josy here to help, well, that's just how it is, I guess.

Most of what we can salvage goes straight to our kitchen or cellar, and the rest me and Daddy load up and take to the market along with a few things that Daddy made during the spring with Josy and them and a few things that me and Mama sewed.

We end up makin' more trades than dollars. The townsfolk are generally real happy to have some fresh vegetables in exchange for a bit of ground beef, and we get some honey and moonshine for Mama's medicine from Mr. Clay ("Shh, don't tell").

I get a glimpse of Margaret Ann at the market, and my heart skips a beat 'cause I see Jenny May with her, and I'm so happy to see her that for a second I have a mind to run over there and hug her neck and ask about Say-Lynn and all the boys. But then my feet freeze right where they are 'cause I see Jenny May doin' the same thing, gettin' ready to run over to me with a big ol' grin on her face, and all the sudden Margaret Ann grabs Jenny May's arm and shakes her head and I can see the word formed in her lips: "No!" And they both just turn back around.

I'm thinkin' about that encounter while I'm mixin' up Mama's cough syrup later, and I'm wonderin' when Jenny May came back and whether all the others came back too, and I'm thinkin' about how pleased Margaret Ann must be to have at least one of her sisters back home with her, and I just wish so much that I could talk to her and we could be friends like we used to.

We could talk about how school's been goin', 'cause I sure miss it, and I'd ask after Miss Glass and all the other kids, and we could have a sleepover again and do our makeup and read grown-up magazines. We could even talk about Jimmy Mack, 'cause I ain't even mad anymore that Margaret Ann shared a soda with him and lied to me about it, no sir, not anymore. I just miss Margaret Ann too much. I'd tell her all about Josy's adventures and how he met Pate and Charlie and how they been helpin' us a lot every time they come home, and how Pate's been real nice to me and Mama, and then I remember that's the reason Margaret Ann ain't my friend anymore – 'cause of Pate bein' colored and stayin' in our house. And then I get mad again.

And I'm thinkin' so hard about all of this that I'm not payin' attention to what I'm doin', and I accidently put I-don't-know-how-many tablespoons of moonshine in Mama's cough syrup bottle 'steada just one, and when I realize what I done, my eyes go wide and I freeze. I take a minute to think about what to do. I cain't dump it all out and start over; that'd be wasteful. I cain't add more honey and lemon 'cause the bottle's already nearbout full. So I put the lid on and shrug my shoulders. It cain't hurt, right? It's just a few tablespoons. I seen ol' Charlie drink way more than that before.

The next time Mama takes some of the cough syrup, she nearbout spits it out, and she hollers, "June! What'd you do different with the cough syrup?"

I tell her what happened, and she shrugs her shoulders just like I done and says, "Well … it can't hurt, right?"

But later that night, Mama's actin' drunk as a skunk, slurrin' her words and repeatin' herself and gigglin' like a schoolgirl. Daddy lowers the newspaper he's readin' and peers over top of it at Mama, real suspicious-like, then looks over at me with his eyebrows all furrowed up. Then Mama dances over to the kitchen to take some more cough syrup, and she turns around and says, "June, I reckon you oughta mixxx up the c-cough syrup like thisss all the time, 'cause I suuure feel gooood."

And we all laugh and laugh, but then I think maybe she's right, 'cause even though she's actin' like a loon, she ain't been coughin' much, and her pale face has brightened up a nice shade of healthy pink.

Josy doesn't come home for my birthday, and this is the first birthday I ever had without him, and it makes me feel real lonely. Mama makes me a cake, but it tastes strange without butter, which we haven't been makin' lately 'cause we're just too tired and too busy. And she gives me a scarf she sewed using a flour sack and some rabbit fur she musta been savin' for a while 'cause I cain't remember the last time I caught a rabbit. But really, the only birthday present I want is for Mama to be well again and for Josy to be home again, and maybe also for Daddy to have his hand back. Life's been real hard for a long time, and I just ain't able to see the light at the end of the tunnel.

Mama hasn't been able to go to church since the doctor told us she has the consumption, so me and Daddy go by ourselves, and every other Sunday evening, Pastor Klein comes out to the farm and prays over Mama and gives her the Holy Communion. She cain't go anywhere now 'cause tuberculosis is real contagious and she might get the whole town sick. So I go to town when we need somethin', and on market days, it's just me and Daddy, and when we're gone into town, I spend the whole time worryin' about Mama.

I spend a lot of time in The Depression Trees, thinkin' about things and wishin' things were different. But then I remember what Pastor Klein says every time he comes to the house: "Don't pray for an easy life; pray for the strength to endure a difficult one." So I do that. I pray for strength.

One day near the end of November, I'm drivin' the wagon to town to see what I can get for Thanksgiving dinner with what little money I have and a couple things for trade. I wrap myself up in a blanket 'cause the only coat I have is too small now. It ain't that cold anyhow, just a chilly breeze. As I'm passin' by the church, I see a lot of folks standin' in a long line up to the church doors. I slow Molly down to a stop, and I watch.

I see some people I know from church and school and town, and others I never seen before. Mostly it's mamas and little kids in the line, and some of 'em don't have shoes on. Or socks. Everybody looks tired and skinny, and it reminds me of The Depression Trees.

As I watch, some people go into the church and don't come back out, but others come out with small bags of somethin', and I focus in on one particular kid who comes out with his mama, and he's diggin' in the bag the mama's carryin', and he grabs a piece of bread and devours it right then and there like he ain't ate nothin' in such a very long time. And that's when I realize this is one of them food lines I read about in the newspapers that Mr. Macafee keeps in a stack in his shop. A soup kitchen.

I snap the reins. "Go on, Molly." And we clomp away, and I'm thinkin' about that food line the whole time I'm in the Piggly Wiggly buyin' canned ham and a stick of butter, and the whole time I'm in Macafee's tradin' some eggs for some potatoes and salt, and the whole time I'm walkin' to the wagon in my shoes that may not fit right anymore but still keep my feet warm and dry. When I ride back by the church, that line is still as long as can be, and I pray that I don't never have to stand in that line.

But sometimes prayers ain't answered in the way you want 'em to be.

After we eat up all our canned ham, along with pretty much everything else, we're livin' on vegetables and eggs for a while. We pick gooseberries in the woods to make jelly, and I've learned to make a stew outa just about anything. Cornmeal can stretch a long way, and we use it to make dumplings, mush, and puddin'. Me and Daddy ain't been huntin' 'cause we been too busy doin' everything else for winter, and takin' care of

Mama. Seems her bad days are startin' to outnumber her good days lately, but I keep prayin' for strength and a cure.

Some men from the city come over sometimes wantin' to hunt on our land, and they pay us in pennies and nickels, and that gives us enough to buy some flour or wieners for three cents a pound. But still, most of the time we're down to just one meal a day. One mornin' the chickens are squawkin' up a fuss and I run outside and there's Daddy with his axe tucked into his left elbow, and with his good hand he's tryin' to catch a chicken, runnin' to and fro, and if I wasn't so shocked, the scene would be downright hilarious.

"Daddy!" I call, runnin' out to the yard. "Daddy! What're you doin'?"

He stops and sags his shoulders, droppin' the axe and heavin' heavy breaths. "June," he says between breaths. "We gotta put these chickens to better use."

"You mean eat them?"

"We ain't had proper meat in a long time, and—"

"But Daddy, if we eat them, what're we gonna do for eggs?"

"Well, we gotta make a choice, now. Your mama's gettin' sicker, and I think if she had more to eat – especially meat – she'd get better."

I look away. I hadn't thought about that, but he's right. Mama's been eatin' the least of all of us, and havin' a hearty meal every now and then, with meat, would probably do her loads of good. And if I'm honest, I'd love to have some crispy fried chicken right about now. But tradin' eggs is how we been gettin' sugar and other things we need, not to mention I may be a bit attached to these silly ol' hens.

"They won't have much meat on 'em. These hens are better for egg layin'." I see Daddy thinkin' on that, and then I

114

have an idea. "You know that the church is givin' out food? Meals for folks who need 'em? Couldn't we get some meat for Mama there every once in a while and keep our chickens for their eggs?"

And that's how it came to be that twice a week, I'm standin' in this line at the church. They give us meat, beans, potatoes, and bread, and we try to get Mama to eat most of it, though her appetite ain't what it used to be. In the food line, folks who know us try to stand as far away from me as they can, 'cause word has spread that Mama has the tuberculosis, and they don't want to take no chances. They're still kind, though, standin' three yards away and hollerin', "How's your mama doin', Miss June?" and "You tell her we're prayin' for her," and wavin' and smilin' as if they were close enough for me to see the caring on their face.

And not a one of them has said nothin' about us bein' friends with a colored person, and I'm glad of that, 'cause after losin' Margaret Ann, I couldn't stand havin' the whole town mad at us.

Josy's and Mama's birthdays and Christmas pass in a slow, cold haze of monotony, with no hope or relief in sight. Until New Year's Eve comes, and we are swept offa our feet. Josy comes home! He doesn't bring Pate and Charlie with him this time, but what he does bring home – hallelujah! – is enough to lift the spirits of the dead.

"Oh, y'all won't believe it," Josy says. "I found the best work out just past Memphis. People are hirin' there for all sorts of things."

He starts pullin' things outa his pack. "Look here, there's enough money here to maybe get caught up on the mortgage and get new coats, maybe new shoes. Set some aside for some meat and groceries, too."

He pulls out a book he brung for me, a book of poems. I flip through the table of contents. "T.S. Eliot, Robert Frost, Ezra Pound, Edward Arlington Robinson. Thank you, Josy!"

But that's not all. Josy gives Mama a box of sewin' needles and a bag of flowery cloth, and he gives Daddy a winter hat and gloves.

Daddy thanks him but holds the pair of gloves up awkwardly with his one hand, and Josy turns real red and says, "Sorry, Daddy, I—I keep forgettin'."

After a spell of silence, Josy jumps like he just remembered somethin', and with a flourish, he pulls out a handful of caramel cubes. And it may just be New Year's Eve, but it feels like a royal Christmas, and even Mama is filled with energy and hope, her eyes twinklin' like they used to, before the sickness got her.

Josy stays home a few days, and the day after New Year's, we hop into the wagon and take a trip into Knoxville to buy some coats and shoes. It's freezin' cold, but that just reminds us how much we need new coats and shoes. Mama cain't come and Daddy wants to stay home and take care of her, so it's just me and Josy, and I don't mind none, 'cause I sure have missed him.

He's lookin' mighty old to me with his growing beard and his face with new lines on it, and that's when I remember his birthday passed. "Josy! You're seventeen now!"

He ruffles my hair and smiles, and even though he looks a little older and rougher than the old Josy, before the train hoppin', right now he looks the happiest I ever seen him.

He must be all kinds of proud to be workin' hard and providin' for the family. And right on cue, he asks me, "Junie June, do you know where we're sittin'?"

116

"Why, yes, Josy, I do!" And then together we say, "We're sittin' on top of the world." And then we're singin' just like old times, all the way to Knoxville.

In town, we look in dismay at some of the shops that have been shut down. Some of them have boards over the doors and windows, and signs written out by hand, "CLOSED PERMANENTLY." But even that cain't dampen our spirits as we go in and out of shops in Knoxville and get most of what we need and some of what we want. We even go into a coffee shop and sit and enjoy hot chocolate with whipped cream on top, and I cain't remember the last time I had somethin' so delicious. We sit and relish the warmth of the coffee shop for a while, knowing our freezin' wagon ride home is gonna be long and dreadful.

"Do you like bein' out on the railroad, Josy?" I ask.

He thinks on that a minute before answering. "It's been hard work, and it's dangerous and scary sometimes. But there ain't nothin' like comin' home with a wad of cash to give you and Mama and Daddy. That makes it worth every bit of hard work."

After a while, he says, "Everything's gonna be just fine, June. I can tell it. I've been hearing stories, and people are real sure the Depression will be over soon and folks'll be able to get back to workin' and livin' right. Don't you worry none, li'l sis."

He's smilin' real big, and I look right into those deep blue eyes that look just like mine, and I memorize his face, this beaming face that I ain't seen this happy in such a long time, and it makes me happy too. And I believe him.

14

Six Months

After Josy leaves, the three of us are ridin' a wave of jubilation the likes of which this family ain't seen in a real long time. With the money Josy brung this time, Mama says we ain't too far behind on our mortgage payments now, and we fill our bellies and pantry with meat, bread, and sweets, and I know they say money cain't buy happiness, but right now I have to say, *Yes it can!* At the very least, it has bought us some relief and peace of mind, and possibly a tad bit of delirium, 'cause we sure are actin' like we're the richest folks in Maynardville. It even seems like Mama's sickness is goin' away, she's so full of joyful energy.

Our first supper after Josy's gone, me and Mama cook up a stew chock full of beef, and we make biscuits and sausages and gravy, and for dessert we make a blackberry cobbler with more than enough butter and sugar and flour, and by the time we're done with all that food, we're lazin' around like pigs. Truly happy pigs.

I look over at Mama, who's loungin' in her chair in the front room, head leanin' back, eyes closed, and lips curved in a smile. Daddy's on the couch with his feet up, and he's unbuttoned his pants and he's rubbin' his belly.

"I do believe that is the best meal I've ever had," Daddy says.

Me and Mama just nod, our senses still savoring the smell of food in the house and the taste of gravy on our lips. My eyes trail over to the kitchen pantry, which is full for the first time in so long I cain't even remember.

Then I snap to attention 'cause I just thought of somethin': "I don't have to stand in the food line no more!" And that's the thought I carry with me to bed that night and fall into a peaceful, dreamy sleep, hopin' that Josy brings home the same amount of joy next time.

Even the weather is in our favor this winter, 'cause it's sunnier and warmer than usual, and we don't get much snow at all, which makes it a whole heap easier to ride the wagon into town. Mama still has her bed out on the porch, even in February. She just covers up with an extra blanket at night and keeps the door open so she can feel the heat comin' offa the wood stove.

All the folks at church and in town ask after Mama and send their best good wishes, though they still try to keep their distance from me and Daddy.

They also ask after Josy, 'cause they've heard what he's doin'. Some folks don't approve and they don't mind sayin' so, ever so politely. *I'm sure if Mrs. Baker wasn't so sick and Mr. Baker wasn't injured, Joseph wouldn't feel the need to risk his life like that.* Or, my favorite: *Maybe next time he returns, he'll stay home and work on the farm like a good son should.* But most folks just tell me they're prayin' for Josy's safe return or they're thinkin' about our family or to let them know if we need anything.

On the few days when it snows, wouldn't you know it, even the snow is more beautiful and whiter white than ever and fluffy and soft, and we cut our work short and play in the snow. Me and Daddy make a snowman right in front of the porch so Mama can see it, and she comes down the steps and helps for a spell before feelin' too tired, and the three of us laugh and laugh like there ain't a care in the world, and the only thing that would make it better is for Josy to be here with us.

One of the things we do, now that our pantry is full, is we get back to sharin' with folks. We pack up a basket of food to take up to the school on Mondays, just like we used to, 'cept now it's just me 'cause Mama still cain't be around people. The best part about it is I get to catch a glimpse of Margaret Ann and Jenny May. They don't come out and say hello like Miss Glass and some of the kids do, but I can see 'em through the schoolhouse door, which the kids always leave wide open when they run down the steps toward the wagon.

Some of the little kids don't have shoes on again and I reckon they've outgrown or worn out the moccasins me and Mama made last year.

Miss Glass looks glad to see me, but her thankful smile doesn't quite reach her darkened eyes. She says they cut her pay again, and almost half the students don't even come to school anymore most days. She's not sure how much longer the school will stay open.

I think on that while I'm ridin' home and I think about how we've had it pretty good for a whole month while other folks are still hurtin', and I wonder when the hard times will end. I look forward to a day when Josy don't have to ride the rails no more and I can go back to school and Mama can go back to church and Daddy can go back to — my heart sinks just a little bit 'cause I remember that Daddy ain't never gonna be able to go back to farming, not like he used to.

Daddy's been havin' a real hard time of it lately. When he first got his whole hand cut off and after the bandages came off and he was all healed up and in no more pain, he was a workhorse, as determined as ever to be able to do everything he used to do. And he did, too, just twice as slow and, I'm sorry to say it, twice as poorly. And I think he just plumb wore himself out, physically and emotionally, 'cause now he's just about given up doin' much of anything.

He ain't doin' his woodworkin' anymore 'cause it turns out you cain't do much woodworkin' with only one hand, and he's tired of gettin' so frustrated and angry. He doesn't chop the firewood anymore – I do that now, but I don't mind none 'cause I don't want Daddy to hurt himself tryin'.

And now that we're gettin' closer to plantin' season again, I don't know what's gonna happen, 'cause one-handed he's darned-near useless on the farm, no offense. The main thing he does now is care for the animals, but even that I have to help with, 'cause milkin' a cow with one hand just don't cut it.

And just as fast as we started livin' high on the hog, we come down with a crash in March when we're out of money and the pantry is nearly empty and there's no more meat in the cellar. Our spirits crash as well, 'cause Mama's feelin' worse again and the only thing that makes her feel better is to mix a little more moonshine into her cough syrup. She's stricken with the chest pains and night sweats again, and her energy is sapped real quick, especially if she's been standin' up doin' any cookin' or cleanin'.

Me and Daddy start huntin' again so that we'll have a little meat to put in our stew, a little somethin' to trade when we need hooch and honey for Mama's medicine, and a little somethin' to sell so we can pay our mortgage. Sometimes we're able to snag a turkey, and once we caught a deer. Daddy makes me hook up Josy's rabbit snares again, and he helps me check 'em and skin and clean 'em when we catch somethin'. We sell almost all of what we catch, and we still don't have enough money. So all of a sudden we're goin' hungry again, and I know what that means. I cain't stop the tears from fallin' as I ride up to the church to join the food line.

About the time I have to start gettin' food from the church again, we start gettin' the letters from the bank, about us bein' behind on our mortgage payments, and about how if we don't pay it all soon they're gonna foreclose on our land. I'm not sure I know exactly what that means, other than we're gonna lose our land, and then where will we go? So when it's plantin' time and Daddy says we ain't gonna plant nothin', I get real scared.

"What do you mean we ain't gonna plant nothin'?" I ask.

"I mean," and he says this real slow, "we ain't gonna plant nothin'."

I stare at him with questions in my eyes, and he finally says, "June, I just can't do it. I can't do another plantin' season with one good hand and without Joseph here and with your mama gettin' sicker."

I start to protest, but he holds up his good hand. "No, June, now I know you want to help, and you are a good helper, but there's just too much for the two of us and we can't do it this season. We need to save every penny for the mortgage or we won't have land left to plant on."

I still have so many questions and worries, but it's no use askin' Daddy. He's got a terrible lot on his mind, what with the bank letters and not bein' able to do this year's plantin' and

Mama gettin' sicker again. I sidle up to Mama's bed on the porch and sit down next to her. She ain't asleep.

"Mama?"

"Yes, baby girl." She strokes my hair and tugs playfully on my earlobe.

"What's happenin'? Why ain't we gonna plant this season, and what happens if we lose our land? And how come you ain't over this tuberculosis?"

Mama closes her eyes. "Shhh, Junie, you don't have to worry about none of that."

"Yes, I do, Mama." I grab her hand and move it away from my hair. "Tell me!"

She shifts herself up into a sitting position on the bed and looks me in the eyes. "Well, we're gonna take a break from farmin' this season and focus on sellin' our sewin' and eggs, and you and Daddy can keep huntin' and sell what you get. That way we can pay the mortgage and we won't lose our land. We just won't. I promise."

Deep down, I know she cain't promise that, but I nod anyway. "And you, Mama? Why ain't you well yet? It's been so long."

She nods. "Yes, it has been a long, long time, and I'm sick and tired of bein' sick and tired." She smiles. "They say for some people it just takes a while to get over it for good, and I guess I'm one of those people. But don't you worry, June. I'm gonna get over it one of these days, I really am. I just know it."

But I look into her eyes and they look the most worn out I've ever seen them; they've lost all their light. And when Mama's light goes out, mine does too, so I don't have the confidence she seems to have. So I'm back to prayin' for strength and a cure.

As plantin' season comes and goes, on top of everything else, we grow more and more worried about Josy, 'cause we ain't seen him since New Year's.

That's almost six months.

Six months.

Six *months.*

And I can no longer sleep.

15

The Whole Town's
Closin' Down

With nothin' to harvest come fall, I got more time on my hands, and I'm gettin' real antsy. I talk Mama into lettin' me go to school, and on a late August Monday mornin', I get cleaned up after doin' my chores and get dressed for school. I ain't got much that fits me anymore, so I put on the only clean thing I have left – a worn-out pair of overalls, which are about two days from not fittin'. My new shoes that we got last time Josy was here are too small now, but Mama says I can wear hers 'cause it ain't like she can go anywhere anyway. I can barely squeeze into them, and the walk to school is hard on my feet. I cain't take the wagon 'cause Daddy'll need it to go to town today.

He's been askin' around to try to find folks who know someone who knows someone else who may be able to find

Josy. He says if he don't find somethin' out soon, he's gonna go hop on every train he can to find Josy himself. I cried and cried when he told me that 'cause me and Mama are sick to death with worry over Josy, and if Daddy goes out hoppin' trains too, then we gotta worry 'bout both of them, and I don't think our hearts can take that.

When I get to the schoolhouse, I don't hear the usual sounds of kids stompin' around and talkin' and gigglin', but the door is open, so I go on in. Miss Glass is standin' at her desk, packin' a box with books and things. "Miss Glass?"

She turns around real fast like I startled her, and her sunny smile is gone, her face fallen like the autumn leaves. "June," she says and then she looks like she don't know what else to say.

"Where is everybody?" I ask, and I should say where is every*thing* too, 'cause the bookshelves and desks are empty, like the place has been cleaned out, and I'm pretty sure I know what that means, but I cain't believe it's actually happening.

"June, the school is closing," Miss Glass says, and when my eyes water over, she says real quick, "Just temporarily, until the economy improves enough."

My head is spinnin' with questions, but I don't think anyone has the answers to anything I have to ask, with everything bein' so topsy turvy nowadays. I want to know how long the school will stay closed and what will happen to Miss Glass and how all the kids gonna learn and why we cain't have school anyway, but all I can manage to say is, "Oh."

Miss Glass reaches her hand out to me, and I step forward and take it, and she pulls me into a gentle hug. "You take care now, Miss June, and I will see you real soon, because this Depression won't last too much longer, I'm sure of it."

I walk home with the weight of the world on my

shoulders, my body saggin' beneath the heavy burden, time tickin' by slow as molasses. Never in a million years could I have pictured all that's gone on since that June day in 1930 when I first saw the line of folks at the bank. Store shelves empty, food lines at the church, Josy hoppin' trains to find work, Daddy losin' his hand and not bein' able to work, Margaret Ann's daddy losin' his life tryin' to find work, Mama gettin' the consumption, and now the school is closin'.

When I get to our farm, I don't turn towards the house. I pass up the barn and the crop fields and the creek and head straight for The Depression Trees, and I sit among them, head buried in my arms, heat beatin' down on my back, and I cry. I cry for all I've lost, and I cry for the people who have lost more than me, and I cry for the future and the fear of what is to come.

Daddy tells me we're drivin' to town later, and he says he got a surprise for me that'll cheer me right up, and I ain't that good with surprises 'cause I just need to know right away, and I pester and pester 'til he cain't keep it secret no more and he finally tells me. He's gonna take me for an ice cream cone at the Sweet Shop!

Now, if I was a better person, I would ask where he got the extra money to do that, 'cause I know we're still behind on our mortgage and cain't waste a penny 'til it's paid up, and if I was a better person, I wouldn't allow him to spend a cent on somethin' as frivolous as an ice cream cone for me.

But on this day I am feelin' so low that just the thought of an ice cream cone, which I ain't had in I don't know how long, is enough to wash my cares away, if only for a minute, so I don't ask where the money come from or how we can afford it or why Daddy's gonna spend that on me. I don't ask, and he don't tell.

Instead, I spend the ride to town with a big smile on my face and my eyes darn-near closed, just enough that Daddy hollers, "Keep your eyes on the road, June!" But I'm just imaginin' a creamy, cold scoop of orange ice cream in a sugary wafer cone that melts in your mouth, and ain't it funny how a person can go from feelin' so way down low to up in the clouds at the snap of a finger?

We pull Molly up to our usual spot outside Macafee's Market, and something's wrong. The market's door is closed, and it's almost never closed, and I see a paper taped to the door.

I climb down from the wagon and race up to the door.

"Closed!" I turn and look at Daddy, who's takin' his time gettin' outa the wagon. "Daddy, the sign says Macafee's is closed!" Then my eyes find the Sweet Shop & Soda Stop sign across the road, then the empty windows where there's usually a crowd of customers, then the boarded-up door, just like me and Josy saw in Knoxville, and I want to cry all over again.

Daddy's lookin' around, and he wraps his good arm around my shoulders and steers me away, toward the feedstore. "Come on, June. Let's go in here and talk to Mr. Clay." At least that's still open. We step in, and Mr. Macafee's in there, talkin' to Mr. Clay.

"Howdy, Mr. Baker," the men say. Then the three of them huddle together and talk in low voices and whispers, while I sit down on a sack of feed and feel sorry for the ice cream I ain't never gonna have, and at the snap of a finger I'm back to feelin' way down low.

I only partly listen to the men's conversation. Mr. Macafee's talkin' about how he cain't compete with the Piggly Wiggly, so his market probably won't never open back up. Mr. Clay is sayin' folks expect things to get worse before they get better. And Daddy's tryin' to steer the conversation toward Josy and does anyone know anyone who might be able to find out where he is and if he's alright. And Mr. Clay got a cousin who befriended a hobo once, and he'll ask him what he knows.

The ride home is silent except for the clomp-clomp of Molly's hooves, the bump-bump of the wagon wheels, the twitterin' of the birds, and my sighin' every now and again. Finally I sigh so loud, Daddy says, "Come out and say what you want to say, June."

The thing is, I don't know how to put into words the things I wanna know and the things I wanna say, so I just sigh again. Daddy shakes his head and looks off at the trees, probably searchin' for the answers that I want to know myself.

Mama's at her sewin' table when we get home, and I want to tell her about the shops closin' down, but she already looks pale and full of worry, so I hold my tongue.

"Come look at what I'm makin', Junie," Mama rasps out, not lookin' up from her work. I drag a dining chair over next to Mama and sit with her, and it's one of my favorite places in the world to be, next to Mama at her sewin' table.

She lets off the pedal and the sewin' machine wheel spins to a halt, and she snips the thread and holds up a small quilted angel, then stitches a loop of twine at the top.

"It's a Christmas tree ornament," she says, through dry coughs that sound more painful than ever. "There's a lot of pain and worry out there, June, and folks need some joy and hope. I figure Christmas ornaments are just the thing to spread it. You and Daddy can sell these at Macafee's."

My face falls, and Mama senses it immediately. "What's wrong, June?"

"Well, Mama, Macafee's Market closed down, and Mr. Macafee said he won't be openin' back up again."

"Oh," she says, and her mouth closes tight and her eyes are lookin' around like she's tryin' to find an answer to the world's problems. "Well, we'll sell them at the farmer's market before it gets too cold, and if not, then maybe you and Daddy can ride into Knoxville. Sell 'em there."

She gets up and heads for the porch. "I think I'll go rest now," she whispers and goes out to lie on her bed.

I think about what she said, and what I think is that every possible solution leads to more problems. Not many people go to the farmer's market anymore, and most that do are lookin' to trade rather than buy, and what we need is money to pay the mortgage. We could ride to Knoxville, but that's an awful long way to make Molly walk just for the few cents that someone might pay for a Christmas ornament.

We do end up goin' to Knoxville near Christmastime, but it isn't to sell ornaments; it's to sell Mama's sewin' machine.

For the past few weeks, Mama's been too sickly to even sit at the sewin' table, and she's coughin' so much she cain't stitch a straight line to save her life, is how she likes to describe it. And we need the money more than ever now, 'cause the bank is threatenin' to foreclose and force us outa our home.

It makes me real sad to see Mama like this and even sadder to be gettin' rid of her sewin' machine. And even sadder still to think about havin' to leave our home and not knowin' where we'd go. So me and Daddy lug that heavy machine outa the wagon and into a shop in Knoxville, where somebody buys it from us for $5.50. Five dollars and fifty cents is all we get for Mama's livelihood. Five dollars and fifty cents for the memories of me and Mama sittin' and sewin' together since as far back as I can remember. And it's like we're closin' the door on a part of our lives, never to be opened again, just like Macafee's.

And all the sudden, even though it don't make no sense, I hate Knoxville and want to go home.

But it's in Knoxville that Daddy runs into a man who knows Mr. Clay, and this man tells Daddy he might know someone at a hobo camp who's heard somethin' 'bout Josy.

16

What happened
to Josy

D addy paces the front room and me and Mama watch, our hands clasped together, knuckles white. "Tell me again what the man said," Mama says.

"He said he heard Joseph got caught by a coupla mean railroad bulls," Daddy says for about the third time. "He may have been taken to jail somewhere out in Memphis, or it coulda been up in Virginia, but he don't know that for sure. That's all the man said, honey, like I told you before."

Mama's still not satisfied. "But how'd he know it was Joseph who got caught?"

Daddy throws his hands up. "I don't know. Like I said, the fella said he was with two other men and one of them was colored." I stay silent and think about what this could mean. It's been almost a year since we seen Josy. If he ain't in jail, then I don't like to think it, but he's probably— well, I'm just gonna hope he's in jail. Ain't no other explanation why he wouldn'ta come home by now.

But now Daddy's puttin' his coat and hat back on and announcin' he's gonna go find Josy himself, and Mama's cryin' and beggin' and pullin' on Daddy's arm. "Please, no, Daniel! You can't leave us to go on some wild goose chase."

"This ain't a wild goose chase we're talkin' about. This is my son!"

"But Daniel, you don't have any idea where he is. Besides, we need you here. Please! Please, don't go, Daniel!"

I'm sobbin', seein' my parents torn apart like this, and I want to find Josy as much as anybody, but I cain't lose my daddy, too. And I cain't stand this cryin' and shoutin' no more, so I run out onto the porch into the cold and wish for all the pain and worry to go away.

We spend the next two months watchin' and hopin' and askin' Mr. Clay every chance we get if he's heard anything, and every so often me and Mama have to talk Daddy outa goin' out to search on his own.

We've done sold everything of value we had, and we finally gave in and ate all but one of our chickens, so now we hardly have any eggs. Broke my heart to do it, but we were gettin' desperate. The church ain't givin' out as much food no more, so I might stand in that line half an hour to get one can of ham or one loaf of bread.

At least we still got the milkin' cows, and I can sell a bottle of milk for the things I need to make Mama's cough syrup. A fat lot a good that cough syrup has done, though. Mama's still sick as a dog, and we've had Dr. Jamison come over at least three times, and he always says the same thing: Get fresh air and plenty of exercise. And I just about want to chase him outa here and see how he does with fresh air and exercise.

And this is the mood I'm in when me and Mama see a truck pull up at the end of the drive and two men hop outa the back, and it's too far away to tell what's goin' on, but we stand up and squint our eyes against the spring sun, and we see the two men are haulin' somethin' and hobbling toward us, and the truck turns around and rumbles off.

"Daddy!" I call as I start down the porch steps. "Someone's here, Daddy!" And he comes outa the barn as I'm walkin' toward the two men, and as I get closer, I see one of the men's colored and I know that has to be Pate, and the other one must be Charlie, and what's that they're holdin' onto in the middle? And I'm runnin' now, and Daddy's runnin' too, and we both get closer, and then I hear Daddy's wail and a high-pitched howl that must be me 'cause the closer we get I can see that what the two men are holdin' onto is Josy and he's beat up so bad he's hardly alive. They're half carryin', half draggin' him, and he don't look like Josy, this cain't be Josy.

"Josy!" I cry, and I look up at Pate and Charlie and they look stricken, damaged, robbed of life, and Charlie says, "The bulls got 'im," and Pate says, "He'll be alright, he'll be alright, he'll be alright," and he keeps sayin' that the whole way up to the porch and into the house and into Josy's room, where Mama's cryin' and shoutin' orders at the same time.

"Lay him down right here. June, make some ginger tea and get the willow bark. Daniel, find some cheese cloth, flour bags, anything we can use for bandages and tourniquets. Charlie, will you take Molly to Maynardville and get Dr. Jamison? Pate, help him hitch Molly to the wagon."

I bring the ginger tea and willow bark into Josy's room, spillin' some as I rush, but then I stop and look at Josy's face, and I don't see how he'll be able to drink. Mama's sittin' by his side and she's cleanin' his bloody face and dabbin' on peroxide, and Daddy pushes Mama outa the way to open up Josy's shirt so they can see what other injuries he has, and I see nothin' but red, black, and blue, and Josy's moanin', and all I can do is stand there and stare.

Josy's right eye is swollen shut, dark blue and gray, and the left one is cloudy, staring sightlessly out at nothin'. His nose is a big glob of blood, and his mouth is swollen, lips busted open, teeth missin'. His hair is matted to his head, and there's blood on the pillow. There is just so much blood, and we don't know where it's all comin' from.

Pate brings in a bucket of fresh water and some towels and I wonder at the sight of him 'cause I'd forgotten he was here. I step back and let Mama and Daddy and Pate get Josy's bloody clothes offa him and clean him up, and I listen to him moan and then I realize that I'm moanin' too.

Dr. Jamison's there next thing I know, and he gives Josy a shot of somethin' for pain and infection, but he leaves the house shakin' his head and sayin' sorry, and everybody's cryin' except for Pate, who's sayin', "He'll be alright, he'll be alright, he'll be al—" until the tears start chokin' him too.

That night we all sit around Josy's bed, just starin' at him and talkin' to him in hushed voices like we're afraid to wake him, and one by one, the others leave to go to bed, but I stay there 'cause there ain't no way I'm leavin' Josy's side, not ever.

Josy sleeps the whole next day, and Mama and Daddy take turns checkin' his pulse and his breathin', just to make sure. We all sit around and tell stories, every once in a while sayin', "You remember that, Josy?" like we think he's gonna answer. And we're sayin', "You remember, dontcha, Josy? Right, Josy? Come on, Josy," until we're practically beggin' him to say somethin', and it gets to be so depressin' I cain't hardly stand to be in there but cain't stand the thought of leavin', neither.

Then the third day, he makes some gruntin' noises like he's tryin' to talk, and we all take that as a real good sign, so we're smilin' through our tears and pattin' him and tryin' to feed him some soup and tea, but he won't take nothin'.

And that night, when everyone else has gone to bed and I'm sittin' there beside Josy, restin' my head on the mattress next to his shoulder, he grunts. It startles me and I look up at him, and he's got his head turned and he's lookin' at me with his one good eye, the one that ain't clouded over, lookin' me right in the eye, and I look at his eyes that don't look like mine no more, and he whispers, "Junie." It's hard to understand him 'cause his mouth is all busted up and he's weak, so weak, but I know he said my name. I lean closer to him, my ear right up next to his mouth so I can hear him, and he rasps, "Take care of Mama and Daddy." And then he ain't breathin' no more.

 Cheryl King

17

Under the
Pawpaw Trees

ake care of Mama and Daddy. Josy's last words. But how
can I take care of Mama and Daddy when I cain't get
rid of the vision of Daddy's knees bucklin' and him
fallin' to the floor graspin' at air and Mama throwin'
herself on top of Josy and kissin' his bruised and damaged face
all night long? And they sat on the edges of his bed, sprawled
out over him like they could breathe their own air into him and
he'd wake up.

Now they're arguin' about where to bury him. Pate and
Charlie have gone to get Pastor Klein, and Mama and Daddy
have to decide, and Mama thinks they should take him to the
cemetery by the church for a proper burial, and Daddy thinks
he should be buried here on the farm so we have him with us
forever, so then Mama's sayin' what about over by the creek,

137

and Daddy says no, that's no good, how about right out front, and Mama says that's not private enough, and on and on they go.

"The pawpaw trees." My mouth is dry and my throat sore from cryin' so much, that when I speak, noise barely comes out. Mama and Daddy turn and look at me, their faces confused, like they've never seen me before.

"What?" Mama whispers.

"The pawpaw trees. That's his— that *was* ... his favorite place." I drop my eyes and force the words out. "We should bury him there."

Pastor Klein brings Mr. Macafee and Mr. Clay with him, and they help carry the box they're gonna put Josy in. A pine box for my Josy. Then they go and dig the hole while me and Mama sit at the kitchen table and stare at nothing.

Take care of Mama and Daddy.

"Want some tea, Mama?" It's a long time before she answers me, and I think maybe she didn't hear me. She just shakes her head, barely moving. I notice she hasn't been coughin' too much, but I need to fill the silence with something, so I ask, "Can I get you some cough syrup?" Another almost imperceptible shake of the head.

They come and tell us when they're ready. I don't watch when they put Josy in the box; I hide in my bedroom, pretendin' to get ready, but how do you get ready to bury your favorite person in the whole world? So I'm just standin' there lookin' out the window. I can see the pawpaw trees from here. The only difference now is the big mound of dirt that don't belong.

Then everybody starts filin' outa the house. Daddy, Mama, Pate, Charlie, Pastor Klein, Mr. Macafee, Mr. Clay. I peer into Josy's bedroom, as though maybe this was all a bad dream and he's really in there restin' after a hard day of work on the farm, and he'd look at me and wink and ask if I want to play marbles.

Marbles! I run to the hutch in the kitchen and open the bottom right cabinet door and grab our jar of marbles. I open it and dip my hand in, fingers playing in the cool, slick smoothness. The purple ones Josy gave me for my twelfth birthday are right on top. I take one out and put it in my pocket, then close the jar. The jar will go with Josy, 'cause I don't think I could ever look at this jar of marbles again, knowin' he's not here to play with me.

It's cool outside, Mother Nature decidin' between the crispness of winter and the fragrant dampness of spring. I don't look when I place the jar of marbles in the crook of Josy's right arm. I close my eyes and imagine the Josy I knew before. The tough and strong and gentle and kind one, the one I will always see when I think of him – not the one beaten and battered by railroad bulls. Mama and Daddy both lay a flower on Josy's chest, and then Pastor Klein closes the box and all the men help lower the box into the ground – all the men except Daddy. Daddy's down on one knee, head sunken, tryin' to hold himself together, and Mama's got her arms wrapped around his shoulders, tryin' to hold him together too.

Practically the whole town comes to pay their respects, even the ones scared of catchin' Mama's tuberculosis. They bring casseroles and stews and homemade bread, and it's funny how a whole town that's been starvin' and standin' in line for free food can come together like this for people that's sufferin'. I welcome the distraction, 'cause greetin' people and carryin' in their dishes and gifts leaves me no time to sit with my sorrow.

Everyone I know and some people I don't know come to visit. Everyone except Margaret Ann, and that hurts almost as much as seein' Josy buried in the ground in a pine box. Mama don't seem to notice, but then again, she's hardly alive herself right now – not because of the tuberculosis but because of the grief.

We live on donated food for a few days, but mostly we just sleep or sit and stare at nothin'. No cleanin', cookin', or washin's gettin' done. Poor Miss Priss is so full of milk she 'bout lets me have it when I finally go into the barn to milk her. It takes me nearly half an hour to milk both cows, and it's awfully quiet in the barn, so I do a lot of thinkin', mostly about how to fulfill Josy's dying wish.

I think about his words constantly in the days that pass in a haze of tears. I cain't think of any way I can take care of Mama and Daddy, other than to do the chores the best I can, but I'm havin' such trouble gettin' outa bed to make myself do anything. I ain't had a bath in I don't know how long. How can I take care of Mama and Daddy when I cain't even take care of myself?

It don't take me long to figure out that what they need, other than to have Josy back, is money to pay the mortgage. So I gotta find a way to make money. We ain't got a sewin' machine no more. I can stitch by hand, but that's slow goin', and I know I cain't make much money hand-stitchin' up rips in folks' britches or whatnot. I ain't got nothin' of value that I can sell, other than bottles of milk from our cows and firewood for fifty cents a cord. I can hunt deer and turkey and maybe try to sell rabbits from Josy's traps. I think on that a spell and wonder if that'll be enough.

I decide it's got to be enough, and the next mornin' I make myself get up and go set the rabbit snares. I use fruit from the pawpaw trees that ain't quite ripe. It's the hardest thing to do, to walk around Josy's grave to get up under the trees. I roll the purple marble between my fingers. I keep it in my pocket all the time, and I think it's how me and Josy talk to each other now.

I take a deep breath and tiptoe up to the hangin' fruit, steppin' gingerly, softly as possible. But I cain't get the image of that pine box goin' into the ground outa my head, and I'm growin' dizzy as I reach up for the fruit and I feel so heavy in my chest, and I cain't breathe no more, and I'm swattin' at the fruit that's hangin' just a mite too high, and I try to jump for it without stompin' on Josy's grave, and I hate it, I hate it, I hate it, and before I know it, I'm on my knees sobbin' and beatin' the ground and tearin' at the grass and screamin', "Josy! Come back, Josy!" And I cry 'til I just cain't no more, and then I lay there on Josy's grave and I pretend I can feel him and hear him.

After I set the traps, I ask Daddy if he wants to go huntin' with me. He's curled up on the couch with I don't know how many weeks' worth of beard growth coverin' his face. He says maybe tomorrow. And then the next day he says the same thing. After a while I stop askin'.

I don't catch much, and it turns out that huntin' is a whole lotta sittin' around bein' quiet. They shouldn't call it huntin'; they should call it waitin'. And all that time spent waitin' is wastin' time.

By the end of April, I only have a couple dollars to show for all my waitin' 'cause most folks would rather trade than buy. I ain't good enough at fishin' to make goin' all the way up to the lake worth my time. Besides, we don't have decent rods, and fishin' requires even more waitin' than hunting does.

I get pretty good at catchin' crawdads outa the spring, and most folks'll trade me some eggs for a good batch of crawdads. Imagine that – we used to be the ones givin' folks eggs; now we gotta ask others for eggs. But still, it's money we need, and no one will pay money for no little ol' crawdads.

Mama and Daddy have slowly come back to life. I think once they saw me workin' so hard, they figured they oughta get up and get back to work themselves. Other than bein' worn down with grief, Mama looks like she's doin' better – not coughin' or havin' chest pains, and I take that as a good sign that she's gettin' over the tuberculosis once and for all. I even get her to smile when I mention how nice it'll be for her to be able to sleep inside the house again and stop doin' all her "exercise" in the fresh air.

I cain't say the same for Daddy, though. He's been mopin' around the house in such a sad state that it scares me somethin' awful, and one day I cain't help but to tell him so. And that's when he breaks down.

Through fits of sobbin' and then apologizin' about it, Daddy says, "It's my fault. It's my fault that Joseph had to go look for work in the first place, and it's my fault he's not here with us today, and that's just a matter of fact."

"No it ain't, Daddy!" I look at him in disbelief, horrified that he felt this way all this time. "It ain't your fault at all. It ain't. You know Josy. He was gonna do whatever it took to help. He'd do anything for our family."

I hug Daddy for the first time in a long time, and it feels strange, like I'm the adult and he's the child. "Don't you even think that no more, Daddy," I say. "Promise me."

He pulls away and nods and then pats my hand. After a moment, he shakes his head like he's shakin' away all the bad thoughts, and he plasters a smile on his face, as fake as it may be, and says, "We're gonna be alright, June," but it sounds like a question, and I wonder if he knows I can see right through him and that his fake smile says, *We're gonna be alright*, but his eyes say he ain't got a clue how we're gonna survive.

Take care of Mama and Daddy.

And that's the moment I realize what I have to do. I have to carry on what Josy started. I have to find work and bring home money for Mama and Daddy. I have to be strong and tough like Josy. So I'm gonna have to hop a train out west. There's no other way. I done tried everything else.

Now that I've made this decision, I'm spurred to action and filled with an anxious but eager energy. I pace my tiny bedroom, walking the four steps from the door to the window and back again, over and over, thinkin' about what I need to do. How will I know where to go? What should I take with me? Should I tell Mama and Daddy? And are there even any girl train hoppers? What's gonna happen to an almost-fifteen-year-old girl in a train car full of men? What if they try to hurt me? Maybe I can find Pate and Charlie and they'll look after me. But I got no clue where they are. What if I cain't find them?

That night it's hours before I can fall asleep 'cause I'm thinkin' and plannin', and I have all these questions and worries and ideas, but I cain't do this by myself. I need Josy. But since I cain't have him, I need a best friend. Just before I doze off, I decide that tomorrow I will go and talk to Margaret Ann.

I walk instead of takin' the wagon, 'cause I have nervous energy I need to let loose, and I need time to think. I'm scared she won't talk to me, let alone help me, but then again, how can she help me? I don't even know what I expect her to do; all's I know is I need to talk to someone, and maybe we can work out a plan together.

I don't want Margaret Ann to get in trouble with her mama, so I sneak around to her bedroom window instead of goin' to the front door. I can hear her and Jenny May talkin' as I tiptoe up and tap on the window frame. Margaret Ann swishes the curtains aside and peers out, her mouth forming a perfect circle when she sees me.

"I came by to talk," I say, not knowing where to start.

"I can't talk to you," she whispers. "My mama—" and she turns to look behind her as if her mama would be comin' up any minute now.

"I have to talk to you. I need your help." I sound like I'm beggin' now, but she's shakin' her head. "Margaret Ann, I'm goin' to ride the rails."

She snaps to attention and stares in silence a long while.

"I just need to come up with a plan, and I …" I cain't think of what to say. "I thought if I could talk to you about it, if you could just— I'm scared, and I'm not sure where to go or how to do this." I look at her, my eyes pleading.

Margaret Ann looks behind her one more time, then leans out the window. "Are you crazy?" she whispers. "Just— Look, I can't talk now. Come over tomorrow at noon. Mama'll be gone to town then."

My chest swells with relief. "Thank you! Alright!" I step away to turn and go back home, still thanking her, and tell her I'll see her tomorrow at noon, and then I practically skip all the way home. I'm happy I got to talk to Margaret Ann after all this time, relieved that she might help me, and excited that I'm gonna be doin' something to help Mama and Daddy. That light at the end of the tunnel that folks always talk about – I'm startin' to see it … maybe just a little, 'cause at least I got a plan. And that makes me smile inside.

"So what's your plan?" Margaret Ann asks the next day. She was waitin' for me on the porch when I got here. Her mama and Jenny May ain't home, and Margaret Ann says we have an hour before they come back. We walk into the living room, Margaret Ann with her fists on her hips.

"Well, I— I was thinkin'—" My shoulders sag. "I dunno."

"Okay, where you gonna go? What train do you get on, and what kinda work you gonna find?"

I have no answers to any of her questions. I just shake my head and sink down into a chair.

"See, June? This is crazy. It's dangerous. You can't be serious about doin' this." She's standin' over me like a parent scoldin' a child.

"Margaret Ann, I have to." I shake my head. "You don't understand."

"What's there not to understand? Train hoppin' killed my daddy and your brother!"

I flinch, stung by her words, and I feel my face gettin' hot. She's right. But so am I.

"Your daddy and my brother," I start slowly, "both risked their lives to make our lives better. Margaret Ann, my mama's sick and my daddy's so depressed it's scarin' me somethin' awful. We might lose the farm if I cain't find work."

Margaret Ann's shakin' her head, but at least she ain't stompin' her foot on the floor no more.

"This is my only choice. I done tried everything else. This is my chance to make things better for my family. And to be strong like Josy. To make him proud." My voice breaks on that last word.

It's quiet for a long time, and Margaret Ann sits down on the arm of the sofa, lookin' down at the floor like she's thinkin' real hard, battling evils in her head.

"June, you may be the youngest person train hoppin', and you'll probably be the only girl. How you gonna protect yourself?"

I been thinkin' about this myself, and the answer is sittin' right there in my barn, with our huntin' gear. "I have a gun. It was a Christmas gift from Daddy, and I been target shootin' and huntin' a long while now. I bet I can shoot just a good as any man."

Margaret Ann's eyes squint up, and then suddenly she stands. "Just as good as any man, huh? Wait here. I have an idea." Then she dashes off into another room. A minute later, she returns with her arms full of stuff, and she dumps it all out on the coffee table. A pair of scissors, a hand mirror, some clothes, a hat, and boots.

"What's all this?" I ask.

"If you're gonna do this, June – and I'm not sayin' I approve – but if you're gonna do this, you need all the protection you can get. We're gonna disguise you," Margaret Ann says. "As a man."

My eyes go wide, and I shake my head and stand up, backing away as though she's gonna attack me with the scissors or somethin'. But then I think, *Maybe this could work.*

"Look," she says, "we'll cut your hair short, you'll wear a hat, and you can wear these clothes – they were my daddy's." She looks down when she says that, like all of a sudden it hurts to say *daddy* out loud. I wonder how long it'll be before I can say *Josy* without being overcome with pain.

She looks up and I think she knows what I'm thinkin', and she looks real sad and sorry. "Anyway, the pants will be too long, but you can roll 'em up. And we can stuff socks into the boots so they won't fall off." We both stand there lookin' at the pile on the table. Lookin' and thinkin' and imaginin' until finally Margaret Ann says, "Well, come on, let's get this done before Mama gets home."

I sit in a dining chair, and she wraps a towel around my neck, then grabs up my hair like she's puttin' it into a ponytail, and without givin' me a second to change my mind, she cuts the whole ponytail off, right at the base of my neck. I reach for the mirror, but Margaret Ann says, "Wait. Lemme finish."

I sit back and relax a little, my eyes glued to the long brown cascade of hair that is now detached from my head and layin' on the floor, and she snips away at each side, around my ears, and in front too, tellin' me to turn this way, look down, sit still, turn that way, head back, like a professional barber. Then I remember she's been cuttin' all her brothers' and sisters' hair for years, and that makes me feel a whole lot better 'cause I bet it'll look good. But anyway, it's just hair.

What gets me the most is how me and Margaret Ann's been separated for so long and yet here we are, best friends, almost like no time has passed at all. It's easy to slide right back into a friendship regardless of the rocky roads you've faced, and that right there is the mark of a real good friendship.

"June," Margaret Ann says, and I think she's gonna tell me she's done, but she says, "I'm real sorry 'bout Josy." I don't say anything 'cause I cain't get my throat to work. "I wish I coulda come to pay my respects, and I wish—" She stops, and I turn to look at her, and she's cryin'.

"I just wish…"

"Margaret Ann, it's okay," I say, putting a hand on her arm.

"I'm just so sorry. I'm sorry."

And I know she means it. I know she means all of it – sneakin' around with Jimmy Mack and lyin' to me, takin' our friendship away, and not comin' to Josy's funeral. And I'm tryin' to think of how to tell her that I forgive her and that I've missed her like crazy, when all the sudden she starts laughin'. "June, you look just like a boy!" I spin around and grab the mirror and cain't believe my eyes. I do look like a boy.

"Alright, now put these clothes on and let's see if we think you could fool a train full of men," Margaret Ann says.

I scramble out of my clothes and put on the men's shirt, and right about now I'm pretty glad to be flat-chested. Then I put on the men's pants, and we roll the legs up a couple times, and Margaret Ann finds me a rope I can use for a belt. I pull the boots on, which are only a smidge too big for me after all, and then put the hat on. We angle the back door so I can see my reflection in the glass.

I turn left and right and try to look at the back, and then I start posin' for Margaret Ann, tryin' to move less like a girl and more like a strong, tough man, until we're both laughin' up a storm, but then Margaret Ann says, "June, you still sound very much like a girl. You're gonna have to deepen your voice."

I try it. I reach way down deep for my deepest manly voice, and my chin's touchin' my neck as I say, "How's this?"

Margaret Ann says, "Maybe you could get away with just not talkin' to no one." I agree.

"What's next?" I ask.

"You say you don't know where you're gonna go? Or anything about hoppin' a train?" she asks me.

I shrug. "Well, yeah. I mean, no."

"Okay, June, we're about to test out your newfound maleness. Come with me." And she grabs my hand and we're off and runnin' down her porch steps and down the road past Main Street and past the school and church.

"Where we goin'?" I ask, but she doesn't answer, she just keeps runnin'.

Then we get to a little ol' house, and she stops and turns to me, adjustin' my hat and straightenin' my clothes.

"Now, when we go up to the porch, I'm gonna introduce you to somebody as— wait, what's your boy name gonna be?"

I ain't thought about that none, and the first thing that comes outa my mouth is, "Joe."

We both stand there a moment and swallow the importance of that name. Then she nods and says, "Alright, I'm gonna introduce you as Joe. Don't say nothin', though, or you'll give yourself away. Let's see if he's fooled."

We walk up the steps of a small, leaning porch, and I stomp my feet and swing my arms like I think a boy would. The door's open, so Margaret Ann raps on the door frame, and who should come to the door but ol' Jimmy Mack. I try to hide my surprise, but my cheeks are burnin'.

"Hi, Jimmy!" Margaret Ann says, and they smile sweetly at each other for a moment before she clears her throat and says, "This here's Joe. He's new in town."

Jimmy Mack nods and I try to nod the exact same way, and we're standin' there all awkward-like with no one sayin' nothin', 'til Jimmy Mack asks, "Where you from?"

My eyes go wide, and then Margaret Ann says, "He's from … N-Nashville originally. But … he moved out here with his family to … to take care of his sick gramma …" and that's when I realize that me and Margaret Ann's been holdin' hands and now Jimmy Mack is lookin' at our hands and then crossin' his arms and lookin' at Margaret Ann with suspicious eyes, so I yank my hand outa Margaret Ann's grasp and move to run my hand through my hair, but I knock my hat off in the process, and then I decide to spit over the porch railin' 'cause that's what boys do sometimes, but my spit don't shoot far at all; in fact it mostly just drips down my chin.

Then Margaret Ann starts laughin' and she decides it's time to reveal the truth. Jimmy Mack looks astonished, plus a little bit relieved that his sweetheart wasn't really holdin' hands with another boy.

We all sit down on the porch, and Margaret Ann explains the reason why we're here. Jimmy Mack has an uncle that's been ridin' the rails for years and comes to visit every now and then, so Jimmy knows all kinds of things, like where I need to go, and how to jump onto a train car, and even the name of somebody who'll help me out.

He tells me what all I need to take and when to jump off and how I'll know if folks are friendly or not, and what kinda work I can expect to find, and I sure am glad we came over here.

Jimmy's still shakin' his head in wonder at my transformation and swearin' that he knew I looked familiar and lookin' at me like he's excited for me and scared for me all at the same time, when Margaret Ann says we need to get back.

"Hang on," Jimmy says, and he goes into the house and comes back out with a leather bag with a long strap. "Here."

He loops the strap over my head, onto my left shoulder, and it drops down to my right side. "Use this to pack all your stuff in. There's a secret pocket inside for you to keep your money and anything else important."

"Thank you, Jimmy Mack," I say, surprised by this kind gift. "Thank you kindly."

And then Margaret Ann is grabbin' my hand and sayin' we got to go. We run all the way back to her house, and I change back into my own clothes and stuff the men's clothes into my pack, and we clean up the mess we made.

"When are you leavin'?" Margaret Ann asks.

"Tomorrow," I say, even though I didn't know that until just now.

"It has to be tomorrow. But don't say nothin' to anyone, please, Margaret Ann?"

She grabs me into a hug. "I won't. But you better promise you'll take care of yourself and come and see me when you come back home. Gosh, June, are you sure you're really gonna do this?"

I look into her face for a long time, and my eyes tear up as I nod and thank her for all her help.

"You just better not get yourself ki—um, hurt," she says, and as I'm turnin' to go, she says, "Wait! Your hair. Won't your parents notice and get suspicious or somethin'?"

She's right! I hadn't thought of that. She races to the wardrobe in the girls' bedroom and brings back a bonnet and fits it onto my head, tying it around my chin. "At least this will sorta hide it," she says. She pulls me in for one last hug and says, "See you real soon, alright?"

And I turn and walk down the porch steps and out into the road and head toward home. I check my pocket and make sure the purple marble is still there, and I hold it, and I think to myself, *See you real soon too, I hope.*

18

Takin' Care of
Mama and Daddy

Dear Mama and Daddy...
I wrote the letter so many times in my head that now as
I put pencil to paper, the words flow freely.

> *I am going out to find work, and I may*
> *be gone awhile but I don't want you to worry*
> *none. I am strong and tough like Josy. I'll be*
> *back just as soon as I can. I love you both.*
> > *Yours truly,*
> > *June*

I glance at the moon outside my window and guess it's
about 3:30. Almost time. It's pitch dark in here except for the

low light from two kerosene lamps, one on my nightstand, and one on my writing desk. I keep 'em turned down real low 'cause I don't want Mama and Daddy to wake up and catch me before I'm even gone.

Now I check my pack again for about the hundredth time. Last night I snuck my pistol in from where we been keepin' it in the barn with our huntin' gear. I can feel the burden of it weighing down my pack as I slip it over my head and across my chest. I set Mr. Murphy's old newsboy cap on my head and check myself in the mirror. In the dim light I can hardly recognize myself.

It's funny, wearin' the bonnet yesterday, Mama and Daddy didn't notice a thing about my hair – forget the fact that I don't even wear bonnets. But to me, I look like a different person. I feel like a different person. For a second I question whether I'm doin' the right thing, but real quick I shake the doubts away. This is the only way. I finger the purple marble in my right pocket, then nod as if convincin' myself. I snatch up the note before I can change my mind.

I turn the knob of each lamp, extinguishing the flames and plunging myself into darkness, then feel my way to the door. I carefully cross the creaky hall floor toward the kitchen, where I place the note in the middle of the table and set the kitchen lantern on it so the breeze from the windows don't blow it away. I take a deep breath and creep toward the back porch, out the door, down the steps and into the moonlight. Then I run out to the lane and past the treeline, wantin' to put as much distance between me and home as quickly as possible.

I have a flashlight in my pack, but I don't need it now 'cause the moon is so bright. Besides, I don't know how long them ol' batteries will last, so I want to save it 'til I really need it. The biggest problem is walkin' all the way to where I need to go, through thick woods and rocky hills. Jimmy Mack told me not to catch the train in Knoxville goin' west 'cause I won't find nothin' out there 'cause of the drought. Nowadays out west they're worse off than we are. He said I have to walk north up to Norris Lake and follow the waterline northeast 'til I get to the big bridge, where Norris Lake meets Clinch River, and once I cross the bridge I'll see a hobo camp set up real close to the railroad. Then I can catch a train headin' up through Virginia, where I'm bound to find somethin' that pays decent.

After about an hour of walkin', my feet are achin' somethin' awful on accounta the boots not fittin' right, and I'm tired as all get out, probably 'cause I didn't sleep a wink last night. I'm hungry too. I made it to the lake a while ago, and I cain't be too far from the big bridge. It's gettin' close to sunrise, but it's real dark in the thick woods that border the lake. I can barely see in front of me as I find a mossy boulder that makes a good restin' spot.

I sit and let out a grateful breath. It feels good to get this heavy pack off of my shoulder. I stretch my neck out, right side, then left, then front and back, and roll my shoulders forward and back. I'm tempted to take my boots off, maybe dip my feet in the lake, but I decide against it. 'Fraid if I do that I won't want to put the boots back on and keep walkin'.

I take out my flashlight, shinin' it into my pack so I can find the snack I brought – a handful of raisins. It doesn't quite satisfy my hunger, and the sip of water from my thermos doesn't quite quench my thirst neither, but it'll have to do.

I turn the flashlight on again and open my pocketwatch – Daddy's pocketwatch, really. I took it from his table by the couch. Almost five o'clock. Mama and Daddy should be up by now. Mama'll probably find the note first 'cause she'd be in the kitchen cookin' breakfast. I wonder how they'll take it. Will

154

they be terribly angry, or just worried? Will they try to send someone to find me?

It hurts my heart how much I must be worryin' them, but it'll be worth it in the end, I just know it. The thought of gettin' work and gettin' paid and bringin' money home to Mama and Daddy gives me the motivation I need to get back up and get back to walkin'.

I notice three strange things when I get to the hobo camp. One, it ain't at all what I was expectin'. Sure, it looks more like a trash heap than a camp, but it feels different. It feels like family. The scene in front of me is a family reunion. I imagine all the mamas and daughters off in a farmhouse beyond the woods, and any minute now, they'll ring a bell and someone will holler that breakfast is ready, and all the men and boys will heave themselves up and smack each other on the back and talk about how hungry they are, and they'll head up to the farmhouse and look appreciatively at their wives and mamas and sisters and daughters and thank them for their hard work.

The second strange thing I notice is that nobody notices me at all. A hobo camp of twenty or so men, and nobody pays no mind to the feminine kid who shows up in men's clothes way too big. I guess they got more important things to worry about, like the train barrelin' down the track right now.

I'm drawn up into the stream of stompin' boots and shoutin' and grabbin', and just when I think I ain't gonna make it, a beefy hand grabs my outreached arm and yanks and I jump and I feel like I'm fallin' backward, but my boots make purchase, and the beefy man pulls me, and I'm in and I stumble forward, bumpin' into the men crowded into the dark train car.

They're sayin' somethin' to me, and I nod and avert my eyes and make my way to the back of the car and sink down into the corner and try to calm my racing heart. I'm in the shadows, and even though the sun has risen now, it's dark in the train car. I watch for a spell as the men and boys find a place to sit – a haystack, an overturned crate, some even sit on the edge, their legs danglin' out of the open train car, 'til someone hollers at them and tells them to scoot on inside, and then they wedge somethin' into the bottom of the door so's it won't slide shut on us. Some of the men roll out bedding and curl up on the train car floor, using their bindle as a pillow, and they encourage the others to do the same. "Gotta long ride ahead," they say.

And even though I'm sittin' on the dirty, hard floor of a train car goin' Lord knows where with a buncha strangers, and it smells somethin' awful in here, I don't have any trouble closin' my eyes to it all. And this is the third strange thing I notice ('cause who in their right mind could sleep in these conditions?) – the rockin' and bumpin' of the rollin' train pitches me into a deep sleep.

I dream about Josy. Josy ridin' in a train car just like this one, except he's not hidden in the corner, he's sittin' out in the middle of the car and everyone's gathered around him, and he's tellin' stories of adventures, and the others are captivated and on the edge of their seats, and Josy's wavin' his arms, animated, exhilarated.

He loves it here. He loves the freedom and the thrill of ridin' the rails, and he's proud, oh so proud. He's in his element here. And all the others respect him and admire him. He's like their leader, their chief. And he's taller and stronger than they are, and he's cleaner, too, dressed in a fine suit and a rich Fedora like a Hollywood movie star.

In my dream, Josy's tellin' a story about a time he saved a man's life, when a giant railroad bull appears out of nowhere and grabs Josy by his shirt collar and throws him up against a wall. All the other hobos disappear and Josy is suddenly alone and has no defense, and suddenly the railroad bull turns into an animal bull with angry, sharp horns, and the horns grab Josy up under his arms and pick him up and the bull's about to throw him off the train when I'm yanked from my dream and it's not Josy bein' thrown off the train, it's me, and it's not an animal bull but a railroad police bull, and he's got me under the arms and he's liftin' me and yellin' and roughin' me up, and now I'm screamin' and tumblin' out onto the dusty ground.

The bull jumps down from the train car and grabs me by the arm and he's hollerin' at me, and I wonder where everyone else is and where we are and how long I was asleep, and now I notice that it's dark out, and the bull has a flashlight that's big as a club, and I feel tears comin', and I'm hurtin' all over.

Then, I don't know if it's because he felt the curve of my hip or the softness of my skin or saw the length of my eyelashes or the tears in them, but his whole demeanor changes and all the sudden his broad shoulders relax and his hard face softens, and I know he knows.

"Why, you're just a little girl!" He lets go of my arm, and I dust myself off and straighten up and stand as tall as I can.

"I ain't no little girl! I'm almost fifteen," and I hope he cain't see that I'm shakin' like a leaf.

And he stares at me, lookin' like he don't know whether to laugh at me or holler at me some more, and so we're just standin' there starin' at each other, and finally I say, "Well, are you gonna arrest me or not?"

He looks like he's thinkin' about that a spell, but then he says, "No, I ain't gonna arrest you. But what're you doin' rail ridin,' a young girl like you? It's dangerous."

I scowl at him. He don't gotta tell me what I already know, and I shouldn't have to tell him what he already knows. Don't he know there's a Depression goin' on, and people are starvin' and desperate? Surely he's seen hobos, there's probably about a million of 'em right here in— I look around. "Where are we?"

"We're in Lafayette. Not too far from Roanoke," the bull says, and I ain't never heard of neither of them, so I ask, "That in Tennessee?"

He looks at me strange and says, "No. Virginia," and I'm workin' out in my head how far away from home I must be, and all the sudden I panic like I gotta get back home right now, and I'm lookin' left to right and back again and I'm breathin' hard and fast and I wish I'd never done this. What was I thinkin', what was I thinkin', what was I thinkin'?

The bull reaches out his hand but doesn't touch me. "Miss, are you alright?"

I'm still huffin' and pantin', and all I can manage to say is, "Mama." And I bend over and put my hands on my knees and try to calm myself, but now the tears are streamin' down and fallin' splat to the ground, and I cain't think.

The bull tucks his flashlight under his arm and takes me by the elbow and leads me over to a small station house next to the train yard, and it's got a light on the outside, and the light is comforting. There's a bench, and the bull pushes me gently down onto it and sits beside me.

"What's your name?" he asks me.

I look up and blink away tears and then realize it's sweat too, and I look down at myself and see that I'm downright drenched, and I figure I must look a terrible sight, just as bad as them ol' bearded hobos. "June," I say, barely above a whisper.

The bull thrusts his hand out toward me and says, "Hello, June. I'm Paul. Paul Burnett. Nice to meet you." I don't take his hand, but I look up at him and I'm surprised to see that he

158

looks young, like Josy – cain't be more than eighteen, maybe. He's broad shouldered and tall with thick arms, but his face, which looked so hard and mean earlier, is soft now, and he surely don't look like no railroad bull. More like Cary Grant in the magazine picture I seen him in with Mae West.

And suddenly I'm nervous 'cause I ain't never been in the presence of such a handsome man alone at night, and right now I certainly don't look like no Mae West, so I snap back to life real quick and remember why I'm here in the first place.

"I'm lookin' for work. I live in Maynardville, Tennessee, but my mama and daddy may lose the farm, and I want to help…" I trail off when I realize I may be tellin' too much. Maybe I shouldn'ta told him where I live.

"You live on a farm?" the bull – Paul – asks, his eyes squinting up.

"Yeah, but we had to sell off most of the animals, and we didn't plant nothin' this year 'cause Daddy had an accident and Mama got sick and—" I stop, wonderin' why I'm sayin' so much again.

"Listen," Paul says, "my father needs some help on our farm, and he'd pay you a decent wage if you work hard enough, including room and board. My mother's a good cook, too. Why don't you come on with me? There's plenty of room for you to stay the night and you can start work in the morning."

I look away, toward the railroad tracks, thinkin' on all the questions and worries I have.

But I'm so tired, I don't resist when he takes my arm and lifts me up off the bench, and we walk around to the other side of the station house, where there's a single car parked, and he opens the door for me and I climb in, holdin' my pack, with my pistol in it, close to my body.

19

The Burnett Farm

T hree remarkable things happen when I go home with this railroad bull – aside from the fact that I'm goin' anywhere with a railroad bull to begin with, especially one that threw me off a train, and to tell the truth, I don't know why I agree to go with him, other than the fact that I'm exhausted and starvin' and don't know where I am or where else to go.

And I know he told me his name is Paul and he looks like a movie star, but I cain't help it, all I can think about is that he's a railroad bull and those are bad people – mean and ruthless for what they done to Josy and what they done to Margaret Ann's daddy. So I keep my pack close to me for a long while, sometimes with my hand on the pistol inside it.

The first remarkable thing that happens is that Paul's family – his parents, Mr. and Mrs. Burnett, his two older sisters, Sadie and Laura, Laura's husband Gregory, Granny and Pawpaw, and two farm hands whose names I forget – they all welcome me like I'm kin. They feed me three good meals a day, even though they're already stretchin' to make ends meet, and they give me a room to stay in, no questions asked.

The Burnett farm is stunning. Rolling hills as far as the eye can see, all different shades of green and yellow, against a backdrop of mountains standin' like sentries guardin' the land. Three huge barns rim the property, and all the familiar sounds of farm life – cows mooin', horses snortin', chickens cluckin' and peckin', birds cawin' and beatin' their wings in flight – both comfort and sadden me, makin' me homesick.

The main house, a large white farmhouse with a wrap-around porch, is almost always echoin' with the clatter of pans and the beatin' of whisks in mixing bowls, sensuous cookin' smells waftin' through the open doors and windows, as Mrs. Burnett and her daughters keep the meals comin' for their hard-workin' men.

The first time I met Paul's mama, Louise, she was cookin' breakfast, and I don't think I've seen her more than once without a skillet or a mixing bowl in her hands since, and another thing I ain't never seen her without is a smile that goes all the way to her eyes. She calls Paul "Sweet Pea," which makes him blush and makes me laugh. Imagine that – a tough railroad bull bein' called "sweet pea." She tells me to call her Louise, but I don't know why, I just cain't call a grown woman by her first name.

That first breakfast with the Burnetts is one thing I will never forget. They got the biggest kitchen table I ever seen, with at least ten or twelve chairs around it. Paul says, "Everybody comes to breakfast. It's the most important meal of the day on a farm."

Breakfast is before sunup, and it's quiet 'cept for the crickets outside and the scrape of the spatula on the pan – until

Mr. Burnett comes in the room, hollerin', "Breakfast, lunch, *and* dinner are the most important meals of the day on a farm." A gruff giant of a man, Jerry Burnett wakes up all of Mother Nature when he drops himself into the chair at the head of the table. And the quiet, peaceful mornin' erupts into a hive of activity and chatter.

It's overwhelming, like a family reunion or church revival. It gets loud fast, and then Mrs. Burnett and Sadie, who always helps with the cookin' and cleanin', plop down plates of pancakes stacked a mile high and a tub of homemade butter and a metal pitcher of maple syrup, and folks start passin' the pancakes and butter and syrup around the table.

While everyone's stabbin' one, two, three pancakes with their forks and ploppin' 'em down on their plates and butterin' and syrupin' them up, Mrs. Burnett and Sadie are cookin' up pork sausages, the little round ones I love so much, and the whole house sizzles and smokes with their spicy-sweet aroma. Then the sausages are passed around, along with a basket of biscuits that just came outa the oven and a jar of jam, and Mrs. Burnett and Sadie sit down and everyone bows their heads and recites the grace all together: "In a world where so many are hungry, may we eat this food with humble hearts. Amen."

And just like that, the commotion vanishes, and every mouth is silent, savoring every bite. I think about that prayer and I think about how lucky I am. What would I be eatin' if I'd stayed on that train? And that makes me think about Mama and Daddy, and I wonder what they're eatin' and if they're alright, and thinkin' about them makes me think about Josy, and I get a sudden swelling in my heart and I feel my eyes water up, and I'm so scared I'm gonna start bawlin' right in front of these nice people.

Laura smiles kindly at me from across the table, like she knows I'm sad or somethin'. Paul says Laura's pregnant and in bad health too, so she don't do much but sit and put her feet up while her husband works on the farm. She takes a likin' to me real fast, Laura does, and I help her whenever she needs somethin' lifted or carried or pulled down from up high. She reminds me of Mama when she was pregnant with what woulda been my little sister, but I was so young then and didn't understand nothin'. I surely hope everything's alright with Laura's baby, 'cause I seen what it does to a person to lose a baby before you even get to hold it.

They let me stay in a little room upstairs that used to be the maid's quarters. It's right off the second-floor porch, and I can sit up there on that porch and look out below at the hills and the animals and the mountains on the horizon and I really feel like I'm sittin' on top of the world, and that makes me think of Josy. Again.

It still hurts so much to think of him bein' gone. But I remember I'm here for him, to do what he asked me to do, to take care of Mama and Daddy. I go out on the porch sometimes at night after supper and after all the chores are done, and I sit in the moonlight and roll the purple marble between my fingers and sing our song in my head.

The second remarkable thing that happens when I go home with this railroad bull is that his daddy gives me a payin' job on the farm. He pays me $3.50 a week to milk the cows twice a day and herd 'em to pasture, clean the barn, feed and take care of the chickens and their coop and nestin' boxes, and wash and brush the work mules. It's an awful lotta work, but it ain't nothin' I ain't done before, and Paul tells me that my pay is just as much as the boy farm hands get, and that makes me feel good.

The only difference between workin' here and workin' at home is they got eight dairy cows 'steada just two, and three mules 'steada just one, and a whole yard full of chickens, and a couple of them hens like to go broody, so I gotta be real good about collectin' their eggs early and fast.

The best part about tendin' the hens is that to the left of the chicken yard there's an expanse of sunflowers, pretty as a painting, and I let myself relax and watch the breeze tickle the flowers and listen to the buzzin' of the bees.

It seems to me that out here, with the clear blue skies and velvety green hills and musical sounds of farm life, you could forget there was a Depression goin' on. Forget that your life is marred by loss. Lose yourself in the beauty and peacefulness of the land.

But that don't last too long, 'cause once you get to relaxin', somebody comes around to tell you what to do next.

And seems like every time I turn around, Paul's there to check on me, and that gets me feelin' anxious 'cause most of the time when he comes around, I'm soaked in sweat or dirt or both. And I'm dog tired.

By the end of the first week, my feet are blistered from the work boots, and my face is blistered from the sun. Paul looks real sorry for me, and he brings me some fresh aloe and smooths it over my nose and my forehead, gentle as a whisper, and I can feel his breath on my face, and my heart beats real fast.

In between my paid work, I find time to wash my clothes, and since I'm washin' my clothes, I may as well wash everyone else's, and since Mrs. Burnett caught me doin' that, she's been givin' me an extra nickel on my pay each week. Sometimes she even gives me an extra helpin' of cracklings with lunch and supper, even though there ain't always enough to fill everyone up.

My hands been real sore from milkin' all them cows twice a day, so Laura massages my hands for me every day after lunch, and I think that's the nicest thing anyone ever done for me, until one day while I'm doin' the wash, Mrs. Burnett comes out and gives me a blouse and a sun dress and a pair of short pants, so's I won't have to keep wearin' the man's outfit that Margaret Ann gave me, and now that's two of the nicest things anyone done for me.

I'm thinkin' about how generous this family's been to me one night after supper when Paul comes up to the upstairs porch to sit with me, and he asks me, "You feelin' at home?"

I think on that a spell.

Home. That's a tricky word for some reason. I remember a couple years back when Miss Glass made us write an essay on the theme "What Home Means to You." I had the hardest time writin' that 'cause home meant everything in the world to me, and how was I gonna write an essay on just one page about everything in the world? So I ended up writin' about the smells and tastes and sounds I love about home – biscuits bakin' in the kitchen, caramel cubes meltin' on my tongue, bullfrogs croakin' by the creek.

So now when Paul asks me if I'm feelin' at home, I think about how content I feel next to Mrs. Burnett in the kitchen that smells like good, hearty food, and I think about the warm feelin' that spreads through my belly when we're all sittin' at the table fillin' up on cracklings and conversation. I think about the way Mrs. Burnett and Laura check on me all the time, like protective mamas, and the way the rollin' hills and sunflowers paint the days with joy. I think about the lowing of the cattle that sing me to sleep before the nighttime billows its blanket of darkness across the countryside. And I reckon I do feel at home. I feel so much at home that it hurts even more when I think about my real home and my mama and daddy all alone, and all at the same time I want to go home, and I don't.

The third remarkable thing that happens – and I never in a million years woulda predicted this – is that I fall head over heels in love with Paul.

20

Marbles

I n the beginning I try to ignore the twinges of excitement
I get every time Paul comes around, the buzzin' warmth
left behind on my skin when he squeezes my shoulder or
when our hands brush together as we pass the jam, and
the kiss of air on my ear when he leans in to whisper somethin'.
I try to ignore those things 'cause it's perfectly silly to be pining
over a grown man like a little schoolgirl, never mind the fact
that he's a railroad bull and if my school was still open I *would*
be a little schoolgirl, just goin' on fifteen. But sometimes there
are things you just cain't ignore.

One morning as I'm puttin' on the ruffled blouse Mrs.
Burnett lent me, I notice a name is embroidered into the inside:
Claire B. It's embroidered with such care, with the gentle and
loving touch of a mother teachin' a child to sew, the way Mama
taught me.

After breakfast, when everybody's goin' on their way,
either to the kitchen sink or out to the crop fields, I catch Paul
as he's headin' out to his car, which really belongs to the

railroad company and Paul only gets to drive it when he's workin'. His eyes, just visible in the light of the early mornin' moon, say he was hopin' I'd walk with him – at least that's what I read in them, and I've always known you can tell how people are feelin' by lookin' in their eyes 'cause eyes don't lie – and the smile playin' on his lips makes my breath catch. We walk and I giggle nervously before I pluck up the courage to ask what I want to ask.

"Who's Claire?" And then I regret askin' it.

Paul's eyes grow dark and he looks down and fidgets with his hat in his hands. "Claire was a cousin of mine who lived with us. Ma raised her from the time she was a little thing. But she died a couple years ago. Tuberculosis."

My eyes go wide. It's scary to hear about someone dyin' from the illness that Mama has. "My mama has tuberculosis." We reach the car, and Paul leans up against the driver's side.

"Not everyone dies from it," he says. "Claire was sickly to begin with."

"How old was she?"

"She was seventeen. Me and her were the same age, so we were pretty close."

I do the math in my head and figure Paul's only nineteen. I knew he couldn't be much older than Josy. I finger the marble in my pocket and think about Josy. I wonder how I'll feel when it's been a couple years since he died, and I feel real sorry for Paul. I ask him if he minds me wearin' the clothes his mama lent me that belonged to Claire, and he says he don't mind at all.

Then he surprises me by askin', "Whatcha got in your pocket that you keep messin' with?"

I blink at him. I didn't realize it was that noticeable. I reach into my pocket and bring out the purple marble and show it to

168

him. "I love marbles," I start, "but this one's extra special 'cause my brother Josy gave it to me." Paul nods, and when he reaches for it, I yank it back, protective, and then feel silly for doin' that. "He died in March," I explain.

"Oh. I'm sorry," Paul says. "That's awful. It's so recent."

"Me and Josy was real, real close. This marble is the only valuable thing I got left." I put it back into my pocket.

"Do you mind me askin' how he died?"

"He was hoppin' trains." I look at Paul, afraid of how he might react when I tell him. "He worked odd jobs to bring home money, but he got beat up real bad by some railroad bulls. His two friends brung him home and he didn't make it." I choke up and try hard not to cry.

Paul stiffens and his eyes squint up, and he looks uncomfortable, like I'm accusin' him or somethin', so I say, "I know you're not like that. Least I don't think you are."

He nods tersely and then leans up off the car and opens the door. Before he slides into the driver's seat, he looks down at me and says, "See? We all got our tragedies, June. Can't escape 'em." And I think on that and it reminds me of Pastor Klein sayin' that we cain't hope to have a life free of trouble, but instead we should pray for strength to get past the troubles.

I don't see Paul for a long time after that, but I think about him a lot and I wonder if he's thinkin' about me. I find my answer when I go to take clothes down from the clothesline and I keep findin' little notes tucked into the pockets of my pants that are hangin' up. Usually it's a quote or a riddle, which makes me laugh, but sometimes it's a line or two of poetry (which he says he wrote himself) – *Hope is found in all places, especially the sea*, or *Never have I seen a thing as lovely as an old oak tree*, or *Laughter is but the music of the land* – and I'm impressed that a tough ol' boy like him could be so sensitive and creative.

Other times it's just a note to say hello, and it's wrapped around a caramel cube, which he's taken to bringin' me from time to time ever since he found out it's my favorite in the whole wide world. I cain't help but laugh every time I find one tucked into my dryin' clothes, and now when I go out to get clothes from the line, I find myself skippin' gleefully and hopin' there's a treat for me, and I feel just the slightest bit let down if there's not, goin' back around and checkin' all the pockets again.

I start seekin' him out while I'm workin' and in between chores, and most of the time, he's gone, but sometimes he lingers in the barn while I'm milkin' the cows before he has to go to work, and sometimes he drops in at lunchtime.

But mostly, after supper we sit on the upstairs porch and watch the red sun sink down behind the mountains. I tell him about my day and he tells me about his. He mainly guards the train yards, but sometimes he has to go onto the trains and look for tramps. He says hobos don't bother him so much 'cause they're decent folks lookin' for work, but it's the bums and tramps that cause trouble, or the young folks just lookin' for the thrill of a free ride.

"Which one was I?" I ask with a wink, and he blushes and says I was the worst kind – a troublemaker and heartbreaker. Now, I know I ain't got any experience at all with boys, and no knowledge about dating, other than what I've read in Margaret Ann's magazines, but I can say right now with about ninety-nine percent confidence that this man is as sweet on me as I am on him, and my heart jumps around in my chest just thinkin' about it.

One time, about the middle of June, I'm in the mule barn brushin' and talkin' to the mules, and Paul comes in. I'm surprised 'cause it's early, before suppertime, and then I see

Paul's right hand is swollen and red, his knuckles stickin' out like tree knobs.

"What happened?" I ask.

He holds his hand up and looks at it. "Oh, just had a run-in with a train-hopper mouthin' off."

I blink at him. "I thought you said you don't get violent with train-hoppers."

"I told you. Only the ones who cause trouble," he says. "Anyway, the sheriff took him to jail and sent me home. Said I should take care of my hand and cool down."

Just then, the mule in the middle starts snortin', and I pat him on the back and rub his neck and coo at him. "You want some attention, D?"

Paul scrunches up his eyebrows. "What'd you call him?"

"What? Oh, I didn't know their names, so I been callin' them F, D, and R, after the president."

Paul grimaces. "Don't let ol' Mr. Burnett hear you say that. Roosevelt's puttin' limits on farm crops, and so far we ain't seen nothing but government control in all his 'new deals.' These mules are Murray," and he pats each one on the side as he says their names, "Max, and Mo."

I nod. "Good to know." And I get back to brushin' 'em so I can get on to my other chores, and by that time I've forgotten all about Paul's busted-up hand until I see it again at supper, and I wonder what or who he musta hit and how hard he musta hit it. And then I start havin' irrational fears about him losin' his hand like Daddy did, and I don't know what's gotten into me.

By the Fourth of July, the sparks between me and Paul are so intense I cain't hardly stand it, and even though he hasn't come right out and said it, I know he feels 'em too.

Turns out they do a big picnic in Lafayette, just like we do in Maynardville, 'cept here everybody in town comes to the Burnett farm. They bring out the horses, and all the kids love to ride the horses 'round the pasture, and there's a feast of ham and apples and watermelon and lemon meringue pie, and after the fireworks, they have a barn dance. They bring in a battery powered light that shines right into the center of the barn like a dance floor, and just like back home, there's a group of folks playin' music.

I feel pretty in Claire's sun dress, and my hair's fillin' out and curlin' up over my ears now, and Sadie gives me a headband with flowers on it to wear, and I'm feelin' more alive than I have in a long time.

Some folks are playin' music, some folks singin', lotsa folks laughin', and there's a joyous feelin' in the air, and I'm smilin' cheek to cheek when Paul comes up and says we should dance. So we do, and I can feel the heat in his fingers as they brush mine, and he smiles all the way up to his eyes, and I cain't tear myself away from those eyes for nothin', and I feel like I got enough electricity runnin' through me to light up the whole farm, maybe even all of Lafayette.

"You're sparkling like fireworks, June," Paul says, and I agree. The only thing that burns that sparkle out is when I see Paul dancin' the same way with some ol' girl from town, and then another and another, but I remind myself that I live here and they don't.

Sundays on the Burnett farm are just about as delightful as Sundays back home, 'cept they don't go to church, they go fishin' on Roanoke River. Sometimes I stay back with Mrs. Burnett and Laura and Granny and Pawpaw, and we laze on the back porch and walk through a trail in the trees out front and make lemonade and make small talk with the chickens, and then when everybody gets back, we fry up the fish they caught. It's real relaxin' and I relish the rest, 'cause I been workin' so hard I'm plumb wore out.

But sometimes, if Paul's goin', I make sure to go too, and we pile into the back of Mr. Burnett's truck with the fishin' poles and tackle boxes, and I like goin' 'cause when folks are fishin', it's real quiet, and I can sit there next to Paul and just listen to his presence. And he smiles at me and lets me help him bait the hooks and when we do that, our hands touch, and that's about enough to make me happy the whole rest of the week.

Then one Sunday in August, insteada goin' fishin', Paul says he wants to show me Roanoke, and I ain't seen a city that big before, so I'm amazed by the humongous movie theater and the Lenox Hotel, which is the tallest buildin' I ever seen, and there are so many cars here, more than I've ever seen in one place, even in Knoxville, and Paul squeezes my hand, and even though it's only for a second, my heart is so fluttery I cain't even look at him or feel myself breathe.

I steal glances as he points out the sights of Roanoke. He's loving showin' me things I never seen before, and I'm loving experiencing this with him.

I start to imagine what our life would be like if we stayed together forever. We could move to Roanoke and live in a little ol' house right here by town, and we could come to the theater and the fancy steak house in the hotel, and the doorman would bow and say, "Good evening, Mr. and Mrs. Paul Burnett," and I'd smile and think about our soon-to-be twin boy and girl, Bradley and Betsy, who I've been dreamin' about for I don't know how long, and I must have this ridiculous dreamy smile on my face, 'cause Paul snaps his fingers in front of my eyes, and suddenly I'm lookin' at him and he's laughin'.

"Whatcha thinkin' about, June?"

The air between us is tense, my longing barely contained, and the only thing stronger than my longing is the fear that in a few weeks I may lose him. The harvest season will come to an end, and I will have to return home.

So I tell him, "I gotta go home to Maynardville soon, Paul."

The thought stirs my insides into a frenzy. I cain't wait to get home and give Mama and daddy the money I've earned, and I'm dyin' to see Mama and make sure she's gettin' well, and I miss them both so much. I also need to go see Margaret Ann and let her know I did it — I hopped a train disguised as a boy and I found work and I'm still alive!

My life in Maynardville, Tennessee, is pullin' so hard at my heart, and I cain't hardly believe it's been over three months since I left home. But I cain't bear the thought of leavin' Paul just when I've discovered this light, like I've been livin' in darkness all this time and he come along and lit me up like a bonfire.

"Well," Paul says, "you can always come back. You're always welcome."

And then he goes quiet, and that quiet seems to last the whole of my last few weeks on the Burnett farm.

I ain't never been good with goodbyes, so I don't plan on drawin' this out. The night I get my final pay from Mr. Burnett, I pack my bag with food I saved from supper, along with my one clean outfit. Just like I did at home, I write a note, tellin' the Burnett family I appreciate all they done for me and that I'll be back to help for the winter.

I write a separate note for Paul. It's a cool September morning when I'm pullin' on my boots and tuckin' my hair up under Mr. Murphy's hat, and there's a lump in my throat that

174

hurts like nothin' before. I imagine Paul tearfully beggin' me not to go, and me beggin' him to come with me, when by the light of the moon I wrap his note around my purple marble and set it in the driver's seat of his car. And then I turn to leave, toward a hobo camp and away from a railroad bull that I have grown to love.

21

Mulligan Stew

The camp is not too far from the train yard in Lafayette where I first met Paul, and I get real good at sittin' far enough away from folks to not be noticed much but close enough to hear the conversation and get important information. The next train, they say, will probably be goin' northeast, but in a day or two, there oughta be one comin' back down toward Knoxville, Tennessee, and that's the one I want.

I figure out soon enough that I gotta make friends with somebody, 'cause the food I packed ain't gonna last two days. I scan the camp the best I can in the pre-dawn light and decide to sit up against a tree near a man that looks so old and frail that there's no chance he'd be able to hurt me even if he tried.

I take a biscuit outa my pack and nibble on it while watchin' the scene around me. Some of the men are still sleepin', and those who are awake are movin' around quietly. I have to avert my eyes when I see a man urinating nearby, and

I panic, wonderin' how I'm gonna take care of my personal business out here for two days with a bunch of men. I look around behind me and decide I'll go deep into the woods, but then I panic more 'cause what if I start my menstruation while I'm out here, and I'm thinkin' about these things when all the sudden the old man beside me starts laughin' like a loon, and I ain't even kiddin', I think somehow he knew what I was thinkin'.

I reach into my pocket for my marble and then remember that I don't have it no more. I left it for Paul. And suddenly I'm missin' Josy and missin' my marble and why'd I leave it for Paul anyway, and for a second I think about walkin' back to the Burnett farm to get my marble back. But then I think about Paul and his eyes and his smile and I can feel the sparks again, and I doze off, thinkin' about how Paul might be reactin' when he reads my note and finds me gone.

When I wake up, there's a train goin' real slow in the wrong direction, and some of the men are hoppin' it. I look around the camp, which is now smaller and cleaner than it was when I arrived. The old man is still there, but he's moved a little further away from me.

With everyone distracted, I take the opportunity to head off into the woods for some privacy. I decide to stay among the trees for a while so's I don't have to talk to no one. These trees are skinny – not as skinny as The Depression Trees, but almost – and they remind me of home.

I find a small brook deeper in the trees and take a bar of soap from my pack and wash my hands and arms and the back of my neck, then take off my boots and socks and wash my feet. It's muggy out here, and hot for September, so it feels good to let the water glide over my feet. As I listen to the birds and the distant hum of conversation from the hobo camp, I wonder if I should start walkin' rather than sit here and wait for the next train. I feel like I'm wastin' time, and I'm real eager to get home. A twig snaps behind me, and I turn, instinctively huggin' my pack to my chest. It's the old man. "You alright?" he asks.

I nod and grunt. I'm afraid to talk and give away that I'm a girl.

The old man nods and grunts too, and then he says, "Chow time," and heads back toward the camp.

I use my pack to dry my feet off and put my socks and boots and hat back on. There's a fire in the firepit and a dented pot hangin' over it, and five or six men are standin' around and throwin' I-don't-know-what-all into the pot. The old man holds his hand out toward me like he's waitin' for me to give him somethin'. I shake my head, not understandin', and he grumbles, "Whatcha got?"

I learn that when you're stayin' overnight at a hobo camp, you're supposed to hand over whatever food you got and they throw it into a stew. Mulligan stew, they call it. Today's stew consists of somebody's potatoes, canned tomatoes, some kinda eggs that ain't chicken eggs, canned beans, plus the ham chunks they want me to give 'em.

I'm hesitant to hand my ham over, 'cause I know for certain I'd rather eat the ham by itself than in a stew with all those other things, and now they're all laughin' at me and promisin' it'll taste good.

Then they start passin' around a cup of what I suspect is moonshine, and when it gets to me, I gotta make a quick decision. It ain't no secret that I'm young, but it is still a secret – at least I hope it is – that I'm a girl, and I want to look as tough as I can, so I take a swig of the hooch and then have to clamp my lips shut so's I don't spit it back out, and it burns so much goin' down my throat that I don't think I'll ever be able to eat or drink again. My eyes are tearin' up and I'm prayin' that they don't spill over in front of these men.

The mulligan stew ain't all that bad, and even though I wish I still had my ham, I'm glad I got to contribute to this group's meal. My ham is the only meat in the stew, and from what these fellas say, it's the only meat they've had other than roadkill in quite a while, and for that reason alone, they seem to take to me and look after me, which I really appreciate later when a bunch of rowdy hobos show up and make a ruckus.

I scoot over to the edge of the camp, closer to the ones who cooked the stew, and closer to the old man, whose name I learn is Rump. That ain't his real name, but the others say they call him Rump 'cause it seems like all he ever does is sit on his rump. I get away with not talkin' 'cause some of these men talk so much they don't mind puttin' words in my mouth, which reminds me of Charlie, and I have half a mind to ask these fellas if they've seen or heard of Pate and Charlie, but I decide it's better to just stay quiet.

The rest of the day is a whole lot of sittin' and waitin'. Some of the men gather and play cards, and the rowdy group go off into the woods and I can hear hootin' and hollerin' and gun shootin', which scares me somethin' awful, but they come back with a rabbit and a couple of squirrels for supper, and they offer to share.

Rump has a beat-up ol' magazine that he lets me read 'til it gets too dark to see, and then he tells me that if I'm aimin' to hop the train goin' to Knoxville, I better get some shut-eye 'fore it gets here. He's got an alarm clock that he winds up, and I swear I ain't been asleep but a few minutes when that thing's ringing and ol' Rump is tellin' me I better get ready.

"What time is it?" I ask, rubbin' my eyes.

"Nigh fo' o'clock," he grunts.

He watches while I fold up the blanket I used as a pillow and put it back in my pack, drink some water and then put my hat on and sit up straight, eyes strainin' to see in the dark.

"You got gloves?" Rump asks me.

I think about the work gloves I used on the Burnett farm and wonder if I shoulda brought those with me.

"You hoppin' trains, you need gloves," he says, and he reaches into his bindle and takes out a pair and holds 'em out toward me. They're rough lookin', dirty and sweat-stained and probably a hand too big, but I take 'em and grunt my thanks and put 'em on. I don't know how this old man knew when the freight train goin' down to Knoxville would be comin', but all the sudden, here it comes, and I stand up to go just as a bunch of the other men do, but Rump stays put.

"Ain't you comin'?" I ask, forgettin' to lower my voice, but there's so much other noise goin' on that I don't think the old man notices.

"Nah," he says. "I'll wait for the next one."

I nod a goodbye, wonderin' if ol' Rump is a bum 'stead of a hobo, and I remember what Paul said about bums and tramps bein' no good, and I decide that cain't be, 'cause Rump is a good person.

Then I turn to go, my heart beatin' faster at the prospect of havin' to jump onto a movin' train again. I find some of the other men who I ate the stew with, and I run up beside the train with them. They spot the open boxcar they want, and they holler at me to throw my pack in first, but I shake my head.

One by one, they start hoppin' on, using the door latch to swing themselves up. This one's goin' slower than the last one was, so it's easier to get on, and I feel the wind just about take my hat off, and as soon as I've got my balance, I pat it down on my head and duck back to a dark corner of the car.

Somebody lights a lantern, and the fellas are sittin' around talkin'. They're tellin' stories about folks who got their legs chopped off jumpin' on or off a train, folks who tried ridin' the rods up under the train cars and fell and got crushed, and folks who got caught by bulls. My ears perk up and I listen real hard, like maybe I'll hear somethin' about Josy. Or Paul. But I don't.

It's a long ride, and it gets so hot in the boxcar I cain't hardly breathe, and this car ain't got no hay or nothin' for us to sit or lay down on, so my bones are bruised up by the time we get close to the train yard where I need to get off, near Norris Lake and the hobo camp I started out at four months ago. Nobody else plans to get off here, so I'm on my own, but they tell me it's best to scoot off when it slows down before it comes to the train yard and then run like the dickens.

"Don't wait til it stops at the train yard, 'cause there'll be bulls," one of the men says.

So I get ready, scootin' up toward the edge on the open side, and I can feel the train slowin' down little by little, and my heart is speedin' up, and all the men are gathered around and tellin' me how to tuck and roll when I hit the ground and to use my pack to break the fall, and I'm huggin' my pack to my body and I'm 'bout as scared as if I was jumpin' out of a plane, but when the men holler, "Now!" the train is goin' so slow I feel like I could just walk on off. And that was a mistake.

My fall is not the easy tuck-and-roll the hobos described. It's a flailin', head bumpin', ankle twistin', pack bouncin' tumble down a grassy ravine, and when I finally slide to a stop and look back up, that train is long gone, but I swear I can hear them hobos laughin'. I'm breathin' hard, and I sit up and check all my limbs and then check my pack to make sure everything's still intact, and then the tears come and I'm just relieved I didn't break a bone, or worse. I get up slowly and stretch out and get my bearings and, using the train tracks as my guide, head toward home.

Before I know it, I'm passin' through Maynardville, past the Piggly Wiggly and the closed-down Macafee's and Sweet Shop, and the closer I get to home, the faster my heart beats and the bigger my smile grows, and the whole time I was at the Burnett farm in Lafayette, Virginia, I never realized how much I truly missed home. When I see the church and the school, I break into a run toward Margaret Ann's. I decide to stop by to see her first since I'm passin' right by anyway. Besides, she can give me an idea of what to expect when I get home.

She squeals and hugs me, but when I ask about home, the look on her face is bleak. She says Daddy came by askin' questions, and her mama went over to help take care of my mama, and now I'm scared to go home. "Oh, June, you gotta get there right away," Margaret Ann says. "Go on. They need you."

And I'm practically runnin' the whole way, worried about what I'm gonna find. My pocketwatch ain't workin' no more, but I reckon it's about four o'clock, so Mama and Daddy are probably gettin' ready for supper. With no more chickens and no more garden, I ain't real sure what they been doin' all this time. Normally we'd be gettin' the farm ready for winter, choppin' firewood, repairin' or repaintin' the barn, fixin' up any gaps in the fences. I don't know if Daddy's been able to do those things by himself.

Walkin' up the lane to our farm, I'm taken aback. It looks so much smaller than I remember. The barn, the field where the goats used to graze, the patch of pawpaw trees, where Josy lies in rest. I get halfway up the drive when Mama comes out onto the porch and is beatin' dust outa the front room rug, and then she looks up, and she drops the rug and she half runs, half stumbles down the steps, and then she's runnin' toward me, and I'm runnin' toward her, and then we're a tangle of arms as we embrace, just barely holdin' each other up.

We're takin' each other in as we walk toward the house, and I'm seein' how much thinner Mama looks and how pale, her face lined with worry and sadness, and now her nose is dripping and she wipes it with the back of her hand and says, "I thought we'd lost you too."

I stop walkin' and drop my pack on the ground and grab Mama in a hug again. "Oh, Mama, I'm so sorry. I wanted to help."

She rubs and pats my back. "I know you did, June. You always were strong-willed."

Just then Daddy comes around from the back of the house with what looks like a dead rabbit in his hand, and when he sees us, he stops and stares. He doesn't move toward us. He doesn't move at all.

"It's been tough on your daddy," Mama says, and she pushes me gently, nudging me toward him. I grab my pack off the ground and take tentative steps toward Daddy. I'm thinkin' maybe I should take the money out, show him right away what I earned for them, but when I get up close I see that Daddy's face looks fiercely mad, and tears are fallin' like waterfalls, and then I'm thinkin' maybe I shouldn'ta gone. Maybe I shoulda just stayed home and we'd all find a way 'cause we're all in this together, just like Miss Glass always said. And then he lets out a sob that he was tryin' to hold in, and I hold my hand out to him. "Daddy?"

He comes closer and strains to smile and says, "Glad you're home," and then with his stump he wipes his eyes, and

I stare. It feels like a lifetime ago that he lost his hand, and I just about forgot.

"Lemme go get this rabbit skinned and cleaned. I'll be in shortly."

I nod and watch him walk toward the barn, and then Mama puts her arm around me and walks me up the porch steps and into the house, and my heart feels so heavy with the burden I put on my parents, the fear and the worry, and me not bein' here to help them and to take care of them like Josy wanted me to. Mama gets the washtub set up with fresh water for me and the lavender soap I always loved so much, and I sink down into the water and I cry and cry and cry.

When I'm clean and dressed I go out into the kitchen and help Mama prepare supper. We dice potatoes that Mama got from Mrs. Porter down the lane, and we season them with fresh herbs. "I've kept up my herb garden," Mama says, proud to share a bit of good news. She's movin' slower than I remember, but I ain't heard her cough yet.

"How are you, Mama?" I ask. "Is the tuberculosis gone?"

She nods, but it's unconvincing. "Oh, yeah, Dr. Jamison cleared me back in June, I think it was. I been goin' to church most Sundays and to town. I mean, I'm not a hundred percent yet, but I do feel better than before." She drops her eyes and focuses on the herbs she's choppin'. "I'm just tired is all. So very tired."

I glance back out at the porch. I hadn't noticed when we came in, but her bed's out there. "You been sleepin' on the porch?"

"Well, you know how hot it gets in the summer," Mama says. "Besides, fresh air can't hurt."

My eyes wander around the kitchen and the front room 'til I spot her handkerchief on the table by the couch, and it's stained a rusty red. I stop and put down my knife. "Are you sure you're okay, Mama?"

She looks at me with red rimmed eyes. "Baby girl, why don't you tell me about you, huh? Whatchya been doin' all this time? Where'd you go? Tell me all about it."

She scrapes the potatoes and herbs into a pot of water and adds a few pinches of salt. Then, without lookin' at me, she takes the pot over to the wood stove and sets it on a cookplate, then opens the firebox and pokes at the sizzlin' woodpile inside. Before I say anything, Daddy comes in with a tin of rabbit meat and dumps it into the pot. Then we all sit down in the front room, me and Daddy on the couch and Mama in her chair, and I tell them everything.

I tell them about disguising myself as a boy and walkin' up toward the big bridge and jumpin' onto a train and gettin' thrown off. "It wasn't movin' at the time," I say real quick when they gasp.

I tell them about workin' at the Burnett farm and how nice the family treated me and about seeing Roanoke. The only thing I leave out is how much I love Paul. I haven't decided when I'll tell them about that.

Then I reach into my pack and pull out my stack of money. I have $67, including the extra nickels that Mrs. Burnett gave me for workin' around the house when I didn't have to, and Mama 'bout passes out when she sees it, and both Mama and Daddy are smilin' and cryin' happy tears now 'cause this will pay for two months of the mortgage with some left over.

I get used to bein' home again real quick, and I savor every smell and every sound, wonderin' if Paul would like it here. I pet and talk to Molly, who I think is mighty glad to see me. Even ol' Miss Priss seems to light up when I walk into the barn.

I sit out by the creek like me and Josy used to and watch baby turtles bask in the last of Mother Nature's warmth before fall's cold weather blows in. I sit among The Depression Trees and remember how me and Josy used to run around and around through here.

I pick the last of the fruit off the pawpaw trees and then sit down and talk to Josy. I tell him how I met a railroad bull who ain't like the mean ones and in fact I love him, and I hope Josy don't mind me givin' him our purple marble, and I tell him how if he could meet Paul he'd like him too. I think the two of them would get along real well. Talkin' about Paul makes me feel alive again, and I start to get excited about goin' back to Lafayette to see him.

For my fifteenth birthday, me and Mama and Daddy ride into Knoxville and have an ice cream cone with the little bit of extra money left over after payin' the mortgage. Daddy says we're still behind, but this'll keep the bank off our backs for a while longer.

"How behind are we, Daddy?" I ask, and he tries to brush it off, tellin' me it's not for me to worry about, but I persist 'cause after what I done, hoppin' trains and workin' for strangers all this time and travelin' with hobos, I deserve to know.

Daddy sighs and his shoulders sag. "About six months."

And I feel my insides go numb and now I'm starin' out the window of the ice cream parlor, starin' out the window but not lookin' at anything, not seeing anything. How are we gonna get out from under six months of debt? I'd have to work at the Burnett farm for a year to earn that much money. And Mama and Daddy can see the worry in my face, so they try to pull me back.

"Hey, Junie," Daddy says. "We're here to celebrate your birthday. Let's not talk about that right now."

And Mama smiles and when she does, a glob of ice cream slips out of her mouth and rolls down her chin, and her eyes go wide in embarrassment, and her free hand springs up to her face to catch the runaway ice cream, and then she laughs, and I laugh, and then we're all laughin', one magical moment of silliness to erase the worry.

22

Gumption

and a Gun

Mama and Daddy are not thrilled about me wantin' to go back on the railroad, not one bit, but they cain't argue with the fact that we need the money. Daddy's been sellin' the rabbit furs when he catches 'em in Josy's traps, and they've been tradin' bottles of milk for groceries and things they need, but they're just scrapin' by and fallin' further and further behind on the mortgage.

Mama says she feels well enough to get back to her sewin', but now she ain't got a sewin' machine no more, and besides, things are still bad for most folks, even with government assistance, so ain't nobody gonna want to buy whatever Mama could sew anyhow. At least that's what she says. I look at her get short of breath just walkin' from the front porch to the kitchen or from the back porch to the outhouse, and I think

188

the real problem is she's still sick, even if she says she's feelin' better.

Daddy seems pretty wore out himself, and I feel a heightened responsibility to provide for them since they cain't provide for themselves no more. I think that hurts Daddy more than anything, more than losin' his hand, more even than losin' Josy, and so when I'm packed to go and I'm huggin' them and promisin' I'll work my hardest to bring home lots of money, Daddy looks downright miserable and won't hardly say a word.

I start walkin' down the drive, but somethin' makes me stop and turn around, and Mama's got her handkerchief up to her mouth and Daddy just looks so glum and pitiful, and I run back to him and take his face in my hands and holler at him, "I love you, Daddy! More than anything. And I'll be back as soon as I can, don't you worry."

He nods and smiles and squeezes my shoulders, and he says it so quietly that I cain't hardly hear him, but I think he says he's real proud of me, and that gives me the courage I need to get on going down the drive and up the lane and past the treeline and up toward the big bridge.

Gettin' on the train this time is somethin' awful. It feels *off* for some reason. The hobo camp was crowded with folks I ain't seen before; I didn't recognize nobody. And now the boxcar is crowded and stinky and some of the men's bein' loud and rowdy, pickin' on folks and startin' fights. The back corner I usually sit in is taken and there's hardly any room to sit, so I scrunch myself up against the wall in the middle of the car and pull my knees up to my chest and try to make myself invisible.

Storm clouds block out most of the sunlight outside, makin' the boxcar feel like it's plunged in nighttime darkness, a small wedge of gray light making its way just about to where my feet are. I try to close my eyes and go to sleep, but there are two obnoxious fellas to my left that are hollerin' at somebody. Then there's a scuffle and they start beatin' on this person, and they're in the shadows, so I cain't see what's happenin' but I can hear it – the poundin' of the punches and the thud as the person falls to the floor of the car and the whoof-crunch of the kicks and the hollerin' and name-callin'.

I put my hands over my ears and duck my head into my knees and try to scoot over, away from the fightin' 'cause it just about scares me to death.

And then I hear somethin' that makes me lift my head and turn my ear toward the sound. It's a distinctive sound, a sound I've known all my life, there in the darkness, a clink and a roll, and somethin' has rolled over to the toes of my boots in the wedge of gray light. I reach out and pick it up, and it's a perfectly clear marble.

Pate!

I turn and look and try to see the fella on the ground, and I cain't see, but it just has to be Pate. I reach into my pack and wrap my hand around my pistol, and then I'm standin' and I'm holdin' the pistol with both hands and aimin' it right at these two mean men, and then I'm growlin', a voice like I've never heard myself make before, "Leave him be!"

And I say it again louder. "I said leave him be!" and I pull back the hammer on the revolver and the click seems to echo in the boxcar, and suddenly the two men are starin' wide-eyed at me with their hands in the air and they're backin' away, but just to be sure, I say, "I'll shoot!" and I point the gun right at their eyes, back and forth, one man's eyes, then the other one's eyes, then back at the first one, and I'm shakin' like mad, and I think they think I'm crazy enough to shoot, 'cause they inch away and scoot around to the back of the boxcar as far away from me as they can get, and I follow them with my aim 'til they're in the darkest shadows of the car.

Somebody whistles and somebody chuckles, but then it's mostly quiet 'cept for the whimperin' and spittin' from the fella on the floor. Then as I'm lowerin' the gun so I can help this man who I think must be Pate, I squeeze on the trigger accidentally and the gun goes off and shoots a hole right through the floor of the boxcar, and I jump and now everybody in the train car is on alert. So I stand up straight and puff my arms out like I did that on purpose to make a point, and I take a moment to send a hateful glare to the back of the train car where the bullies went.

And then I put the gun in my waistband and kneel down close to the beaten person, and when I get up close, I can see that he's got skin the color of chocolate puddin', and he's bleedin' from his lips and he's bruised up, though not as bad as Josy was. I turn his face so I can see his eyes. "Pate?"

He looks at me, confused, and his eyes narrow up. "J-June?"

I nod and nod and nod, and I smile and then I'm helpin' him sit up and I'm helpin' him scoot to a wall and I'm reachin' into my pack for the few first-aid supplies I have – peroxide, a small bit of gauze, and willow bark. I hand him the willow bark and he pops it in his mouth and clamps his teeth down on it. Then he points toward his bindle, and I scoot over to get it. He's got more gauze and bandages, and water and aspirin.

Once we start cleanin' the blood off, we see he ain't that badly beaten, and we get bandages over the worst wounds and then sit back against the wall and try to calm down, and I keep one hand on my pistol, just in case.

It takes a few deep breaths for my heart to stop poundin', and we're sittin' in silence for a spell, the steady clickety-clack of the train and the low hum of talkin' comin' from the other end of the car.

"What're you doin' here, June?" Pate asks.

"Same as you. Same as Josy was. Goin' to find work." And then I realize Charlie ain't here. "Where's Charlie?"

Pate looks away and fidgets with a piece of gauze in his hands. "I lost track of him one night when some bulls was chasin' us and a bunch of guys got arrested. I ran and hid, and I ain't seen him since."

"How long ago was that?"

He looks at me. "April."

The reality of what musta happened to Charlie hits me, and I think of Josy, and I reach into my pocket, almost surprised to feel the silky sphere of a marble, and then I remember it's Pate's clear marble. I hold it up and smile, and he takes it from me and rolls it around in his fingers.

"I found this in my pack right after that night I lost Charlie," Pate says, "and it reminded me of Joseph and you, and ... I dunno ... it sorta helped me, ya know?"

I do know. I know exactly what he means, and it makes my heart real happy that the marble I snuck into his pack actually meant somethin' to him.

"I'll look after you now," I say, "since Charlie ain't here. Or Josy. We'll stick together." And I nod toward my gun, my eyes sayin' ain't nobody gonna mess with us since I got my gun. And it's true, too. I look around at the train car, and everybody has moved as far as they can toward the back end of the car, leavin' the whole front side to me and Pate. That makes me laugh.

Later I learn that all those hobos got a mind to steer clear of me 'cause "that girl's got gumption and a gun," they say. That's when I realize I wasn't foolin' nobody with the men's pants and boots and hat. They knew I was a girl from the moment I opened my mouth and said, "Leave him be."

I tell Pate about my job at the Burnett farm and I tell him that's where I'm goin' and he should come with me 'cause they got a big ol' farm and they're short some farm hands.

Then I get to talkin' about Paul, and I don't know if it's the way my eyes shine when I say his name or the way I talk a mile a minute about Paul this and Paul that, but Pate gets a smirk on his face and says, "You in love or somethin'?" And my face burns like a wood stove, and I guess that's answer enough for Pate, 'cause he don't ask nothin' more.

It's rainin' now, and the drops echo on the roof of the train car, and wind whips the water into the open side, and it's cool, and we hunker down and shiver until it's 'bout time to get off. Another hobo who wants to get off near Lafayette tells us when we oughta jump, about half a mile before the train yard, and this time the jumpin' is easier and I don't go tumblin' all over the place. Instead, I slide 'cause the grass is wet, but that's better than fallin' and sprawlin'.

It's about an hour's walk to get to the Burnett farm, but it ends up takin' longer 'cause I don't exactly know the way, and we cain't see that good 'cause it's rainy and dark. We stop into a little store and ask somebody, and sure enough, they know the way and give us directions.

When the downpour fades to just a sprinkle, I tell Pate about the farm and the house and the animals, but mostly about Paul.

"How'd you meet this Paul, anyhow?" Pate asks me.

I clam up real fast. I don't want to tell him how I met him. I don't want to tell him Paul's a railroad bull.

"Oh, I—well," I stutter. "I got off a train at the Lafayette train yard, and, well, I didn't know where to go, and he was there, and turned out his mama and daddy needed help on their farm. So it was real lucky that I found him."

Pate agrees. "That's some luck, June."

When we get to the narrow dirt lane that leads up to the Burnett farm, my heart beats faster and I'm itchin' to see everyone, and it almost feels like I'm comin' home. It's gettin' dark, probably 'bout six or seven o'clock, so they're probably all at supper, and I think that's perfect timing.

I don't see Paul's car when we walk up the muddy drive, but I know he sometimes works late. We step up onto the front porch and wipe our feet on the rug, and the sounds of family conversation and forks and plates dance out through the screen door, and familiar smells fill my nose.

I knock on the door frame and call out, "Mrs. Burnett?" and then she's shufflin' over to the door, wipin' her hands on her apron, and squintin' to see who it is, and when she recognizes me, she swings the screen door open and squeals and pulls me into her arms.

"June! I'm s'glad you made it back!" Then she hollers into the kitchen, "June's back, everyone!" Then she looks at Pate, squintin' her eyes at his bandaged face, and says, "And who's this that you brought with ya?"

He nods tentatively and real quiet says, "Pate," and Mrs. Burnett leans in closer like she didn't hear him.

"This here's Pate, Mrs. Burnett, and he's lookin' for work too," I say. "He's my friend and he took care of my brother Josy when he was ridin' the rails, and I was hopin' he could work here too this winter, with me."

And all that comes out so fast I don't know if any of it made any sense to Mrs. Burnett, but she nods and says, "Y'all come in and get a bite to eat and talk to Jerry 'bout it."

It's so good to see everyone, Laura and Granny and Pawpaw especially. We all hug and then they're makin' room for me and Pate at the table and Mrs. Burnett is makin' us a plate of pork sausage and beans and cornbread and cracklings, and we eat like we ain't ate in a real long time.

Mrs. Burnett sees me cranin' my neck around to look out the front door, and she chuckles and says, "Paul'll be about shortly. He's workin', but we expect him before it gets too late."

I duck my head and smile, and then I listen while Mr. Burnett talks to Pate. It sounds like he'll let us both work for him and Pate can stay in one of the barn lofts with the other farm hands.

I'm beamin' at Pate and he's grinnin' wide when we hear stompin' up the steps and Paul comes in, and the whole kitchen erupts in cheer as everybody gotta point out the obvious: "Look who's here, Paul!" "June came back!" and on and on, and I look at Paul, expectin' him to be so happy to see me, but he's straight faced and looks almost like he seen a ghost. I turn around to see what he's lookin' at, and Pate looks like he's 'bout to explode, and his face is all red and he's shakin' his head like *No! No!* and then he's up from his chair and he's runnin' past Paul and he's runnin' out the door, and I'm hollerin' after him and I'm lookin' at everybody like I have no idea what's goin' on, and I get up and run out after Pate. Mrs. Burnett hollers after me, and I hear somebody say, "Let her go."

"Pate! Pate, what's wrong? Where you goin'?" And I run in the chilly rain to catch up with him, and by the time I do, he's all the way out the gate and runnin' down the narrow lane, and it's dark and I'm all wet now and I'm scared and I don't know why he's runnin' like this, and I grab his shoulders and make him stop and look at me. "Pate! Tell me what's goin' on!"

Pate is cryin' and pantin' so hard like he cain't catch his breath and he looks half scared to death, and it's makin' me feel real worried for him, and he says, "That fella—that big fella that just came in…" and he's shakin' his hands like they're on fire, and he's cryin' and spittin' tears and he hollers, "That's one of the bulls that beat up Joseph!"

23

We All Got Our Tragedies

I don't understand. It doesn't make sense what Pate's tellin' me. It's rainin' harder now and maybe I didn't hear him right. "What are you talkin' about?" I'm all questions and disbelief and scrunched-up face.

"June, we gotta get outa here," he hollers. "That's him! He beat up Joseph."

But I still don't understand 'cause that cain't be. Not Paul, who brought me into his family and watched after me and took care of me and was so nice to me. Not Paul, who I love like I ain't never loved no one before. "Are you sure?"

Pate's noddin' his head so hard, and his face – his face looks like he's in agony. "Yes, I'm tellin' ya! He killed Joseph! He killed your brother!" And there's no way I cain't believe him now, and he's draggin' me by the arm and we're runnin' away, off toward the train tracks, and I look back behind me, and no one's comin' after me. *Paul. Paul killed Josy.* And the full meaning of that knocks the breath outa me, and I run and I sob and I wail, but we don't stop runnin'.

I don't know where we're goin', but Pate seems to know, so I follow him, and we leave Lafayette behind. And then, when we're outa breath and we're far enough away that Paul cain't come find us, we stop, hands on our knees, heavin', pantin', still cryin', til our hearts calm down, and then we sit up under some trees. Pate reaches into his pack and brings out a towel and wipes his face and his head, and that's when I realize I've left my pack in the Burnetts' kitchen, and I drop my shoulders and hang my head.

And Pate says, "I'll look after you now." He hands me his towel and I dry off the best I can, and we drink big gulps of water from his canteen, and I feel grateful.

We sit in silence. The only sounds are the crickets and rainwater drippin' from tree leaves, and I think about what Pate told me, and I have to know exactly what Pate saw. I have to know for sure. And then when he starts describing that day – how the bulls accused Josy of smart-mouthin', and how one of them knocked Charlie out and then held Pate by the neck so he couldn't help Josy while Paul knocked him to the floor of the train and beat him in the face over and over and over and then dragged him off the train when it stopped at a train yard and kicked him with his boots and stomped on him and wouldn't give him a chance to get up or to defend himself, and then they dragged him off to jail and beat on him some more for a few weeks before they finally let Pate and Charlie take him home – I wish I hadn't asked.

I'm holdin' my knees and I'm rockin' and I'm cryin' out loud and I'm picturin' Paul, "sweet pea" Paul, doin' these things to my Josy, and I cry until I ain't got nothin' left inside me.

At daybreak, Pate pulls out a can of beans and a knife and two spoons, and we eat, both exhausted and empty. My heart is heavy with sorrow for what happened to Josy, and devastation that Paul was the one who did it.

Why did it have to be Paul? And I keep goin' back and forth in my head, trustin' what Pate said and then thinkin' there's no way it was Paul, and as we pack up and head out and as we're walkin' and walkin', I make Pate describe the bull, again and again – what exactly did he look like, what was he wearin', what did he sound like, what did he say – until he's tired of tellin' it.

We make our way to a hobo camp at the base of a steep rise of trees, and we mostly keep to ourselves 'cept for one fella that Pate knows and is friendly toward us. They talk about when the next freight's expected to be comin' along and where there's work to be had, while I sit and sulk and think about Josy and Paul. It just hurts so much.

I replay in my mind every moment I ever spent with Paul, how my skin felt electric with just a whisper of a touch, how my eyes burned every time they found his, how much I wanted him to love me.

Did he? He left me notes, he brought me caramel cubes, he danced with me, he watched the sunset with me, he took me to see Roanoke, he checked in on me all the time while I was workin' on the farm. How could he not love me?

I think back to the conversation we had about Josy, when I first told him how he died, and now I remember, I remember! I remember how strange Paul acted, how he clammed up and wanted to leave real fast and how he said … what was it? *We all got our tragedies, June.* Did he know then? Did he realize who I was talkin' about and that he was the one that done it?

And now I fill with rage, my body burnin' from inside out, because if he realized, if he knew, then how could he go along like nothin' ever happened, and how could he pull me in like low tide of the ocean and make me think he cared about me? How could he do that?

And just as fast as I fell in love with this railroad bull from Lafayette, Virginia, I hate him with all the life that's left in me, and I reach instinctively into my pocket, and then I grow dizzy with the realization that this man has my purple marble. Josy's purple marble. And I'm crying again.

Soon Pate's scootin' over to me and checkin' to see that I'm alright, and he says he got a plan. We're gonna hop onto the next train goin' southwest. There's a little town by the name of Independence, and that's where we're gonna jump off, and then we're gonna walk down across the border into North Carolina, where there's some farms that the hobos say are friendly and lookin' for workers.

I wipe my tears and nod, but I sure don't feel no motivation to go work on a farm. I don't feel no motivation to do nothin' but sit here and hate myself, and all the sudden, as if he done channeled Josy and knew just what I needed, Pate pulls his clear marble from his pocket and he holds it up and the sun shines just right on it, and somehow I don't see a plain clear marble no more, I see somethin' special, just like Pate said the first time I met him, and I smile and a laugh spills out.

"I think you need this more than me now, June," Pate says, and he places the marble in my hand and folds my fingers around it, and I hold it there and think of Josy and our jar of marbles and the game we used to play, and I take a deep, deep breath, and I feel like I can feel him right here next to me.

I keep that marble in my pocket now, and I reach my fingers in and hold it every time I get lonely or sad or angry about everything that's happened, and it calms me, and I'm so grateful to Pate for givin' it back to me, so grateful.

We follow Pate's plan, and we work on a farm just inside the northern border of North Carolina, and I try not to think about the Burnett farm, and I try not to get attached to the folks who own this farm.

We stay through the fall and into the winter, Pate workin' on the tough projects like choppin' wood and fixin' fences and workin' on the barns, and I help the lady of the house with cannin' fruit and sewin' up clothes.

It reminds me of Mama, and I get homesick and wonder what Mama and Daddy are doin' and if they're keepin' warm this winter. I take to pretendin' I can send messages to Mama by holdin' the clear marble and talkin' to her. I tell her I'll be home real soon and that I ain't in Virginia no more and that she don't have to worry 'bout me 'cause Pate's lookin' after me.

The Rogers – they're the owners of the farm – pay me fifty cents a day for my work, and since we don't work on Sundays, it comes out to $3 a week, and that's alright with me since I ain't doin' all the hard work I was doin' at the Burnett farm. Cannin' and sewin' is real easy work for me, and I enjoy it, but I do get scared every now and then that I won't have enough to give Mama and Daddy to keep our farm.

I shake that thought outa my head real fast, though, 'cause I've just had too much to worry and be sad about and I don't think I can take anymore worry or sadness. Mrs. Rogers seems to know that, 'cause she's real calm and gentle around me, and it makes me feel safe.

About the middle of December, Mrs. Rogers tells me that I oughta go home so I can be with my family at Christmas, and

I agree, so me and Pate make a plan and head on out to a hobo camp, his pack filled with food Mrs. Rogers gave us, and a wool blanket to wrap around us.

Pate says it should take about four hours, maybe a little more, on the train to get back to Maynardville, depending on how many times the train stops and how slow it goes.

He says he'll ride the whole way with me and then continue on out west to find another job, even though I beg him to come home with me for Christmas 'cause Mama and Daddy sure would be glad to see him. He shakes his head and says no, but ends up sayin' he'll think about it, and we eat some of Mrs. Rogers' food and go to sleep, huddled under the blanket as close as we could get to one of the firepits at the hobo camp.

In the mornin' there's a commotion as a coupla new campers come walkin' up, and they're hollerin' for somebody, and I see other fellas gather around the men, and they're talkin' and shakin' their heads, and then somebody's pointin' over in our direction. Me and Pate are eatin' some biscuits and sausage under the warmth of the blanket and we watch as these men come walkin' up toward us.

"One of you named Baker?" one of the men says.

I swallow and look up. "Yes?"

They come closer. "You Baker?"

"Yessir, I'm June Baker," I say.

"I gotta message for you to go home. Real urgent."

And my head gets fuzzy and my ears close up. "What? Why?" I got so many questions I don't even know what to ask.

The man holds his hands up and says, "I don't know nothin' but that somebody says you need to get home now."

It's Mama. It must be Mama's sickness come back. And I'm up and I'm shakin' my hands like mad and I look at Pate and he looks about as scared as I feel, and I throw my arms around him and I'm cryin' and I'm hollerin', "I gotta get home. Mama!" Daddy musta gotten a message out just like he did back when he was lookin' for Josy, and for him to do that it must be real serious. *My God, what if Mama's dyin'?*

Pate says I cain't wait for the next train 'cause it might be hours 'fore it comes along, so somebody shows me a map and tells me where to go to get onto a road where I can hitch a ride, says it'll be faster than waitin' here. And I take off before anyone says anything else, and I'm runnin' and runnin' 'til I get to the road.

It don't take long before I start to see cars drivin' up and down the road, and I hold out my thumb like I seen folks on the side of the road do, but I keep walkin' 'cause I ain't got time to slow down and wait. And it don't take long before a car sputters up beside me and the folks inside – a man and a boy about my age – ask if they can help me. They say they can take me as far as Kingsport, so I climb into the back seat, and I pray and pray that I can get home in time to tell Mama I love her.

In Kingsport, I get out and walk some more, and it seems like I'm walkin' forever, and I'm tired and I'm so scared for Mama, and now I cain't breathe, and I'm thinkin' maybe I shoulda waited for a train, and I plop down on a boulder and cry all the tears I thought I had already gotten rid of.

My head is in my hands and my face is a red, slobbery mess when a truck pulls up and an old fella asks me if I'm alright. I know he's a stranger and all, but I pour out my soul and tell him everything about Mama bein' sick with the tuberculosis for so long and gettin' weaker every time I see her and how I gotta get home just as fast as I can.

He pats me on the back and says, "Don't you worry, honey, I can take you to Maynardville." And my heart leaps with hope.

I don't even know how long I musta been asleep, but the old man shakes my shoulder and I look up and we're in Maynardville, right outside of the Piggly Wiggly.

I thank him and jump out as fast as my hands can fumble the door open, and I'm so tired, but I half walk, half run all the way home, and I'm prayin' the whole way there and talkin' to myself, sayin', "She'll be okay when I get there, she'll be okay when I get there, she'll be okay when I get there."

And when I get up the lane and to the drive, I see our barn, and I see Molly and the wagon, and I see a car up in front of the house, and I'm runnin' toward the porch and I'm hollerin', "Mama! Daddy!" and just when I get to the porch steps, Mama comes runnin' out with her arms outstretched.

"June!" And I just about collapse in relief. I reach her and grab for her. "Mama! You're alright!" and I'm smilin' and then I back up and I look at her and see that her eyes are dark and red and her face is shadowed with pain. "Mama?"

"Oh, June," Mama says, and the tears fall. "It's Daddy."

"Daddy?" I think about him workin' and everything with only one hand and think he musta gotten hurt again. "Did he hurt himself? Is it his hand?"

"No, no," Mama says and now she's clutchin' me and she lets out a sob and says, "No, baby girl, Daddy's gone, Daddy's gone, I'm so sorry, Daddy's gone."

And I don't understand until Mama's fallin' to her knees in front of me and she's sobbin' and then I see Pastor Klein comin' out onto the porch.

24

Let the Memories Fill You and Heal You

It seems Daddy couldn't take the pain of losin' his hand to infection and losin' Josy to the bulls and losin' me to the railroad and the possibility of losin' his wife to illness and his land to the bank, 'cause all that loss made Daddy hang himself from the barn loft. It happened about two weeks ago, and I can only imagine what Mama went through when she found him swingin' from a rope, blue in the face, and I think maybe if I'da been here ... and at the same time I think I'm awful glad I wasn't here.

Mama got the message out to me as quick as she could, through Jimmy Mack and Mr. Clay and all the folks they know who could get word out to all the hobo camps from here to the ocean and back again.

Pastor Klein helped Mama bury Daddy up under the pawpaw trees next to Josy, and then he came every day to check on Mama 'til I made it home so we could have a funeral. When Pastor Klein leads the private ceremony on the hill next to Josy's grave, my heart is full of questions for God, 'cause how can he put so much loss and so much pain onto our family?

And then Pastor Klein says, "While no one can heal the heartache of the tragic death of a loved one, no one can steal the memories of their love. Let the memories fill you and heal you." And that's what me and Mama try to do. Every morning, we read from the Bible together, like Daddy liked to do, and all the time, we talk about memories, and we cherish them and we cherish each other. Mama, as amazing as I always thought she was, grows even stronger and more amazing as she holds me up when I cain't stand no more.

"You took care of me for so long, Junie, when I was sick," she says. "Let me take care of you now."

But that feels like a sham. The readin' and the prayin' and the pretendin' like we're strong. 'Cause we're not. Most of the time we move around the house in silence, and that silence is the loudest thing I ever heard. Without Josy and without Daddy, we don't know what to do. We get lost in our own house. And as good as our Maynardville friends are, ain't no amount of friendly people can fill the hole that's left in our family. It feels like we ain't got a family no more.

The days drag on like that endlessly, our grief stretchin' out around us like tendrils of smoke so thick we can touch it. Sometimes it feels like weeks have gone by and I look up at the clock and it's only been an hour. I look out at our land, the land that used to be so fruitful, so productive, the land that provided for us at Daddy and Josy's hands, and all the sudden I hate it, and I hate them. I hate them for what they done, especially Daddy, 'cause Josy at least couldn't help what happened to him, but Daddy— what was he thinkin', leavin' his wife and daughter on purpose like that? Like he meant to hurt us. He meant it. That ain't what a man's supposed to do. That ain't what a father's supposed to do.

I lie to myself a lot, try to trick myself into believin' that Daddy's death was an accident. The infection came back and spread throughout his body, or ol' Molly threw him off and he got stomped, or he fell from the roof of the barn tryin' to patch it. Anything but the truth. Anything at all but the truth, because the truth is what kills.

And then sometimes my anger is a gift, 'cause it's my anger that gives me the resolve to go on livin'. I know I gotta be there for Mama, and I know I got my whole life ahead of me, no matter how lonely I feel. So I try. I don't even try to put on a happy face, 'cause that would be the biggest lie of all. But I do try to live each moment and cherish what I got left: Mama.

We use the little bit I earned at the Rogers farm to pay on the mortgage, and we sell the cows, not just 'cause we cain't keep up with them by ourselves, but also 'cause we got in mind to seal up that barn and never go in there again.

We get by with little to nothin' for a while, but just before springtime, we get a little ray of hope when the government assistance promised to farmers and to people strugglin' in rural areas finally comes to us, and we start to believe that we might just make it.

Me and Mama both know nothin' comes easy, and especially now that we're on our own, we have no earthly idea how – or if – we're ever gonna get the farm back up and runnin', but I tell you what, when we get that first assistance check, we almost giggle like giddy schoolgirls, until we realize it's the first time we've laughed since Daddy died.

Pate comes by one Saturday, and, boy, ain't he a sight for sore eyes. He says he's just passin' through, that he found steady work as an apprentice at an auto mechanic shop over in Memphis. Mama tells him to stay for lunch, but he says he cain't stay long, just wanted to check in on us.

He's overcome with sadness when I tell him Daddy died, and I don't know if it's 'cause I don't want Pate to think poorly of Daddy or if I don't want to burden him with such horrible thoughts, but I don't tell him how Daddy died. Pate deflates all the same and goes real quiet for a long time, so long I wonder if he's gonna be alright.

"Pate?" I reach into my pocket and pull out Pate's clear marble and hold it out to him. "Maybe you need this back now?" And his eyes go from the marble to me and back again, and he smiles, and then he takes his marble and puts it in his pocket.

"You're a real good person, Pate," I say. "Thank you for … everything."

Pate nods and just says, "You too, June." And then he's gone.

I spend a lot of time with Margaret Ann and Jimmy Mack. It feels good to be among friends these days, to let myself lean on them, even if I am the third wheel. They don't mind none, and we sit around a firepit behind Jimmy's house and tell stories, or walk down Main Street and talk about all the things we'd do if we were rich.

"I am gonna be rich someday," Jimmy says. "Y'all just wait. I'll have a big ol' house on a hill."

Margaret Ann bumps his shoulder with hers and agrees, "Me too! We all are, ain't that right, June?"

I look down at the dusty road and think about what rich even means. I think on that a good while, and I decide that I don't need money to be rich. I don't need nothin' but happiness.

Later that spring, me and Mama learn about a government work program, where they're helpin' people get decent-payin' jobs, and we sign up to work in a small clothing factory in Knoxville, and I don't know if God finally decided we needed somethin' good in our lives or what, but this job comin' open for us is just about the best thing to pick us up outa our depression.

It's right up our alley, 'cause we get to sew up clothing for children, and we already know how to use the machines, and I'm tellin' you, me and Mama could do this job with our eyes closed. And it pays enough for me and Mama to live on, along with the assistance we're gettin', and before long we even get caught up on our mortgage, and then we start stashin' money away to save. I cain't remember a time we were actually able to save money, 'less you count the pennies I had in my piggy bank so long ago.

The best part is that the work program also helps folks get a used car for travelin' to work, and with Molly gettin' on in age, goin' all the way to Knoxville every day ain't good for her. The day Mama signs the papers for our very own 1925 Ford Model T, I will never forget, 'cause she looks just about as proud as I ever seen her. Now, honestly that ol' car don't go much faster than Molly, but I don't mind none, and neither does Mama, 'cause it gives us time to talk.

Mama teaches me to drive, and we take turns drivin' each other to and from work every day. We take turns with a lot of things nowadays – cookin' breakfast and dinner, tendin' our herb garden, cleanin' the house. We go to town together every Saturday, and Macafee's may still be closed down, but there are some signs of new life around Maynardville. A hair salon has opened up, and rumor has it that the Sweet Shop'll be openin' back up real soon.

Me and Mama been takin' some of our herbs to trade or sell, along with some eggs from the hens we got after we fixed up and repainted the ol' chicken coop. And the best part is, we got a sewin' machine on loan from the factory, and we brung it home and been sewin' aprons and bonnets and things, and soon as folks get back on their feet, we'll be sellin' these just like old times. We're a real good team, Mama and me, always have been.

On quiet Sunday evenings, as we sit out on the porch swing and watch the sunset, and ol' Bug hops up into my lap, I think about Josy and Daddy and hope they're watchin' us and are proud of us. Our lives may be missin' a whole lotta things that are supposed to still be with us, but one thing we ain't missin' is love for each other, and when I think about that, I think about all kinds of possibilities for the future.

Me and Mama climb into the ol' Model T on Monday mornin' to head to work, and sittin' up there in that seat high above the ground makes me think of Josy and our trips to town in the wagon, and I say, "Mama? You know where we're sittin'?" And she just looks at me with questions in her eyes, and I say, "We're sittin' on top of the world."

And we smile and smile and smile.

25

Josy's Marble

June 1934

It's a beautiful June day, and like I said before, June is my favorite month, even more favorite than September. I fetch ol' Molly from the little mule barn we had built for her, and I hitch her up to the wagon. Mama's got the car and she's at work at the clothes factory in Knoxville. I don't work there no more 'cept sometimes when they're short-handed. Now I'm helpin' Miss Glass up at the school, which reopened not too long ago. I'm teachin' all the little girls how to sew, and I'm lovin' it and so are they. The kids come runnin' when they hear Molly clompin' up the drive. I smile and look up at the schoolhouse porch, suddenly so much smaller than it used to be.

As I grab my bag of sewin' supplies and ready myself to climb down from the wagon, I hear boots shufflin' down the porch steps and across the dusty ground toward me, and then a hand is on my waist, helpin' me jump down, and then a deep, calming voice is sayin' hello.

I reach out and hug him. "Hi, Jimmy Mack." It was his idea to have a "skills for living" class at the school. I teach the girls sewin', and he teaches the boys huntin' and safety. Our pay ain't much, but we enjoy the work a whole lot. Besides, I ain't even sixteen yet, still doin' high school studies. But Miss Glass lets me do my schoolwork at my own pace. Lotsa folks have been real understanding toward me, knowin' what all I been through in the past year. I lost my Josy and my daddy in the same year, and it ain't but God's blessing that I didn't lose Mama too, with how sick she got. I praise the Lord she's on the mend, 'cause I don't know what I'd do if she left me too.

Speakin' of folks leavin', Margaret Ann and her mama moved out to Nashville to be closer to all their other family. I think if I wasn't in such grief over Daddy's death, I'd have been beside myself with sadness when Margaret Ann told me she was leavin'. But with everything … I guess I just run outa energy to be upset. Me and Jimmy Mack spent the day with her before she left, and then it was just me and him, and we been inseparable ever since.

"I got a letter from Margaret Ann today," Jimmy says. "She and her family's doin' well in Nashville, and she said to tell you hello. She's real happy for us." Jimmy blushes, and I blush, and then we clasp hands as we walk up the steps to the schoolhouse for the last day of class before the kids get a summer break.

One Saturday I'm in overalls and a summer hat, paintin' the outside of the new washroom we had built onto the back of the house, just off the back porch. *No more outhouse!* Now,

I'm usually mighty good at things like this, but for some reason, I got blue paint just about all over me, includin' on my face and on my hat and in my hair, and Mama's on the porch tendin' to our herbs and laughin' at me. And then we hear the rumble of a car.

"You expectin' someone, Mama?" I ask, and she shakes her head and shrugs, and she keeps on workin', and I keep on paintin' 'til I come to a stopping point, and then I say I'll go see who it is. I walk through the house out toward the front porch, and a familiar black car is drivin' away on up the lane. When I push the screen door open, it hits somethin', and I look down. "That you, Bug?"

But it ain't Bug. There on the porch is my pack, the one I took train-hoppin'. The one I left in the Burnetts' kitchen so long ago, and I flinch, and then I'm dizzy and I'm lookin' back out at the road, but the car is long gone.

I bend down and pick up the pack and lower myself into a chair. I reach in and pull out my things – my clothes, my pistol, an almost-empty bottle of peroxide, some gauze, my thermos, and then in the inside pocket I feel somethin' that doesn't belong there. An envelope with a little bulge in it. I open it and tilt it toward me, and my purple marble falls into my lap. Josy's marble. I can't stop the tears as I look at that marble. I pick it up and hold it and then bring it to my lips and I cry and cry.

I hear Mama holler, "Everything alright, June?"

I clear my throat and try to holler back without my voice shakin'. "Yes, Mama."

And I look back at the envelope and notice a folded piece of paper inside, and now it's more than my voice that's shakin'. My hands tremble as I pull the piece of paper out and unfold it.

Sitting on Top of the World

Dear June,

You deserve to have this back. You deserve a lot of things, including an explanation. But I can't give that to you because I don't understand myself. All I can tell you is that I'm sorry I never told you the truth, but you must know that there is always more to the story than what you think. I hope you can someday forgive me. You, June, are truly a light in the darkness, and you shine just like this marble. Please don't ever let your sparkle die.

Love,
Paul

I try not to read it a second time and a third time, 'cause I'm not rightly sure a note written by him deserves my attention. But as I fold it back up and return it to the envelope, I look out toward the road and I finger my purple marble, and I look out at our land and our car and the space by the pawpaw trees where the barn once stood, and I vow that I will never let my sparkle die.

Discussion Questions
for *Sitting on Top of the World*

1. Explain the significance of marbles in the story.

June and Josy's jar of marbles is one of the ways the two bond. It's a comfort to June after her father's accident, and she, in turn, uses their invented marble game to try to comfort Pate during his first stay at the Bakers' home. Her decision to sneak the clear marble into Pate's pack shows her empathy and her hope that the marble may be a comfort to him during tough times. When Josy dies, June can't bear the thought of keeping the marbles while not having Josy around to play with, so she buries the jar with him. She holds onto one marble, though – her favorite of the purple marbles Josy had given to her for her birthday. That marble becomes June's spiritual connection to Josy. When June later gives the marble to Paul, it shows just how much she thinks she loves him. Meanwhile, the clear marble, we learn, did in fact serve as a comfort to Pate, and it subsequently gets passed back and forth from Pate to June and back again as the two take turns watching out for each other as their friendship grows. The return of the purple marble to June in the end is a relief and closure for her.

2. Chapter 3 characterizes June and Josy's relationship and how they work together on their family's farm. Describe their relationship and how it changes throughout the story.

June looks up to Josy and thinks of him as the best big brother, and he is. He teaches her things, helps and supports her, dispenses wise advice, shares secrets with her, and entertains and plays with her. Most importantly, as June says, he makes her feel like a giant, like she's capable of anything, during a time in history when girls were generally not looked upon as being capable of much. June is devastated when she learns he plans to ride the rails. They've never been separated for long. When Josy's out looking for work, June is both terrified she will lose him and proud of him for taking such a risk for the family. She is in awe of him, even though she feels they've grown distant. When he dies, she feels like part of her has been stolen.

3. What is the significance of the pawpaw trees?

The pawpaw trees serve as a connection between June and Josy. It's a place they enjoy going, sitting under them and eating their fruit. June says it's one of Josy's favorite places to go – they pretend they're on a tropical island, making the pawpaw trees a sort of escape. Later, the trees become more significant, as that's where Josy and then Daddy are buried.

4. In Chapter 3, the reader learns where the title of the book came from. Explain the title.

"Sitting on Top of the World" is a song by the Mississippi Sheiks that June says is her and Josy's favorite song. They sing/hum it together, and it becomes routine for them: Whenever they climb up into the wagon, and they're sitting up there high off the ground, Josy says, "You know where we're sitting?" And June answers, "We're sitting on top of the world." It's a symbol for their joy even during hard times. Later in the story, June thinks of that song when she thinks of Josy. At the end of the story, when June and Mama climb up into their car, June is reminded of climbing into the wagon with Josy, and she shares the routine with Mama, a signal that June and Mama will find happiness even after all that they've lost.

5. How are June and Margaret Ann different? How do their differences affect their friendship?

Margaret Ann lives in town, and even though it's the tiny town of Maynardville, she's still a "city girl" compared to June, who lives on a farm. Margaret Ann's family is not rich, by any means, and they have a large family to provide for, but in June's eyes, Margaret Ann has everything she wishes she had – a car, a nice house, an icebox, movie star posters, magazines, and makeup. June does not show envy, though, and conversely, Margaret Ann does not exhibit superiority. Indeed, they help each other out where there is a need, and they share things and support each other. They are best friends until June catches Margaret Ann in an inexplicable lie, and then Margaret Ann's mother won't let her be friends with June anymore. Even after that huge and lengthy rift, the girls come back together almost as if no time has passed, their differences not making a difference at all.

6. What is the significance of Daddy's accident in Chapter 5?

The Bakers run a farm – that's their livelihood. If Daddy is only able to use one hand, that will significantly hinder his productivity on the farm, which in turn will hurt the Bakers' income. Because they're in the midst of an economic Depression, they cannot afford such an accident. As the story progresses, the reader sees that the accident also puts a big gash in Daddy's pride and self-respect.

7. What events cause June to mature quickly after she turns 12?

When Josy leaves to find work, June feels a responsibility to help her parents, especially to cheer her mother up. Then, when Mama has to take Daddy to the hospital in Knoxville and June is left alone for a few days, she takes it upon herself to prepare the house for Christmas. Chopping down a Christmas tree, decorating, and arranging for the big Christmas dinner all by herself makes her feel like a responsible adult. As the story progresses and the family faces more setbacks and tragedies, June is thrown into the position of taking care of her parents.

8. How does Daddy feel about Josy riding the rails?

Daddy feels quite a bit of shame about the fact that he has to count on his 16-year-old son to provide for the family. Like the rest of the family, he's worried about Josy getting hurt, but the family needs the money, and Daddy blames himself for that. When Josy comes home the first time with a pair of hobos and a wad of cash, Daddy is suspicious at first, but then feels terrible that he had those negative thoughts. He is all at once incredibly proud of his son and pitifully ashamed of himself.

9. Describe The Depression Trees. Why might trees play an important role in this story?

The Depression Trees are a group of trees with trunks so thin June can close her hand around them. She and Josy call them The Depression Trees because the skinny trunks remind them of how the Depression has caused many people to go hungry, and folks are skin and bones. While that's a depressing thought, this clump of trees is a place June likes to go when she's feeling down, and when she sits among them, she feels at peace. One of the major themes in this book is that family stick together and help each other. The importance of family is symbolized by trees and their roots. Trees can also symbolize strength, which is another important idea in the story.

Cheryl King

10. What are June's reasons for taking the risk of train hopping?

Right before Josy died, he told June to take care of Mama and
Daddy. There is no way June would not try everything to
fulfill her beloved brother's dying wish. She wants to do this
for him as much as for her parents. She has already tried
hunting and selling what she could, but it wasn't enough. Her
only choice is to go find a decent paying job, and the only
way to do that is to get out of town. She has to pick up where
Josy left off.

11. In Chapter 19, why does June feel like she wants to go home but also does not want to go home?

June has grown comfortable on the Burnett farm, and so
much about it reminds her of her own home. The Burnett
family is kind, generous, and compassionate toward June, and
of course there's the fact that she's falling for Paul. So June
wants to get home and provide her parents with the money
they so desperately need, but she also wants to stay and
continue the new life she's building on the Burnett farm.

12. Before leaving the Burnett farm, June leaves a note for Paul, just like she left a note for her parents when she left to ride the rails. What does this tell you about June?

One of June's flaws is that she is no good with goodbyes.
Perhaps she doesn't want to face the emotions she'd have to
deal with. Perhaps she doesn't want to disappoint anyone.
And perhaps she is so headstrong that once she decides she's
going to do something, she just has to go ahead and do it
without anyone else's say-so. The fact that she left Josy's
purple marble with the note for Paul tells the reader she is
also sentimental and trusting.

13. In Chapter 22, June learns that the other hobos know she is a girl. Do you think they were ever fooled by her disguise? Do you think it mattered?

Answers will vary, but it's important to know that it was not uncommon for women to disguise themselves as men and go train hopping. It was safer that way. That being said, during the Great Depression, there were also women who traveled the rails with their children (and guns to protect them). With June being a young teen, it's understandable that she would fear riding the rails with men and would think she'd need to disguise herself as a boy. It is also reasonable to think the hobos would see right through her disguise pretty quickly. However, at that time in history, if the other hobos knew she was a girl, the consequences could have been severe, so perhaps no one knew until the scene when she drew her gun to protect Pate, and, since she had a gun and proved herself courageous enough to use it, no one would mess with her.

14. What secret was Paul keeping from June? How might the story change if he had fessed up sooner?

Paul was involved in the beating that ultimately killed Josy. If he had revealed this to June early on, she probably would not have stayed at the Burnett farm at all. Perhaps she may have attempted to get even. Perhaps she may have gone back home, devastated, and then she'd be back at square one, with her family still needing money and no way to get any.

15. Why doesn't June tell Pate how her father died?

In Chapter 24, June indicates that she's not sure if it's because she doesn't want Pate to think poorly of her father or if it's because she wants to spare him that grief. But perhaps she's also a bit ashamed, and perhaps she feels partly to blame.

16. In Chapter 25, Paul (presumably) returns June's pack, along with a letter and her purple marble, leaving the pack on her front porch. What does this scene tell you about Paul?

Clearly, Paul feels some guilt and wants to apologize. He also may feel that he doesn't deserve to keep June's precious purple marble. He may have some feelings for her, although probably not as strong as the love she felt for him at one time. But this scene also reveals him to be a coward, for he didn't attempt to apologize face-to-face; instead, he wrote a brief note, left June's pack on the porch, and drove away.

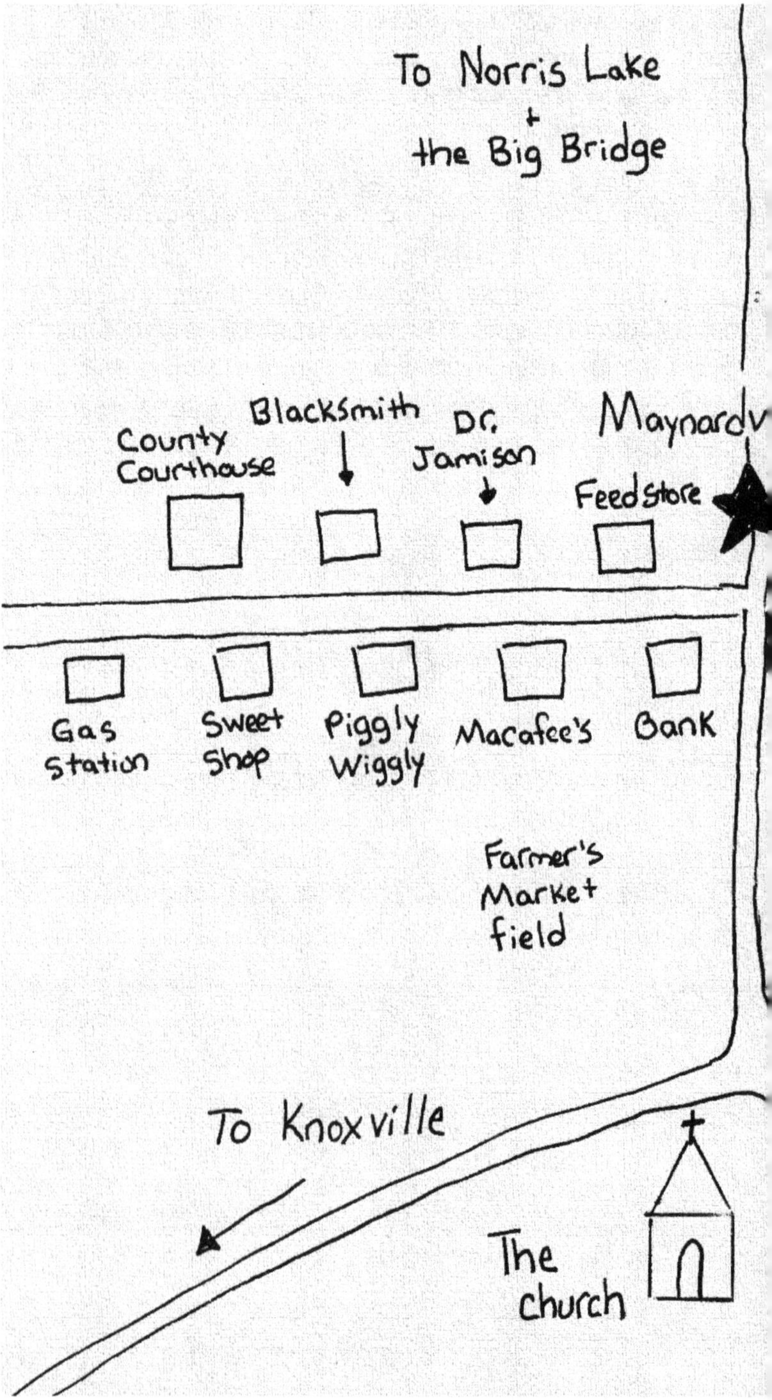
To Norris Lake
+
the Big Bridge
Blacksmith
County
Courthouse
Dr.
Jamison
Maynardv
Feed Store
Gas
Station
Sweet
Shop
Piggly
Wiggly
Macafee's
Bank
Farmer's
Market
field
To Knoxville
The
church

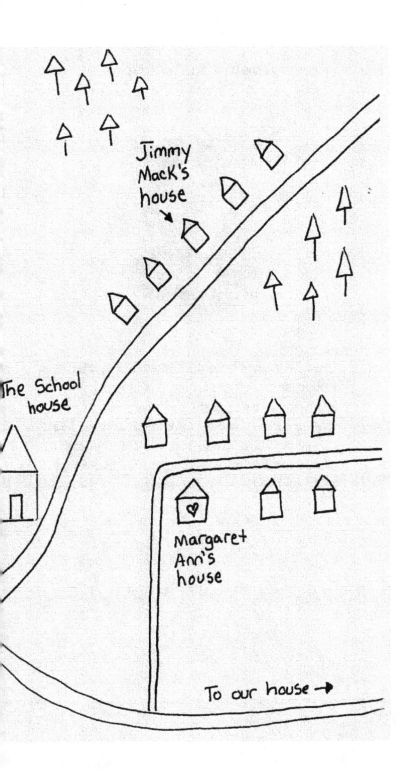

About the Author

Cheryl King is a born-and-raised Texan, Harry Potter fanatic, chocolate lover, and word nerd. She enjoys writing flash- and micro-fiction for writing contests like NYCMidnight and has had two of her short stories accepted for publication. This is her first published novel. She lives in Mansfield with her husband and two teen sons.

Acknowledgments

There are many people without whom this book would not have been possible. From what I hear, life with a writer can be a bit difficult. Try life with a writer who is also a full-time educator, a mom of teen boys, and a hot mess because of menopause. So my husband, Chris, is a saint for putting up with me. My amazing mom, Melody, read my first draft chapter by chapter as I wrote it, and her input was invaluable. My totally awesome 13-year-old son, Carson (get rekt, noob), allowed me to read an early draft to him aloud before bed every night – and what a fantastic revision tool that was. My first-born baby, 17-year-old Hayden, was way too cool to read early drafts, but he promised he would read it once it's published, so I am here now to hold him to that. My lovely mother-in-law, Linda, also read an early draft and offered support and encouragement. I only wish with all my heart that my dad, who was a superb writer himself, could be here today to read my published book.

I must mention NYC Midnight, whose creative competitions helped me rediscover my love of writing and whose prompts gave me the inspiration for this story. Had I been assigned historical fiction for my genre in any of NYCM's writing contests, this book may have been merely a 1,000-word flash-fiction story or a 250-word micro-fiction story. Instead, the idea ruminated in my head as I wrote practically every other genre, and I finally just had to write this story, contest or not.

I had an awesome group of dedicated critique partners who supported me in all of my writing endeavors and gave me invaluable feedback: my pal jimiflan (James Flanagan IRL), Kelly Swan Taylor, and Matt Rigg and the whole 11:59 Workshop on Discord.

A huge thank you goes to Jamie Hitt, who reworked my cover art when I was down in the dumps about our publishing situation. She hand-drew a gorgeous illustration that is a million times better than the first.

And to Emily Joy Brown, the best hairdresser ever, thank you for listening to me and encouraging me and, of course, making my old hair look fabulous every four weeks.

To the CLP Survivors group: We will triumph!